For Ginny, Hannah and Sam

Also by Garry Kay

The Door
Don't Fear The Reaper

ISBN 978-1-291-00806-7

Published by Lulu 2012
3101 Hillsborough Street, Raleigh, NC 27607, USA

Back cover photo by Ginny Kay

Chapter 1

Honest mirror

October 4, 1983: Andrew Leopard had a few spots. Not many and not something that would worry most people, but for Andrew it was the one thing that stood between him and romance. It was not the spots but the strength of this belief that was his downfall. He was a very average 18 year old in many ways, five feet and nine inches with green eyes, but he had very little conversation. As an only child he had been expected to sit quietly in the corner while the adults spoke on 'important matters'. This passive role had extended into his school life and he had grown used to only speaking when spoken to. He lacked self confidence and what he did have was about to be threatened. Andrew Leopard was going to Southside University.

He took with him the burden of low expectations from his father, Frank Leopard, who had always told Andrew that he would never amount to anything. His father was like many people who endured the Second World War as a child. They had seen 'real suffering' and nothing in Andrew's childhood could be challenged. 'You don't know how lucky you are boy. Have you ever seen a dead body? No. And you probably never will.' Frank's words were etched in Andrew's mind. 'All I ask is gratitude. Nothing else. And all I get is "can I play in the park?" Where's your appreciation? I worked hard all my life for what I provide for you. I've bought a dinghy to take you fishing on the canal and you'd rather go to the park and play with your friends?'

This repeated theme of 'no gratitude' was a stick which Frank Leopard used to beat his son with whenever Andrew 'stepped out of line'. Andrew tried not to step out of line, but it was never easy as his father was very particular about what should be done and when it should be done. He wanted everything 'just so' and often told his son 'a place for everything and everything in its place'.

Frank Leopard was a narcissist. He was never able to put Andrew's needs ahead of his own. He had a highly inflated opinion of himself and often spoke of encounters he had had with others where he had 'corrected' them or had to 'put them in their place', a contempt for others that helped raise his own profile in his own mind even to the detriment of his own family. Andrew's mother Maureen had long ago given up trying to share her opinions or needs with him. As the years passed she became subservient to him and acted in the way he expected her to. It made for an easier life. However, this submission compounded Frank's belief that he always knew best. Andrew had gone the same way as his mother, but he was half aware that under his simple façade, there was a fun-loving, ambitious young man trying to break through.

Although he had wanted to go and play with his friends in the park, the truth was he had very few friends. This was partly due to the lack of confidence his home life had created and also partly due to his father's corporate career. They had often moved around the country as Frank had accepted promotions within the company. Andrew often wondered if he had only been born as an accessory. Family men were more likely to succeed in business, his father had told him.

So when his father was away at conferences, his mother would send Andrew to the park and he would sit on his own while other children played together. One particular summer at the age of 12, Andrew had tried to join in with some boys playing football, but a scruffy boy told him 'the sides are already even. Why don't you go and catch fish with your dad?'

Later that day his father returned from a conference and expressed his anger at Andrew. 'What's the matter with you boy? I haven't slept properly for three nights and have worked tirelessly to put food on the table for you and when I get home I have to look at your grumpy face. You're going to have to buck your ideas up. What's the matter with you?'

'I'm sorry. There's nothing wrong.'

'Don't give me that. You look like a wet weekend in Blackpool. What's wrong?'

'I'm fine.'

'No you're not and if you can't tell your old man, who can you tell?'

Frank Leopard was the last person Andrew would confide in but his continued pressure made it difficult for Andrew to refuse.

'Okay. There is a bit of a problem.'

'Go on.'

Andrew really didn't want to tell him but after pausing briefly, he began to feel that a further pause would be rebuked as wasting his father's time.

'I haven't got any friends.'

Without reflecting on what Andrew had said or asking for more detail, Frank replied 'don't worry. You're in a new school. These things take time.' With that he handed Maureen his coat, without looking at her, and walked through to the sitting room. Again without looking at Maureen he announced 'I think I'll have a small whisky before dinner.' Maureen hurried off to pour the whisky.

Andrew went to his room to pack. They were going on holiday to Wales with the caravan the next day. Besides, he didn't want to go in the sitting room. His father was watching the news on the television and if you made the slightest sound during the news, there was trouble.

The next day, Maureen and Frank were hurrying all over the place in preparation for the caravan trip. At Frank's insistence, there was a very specific list of things that had to be taken and they had to be in very specific places and they had to set off at the planned departure time. No room for error. 'If it's worth doing, it's worth doing properly', he would remind them both and properly to Frank Leopard meant in a military manner. Frank had done National Service so he knew how to 'do things properly'.

'Have you pumped up the caravan tyres Andrew?

'Sorry. Not yet.'

'Well get on with it and look sharp about it. They won't pump themselves up will they?'

That was always a difficult one to answer. If you replied that they would not pump themselves up, you were told off for being cheeky and if you took the question as rhetorical, it was repeated louder with the inference that you were impertinent for not responding.

Andrew took the first choice but got the tone wrong. 'No they won't.'

'Get on with it boy and less of your cheek.'

Andrew pumped the tyres up and put the pump back in its place in the garage. 'A place for everything and everything in its place.'

After 150 miles, Frank started to struggle with the steering. After 200 miles he pulled into a service station and went to inspect the caravan with the hope that redistributing the load would improve his steering. Everything was as it should be and Frank's annoyance was growing. He had been planning this trip for months and steering problems were not on the agenda.

Like most narcissists, he was now looking for somebody to blame and the chance came when he spotted that one of the caravan tyres looked a bit flat. 'Andrew. What pressure did you put in the tyres?' he demanded.

'The same as usual.'

'Well that doesn't look like 33 pounds per square inch does it?'

Another one of those questions you don't know whether to answer. Before Andrew could make his choice, Frank continued. 'Get the pump boy and we'll put some more air in it.'

This presented Andrew with a further dilemma. The pump was in the garage. 'A place for everything and everything in it's place.' His father had not told Andrew to pack the pump. It had not been on his list, but pointing this out would trigger further anger.

'Sorry. The pump is at home in the garage.'

Frank now had the chance to place the blame firmly on his son's shoulders but he needed more than that. He wanted his pound of flesh and he genuinely believed Andrew was at fault and his snapped response was so cutting that it was to emotionally scar his son for years.

'You didn't pack the pump. You stupid boy. What were you thinking? No wonder you haven't got any friends. You'll never amount to anything.'

Andrew knew he was in a no-win situation and said nothing while making a mental note that under no circumstances would he ever confide in his father again knowing that it would merely provide him with ammunition the next time he lashed out.

And now for the first time he was going to live away from home. He arrived at Southside University at the same time as everyone else, or so he thought. There were hatchbacks and estate cars everywhere, with the odd van. Boys and girls walked in all directions; arms full of sleeping bags, clothes, audio tapes and cassette players. Frank was in a hurry to get home. He had a conference to prepare for.

'I told you not to use this old grey rucksack boy. People will think I can't afford to provide for you.' With that, he threw the bag in the direction of a large white van which had just pulled up. Before Andrew could pick it up, the door flew open and a tall bald student climbed out and stood on the rucksack. He looked as if his natural expression was an angry snarl and Andrew apologised as he stooped for his bag and quickly retreated hoping that his path would never cross with the fierce bald student.

Frank drove away as soon as the car was emptied onto the footpath and left his son with a firm handshake and the words 'make me proud boy'. Andrew thought to himself that his father would be most upset with him if he were denied the chance of boasting to work colleagues about Andrew's academic achievements. Andrew believed his father had even chosen which subjects Andrew would study based on how the words would flow from his tongue in conversation with his work-mates.

He got the key to his room and spent an age finding it but was determined not to ask for help. He was independent now. When he got there, he piled everything on the bed and sat in the soft chair with the door locked. He was in room two on floor three of Dickens Court, block F.

The room was naked and lifeless. The walls were spotted with Blu-tac stains and drawing pin holes. The only things on the wall apart from a light switch and a very honest mirror were a set of house rules and a list of instructions that were to be followed in the event of a fire. The floor was carpet-less and cold. Every sound he made lingered. Andrew Leopard felt as empty as the room.

After collecting his thoughts for some time in the chair, he set about the task of organising his room, which he did with clinical efficiency. Socks and underwear were stacked neatly into a newspaper-lined drawer. In the drawer above was a collection of very sensible, slightly conservative shirts and trousers his mother had lovingly selected for him at British Home Stores. He pondered briefly before carefully positioning these items in the drawer and thought for a moment about his mother. Maureen had always been there with a comforting smile to share his troubles and pick him up after his father had emotionally knocked him down. A quick glance around his empty room came as a solemn reminder that he could no longer wallow in the protective sympathies of his mother, at least not for the next ten weeks of term anyway.

On the other hand, he had been looking forward to time away from the regime of his father, but was later to discover that even the rigid constraints imposed upon him by Frank were in some respects a form of security blanket shielding him from the real world.

His line of thought was broken by raucous laughter coming from the kitchen, which he would be sharing with seven other boys. These were the people that he hoped would become his new family; the real friends he had always craved. Now would be a good time to meet them. He was nervous. It was important to make a good impression. Andrew checked his face in the mirror. There were a few spots and the odd red lump, but he'd been using the cream and tablets. He could do no more. Time to be brave.

He locked his door and walked down the bare corridor, white painted concrete block walls, his footsteps echoing on the hard floor. He waited for a moment outside the kitchen door. His mouth was dry. He would be spending his first year at college with these students he was about to meet. He was full of hope but feared he may not fit in.

Andrew slowly opened the door not expecting anybody to notice him walking in, but they had been equally anxious to check out every new face that joined them. All heads turned and the buzz of energy switched to pause. Andrew scanned the faces and stopped when he got eye contact with a charismatic young man with a lively face, who had been entertaining the other boys with stories and jokes. Brian Hill, as he later discovered, was sat in one of the four soft chairs which surrounded a white plastic coated chipboard coffee table in a corner of the large square room. The room measured around 20 feet by 20 feet and the corner with the coffee table had been covered in a hard wearing brown cord carpet. The two walls which met in the opposite corner were lined with kitchen units, cupboards, two sinks, two small cookers and one large fridge. Between the units and the carpet was a long white plastic coated chipboard kitchen table with metal tubular legs surrounded by eight plastic moulded chairs.

A third wall was almost filled with windows which overlooked a tree-filled paved courtyard, which was overlooked by every kitchen of every floor of Dickens Court. The final wall was covered with a large noticeboard and that in turn was covered by further instructions on what to do in the event of fire, house rules and posters from just about every society and club imaginable inviting new students to sign up for the coming year. There was the camera club, the hockey club, the society against animal testing, another against apartheid in South Africa and a prayer group. The rugby club poster partly obscured the football club, probably not by accident, while the young Conservatives had been blocked by the poster from the young Liberals.

Andrew was still looking at Brian, waiting for him to speak. Andrew rarely spoke first.

Instead of greeting the newcomer with a smile or a shake of the hand, Brian asked, 'Why did the architect have his house made backwards?'

Brian and three other students all looked at Andrew waiting for his answer. Andrew knew they would judge him on his response, but he didn't have one. He didn't know Brian. He couldn't tell if it was a joke or a serious question or if he had been mistaken for somebody else.

'I don't know,' he stammered nervously, quietly. He didn't know. It was an honest answer. He felt instantly deflated. He could only make a first impression once.

It was a joke and Brian's smile widened as he completed the punch-line, 'So he could watch television.' There was hearty laughter from the three students, mostly in response to Brian's own laughter. He was enjoying the attention. But Andrew wasn't. He didn't understand the joke. He blushed.

It was difficult to remain composed while the joke triggered such a reaction from the others. He thought quickly. Should he pretend to get the joke and join the laughter. Too late. Brian had noticed his blank expression and followed with a visual explanation. He held out his arms as if grasping a pair of imaginary hips and made a few pelvic thrusts.

'Housemaid, as opposed to house made,' Brian said. 'As in au pair girl … backwards.' There was more laughter from the other three boys.

'Oh,' whispered Andrew sheepishly, now fully understanding, although to his limited knowledge it was only cows and dogs that 'did it' backwards. He could see that Southside University was going to be an education. He looked down at his feet with his hands in his pockets. As Brian's attention returned to the others, Andrew took the opportunity to slip out of the room.

On his way back to room two, he passed number five and noticed the door was ajar. Following his setback in the kitchen, he was keen to regain the lost ground and considered going in and introducing himself. He debated with himself for some time before tapping weakly on the door.

It was pulled open assertively. A tall student with short black hair and a warm friendly smile thrust out his hand. 'Pleased to meet you. I'm Tom Hill.'

Andrew's spirits were lifted immediately. He introduced himself and was offered a seat. This was his first friendly encounter. He beamed inwardly but maintained his outward calm, as well as he could. 'I'm in room two.'

'Good. We're almost neighbours. Have you been in the kitchen yet? You'll need to grab what's left of the good cupboards before everyone else jumps in.'

'Actually I've just come from the kitchen. Did you hear all the laughing?'

'I heard something.'

'Well, I think they were laughing at me a bit. A really loud boy told a joke and I didn't get it. He made fun of me. You'll have to watch out for that one.'

'Ah yes. What did he look like?' Tom asked, but he knew it was probably his brother. Tom could see Andrew was timid and he knew Brian would play on such weakness for his own amusement; not maliciously, but with limited concern for Andrew's feelings.

'He looked a bit like you in some ways, but not so tall and his hair was all over the place … it was.'

Tom noticed the quiet, almost silent addition of 'it was' at the end of the sentence after a brief pause, as if to confirm what Andrew had said. Tom had been distracted and not replied instantly. He thought Andrew must have thrown in the 'it was' to fill the silence, sort of like a comfort echo.

'Was he wearing a black denim jacket?'

'That's right. Have you met him?'

'Well actually …' Tom changed his mind. It could wait.

The window was open. A gust of wind filled the curtain and it swelled across Tom's desk pushing over a jar of pens. The contents spilled. One pen fell on the floor and rolled near Andrew's feet. He picked it up. It was one of those novelty pens featuring a girl in a swimsuit who undresses when you turn the pen upside down. Andrew was embarrassed. He turned the pen the right way up and the girl's swimsuit slid back up her body. Tom put the pens straight and closed the window. It had started to rain. 'She's got a nice body hasn't she?'

'Sorry?'

'The girl on the pen.'

'Oh yes. Lovely.' Andrew's red face gave him away. The girl on the pen was the first he had seen with no clothes.

Tom saw a new subject would be appreciated. He was a kind young man and, unlike his brother, chose a more considerate path when it was clear that another person's feelings could be hurt. 'What course are you on?'

Andrew was grateful. 'Economics and politics. You?'

'Sociology.'

'Ah. I think I will be doing some sociology in my first year … I will.'

Tom noticed the soft echo again. He liked Andrew. He had always kept an eye out for weaker people. He didn't like to see anybody picked on and always favoured the underdog. 'Do you fancy a beer later?'

Andrew was delighted to have been asked and said that he would. A visit to the pub would be an excellent chance to build on his new friendship and maybe even meet a girl. They agreed a time to meet and Andrew pulled the door open. As he walked out, Tom shouted after him, 'My brother will be joining us.'

'I look forward to meeting him,' Andrew replied with fresh composure.

'You already have. He was the loud one in the kitchen.'

Chapter 2

Brian's testicle

Same day, October 4, 1983: It was Brian Hill's 19th birthday and he had just started a sociology degree at Southside University near London. His thoughts were far from his studies as he sat in the waiting room. He was going to show the doctor a rather embarrassing irregularity to his left testicle. He would have kept it to himself as there was no pain, but he feared it may effect his sexual performance.

He was a virgin but not for lack of trying. But now he was a college boy, his expectations were sky-high. Brian Hill was ready with his packet of condoms which had been in his wallet for two years. One of the three had been used when he tried it on to avoid mistakes on the big day.

He was a good looking young man, slightly above average height with sharp features and broad shoulders. He had thick, fair hair. The style depended on how many times he rolled over in bed the night before. His blue jeans, black denim jacket, white T-shirt and black Dr Marten shoes were a neutral fashion statement and his lively face gave him an air of youthful confidence.

He didn't like the idea of showing the doctor his penis and his mind was racing with thoughts of what might happen. 'The doctor might touch my dick. What if it's a female doctor? Potentially good. What if there's a window facing a busy office?' Brian knew what he liked and the idea of the female doctor was his favourite scenario. Now he had a new fear. 'What if I get an erection?' His fears had been partially realised which led to a new concern. 'What if it's a gay old man and I drop my pants to show a fully erect willy?'

Brian quickly looked around the empty waiting room and concentrated on posters warning against smoking and sexually transmitted diseases. To his relief, the posters had the required effect and his erection faded. As he regained his composure an attractive girl wearing a short green cotton skirt, cut just above the knees, entered the waiting room and sat opposite.

She crossed her legs and straightened her long black hair with her fingers; nail varnish to match the skirt. She pulled out a packet of Silk Cut cigarettes and lit one. Brian wondered what she was in for and considered the posters on sexually transmitted disease. While watching to see if she scratched herself, his eyes were drawn to the curves hidden beneath her slightly-too-small shirt, which featured the word Puma in capital letters across her chest. His eyes traced the outline of her breasts. Again his consulting room fears were aroused and he quickly looked back to the herpes posters. Now there was conflict in his mind. Visions of seeping genital sores fought for supremacy over ample breasts and crossed legs.

Although it was a warm day, the waiting room was cool. It was on the dark side of a stark Sixties tower block, hidden from the warming rays of the late morning sun. A window at the end of the long thin room was wide open. A light breeze snaked its way behind the accusing posters. The rustle of paper was the only noise, although Brian could hear the occasional car manoeuvring in the parking spaces six floors below.

The light wind tangled with the girl's cigarette smoke and caught Brian's attention. His eyes returned to her shirt. The chill in the room and the gentle breeze had had a pleasing effect on the contours beneath the deep red cotton, which was now stretched to a point behind the P of Puma and a similar point behind the A.

Without considering the merits of approaching potentially diseased girls, Brian boldly made his move. 'What a lovely day for visiting the doctor.' No answer. But she did afford him eye contact for the first time, if only fleeting. Brian very rarely considered the merits of anything he did before acting. He often made inappropriate comments.

'Do you come here often?' Brian knew it was crass but he wanted to provoke conversation. It didn't. But she stared aggressively into his eyes for long enough to make him feel uncomfortable. She reached for a magazine and flicked through, looking at the pictures. Brian was inspired by a baby on the front cover and tried to shock her into talking to him. 'Are you here for a pregnancy test?' He immediately regretted his rudeness. She placed the magazine back on the rack, leant in Brian's direction and with a tone of assured contempt, shot him down. 'I'm expecting twins young man and I'm here for a refund on my contraceptive prescription.'

Brian was extremely thick skinned and barely noticed the patronising slant preferring to see her reaction as a victory in breaking the ice. The girl settled back in her moulded plastic chair, re-crossed her legs and continued to groom her silky black hair. It was long and wavy. It fell forward now and then as she pulled it from side to side. Brian kept his fingers crossed. He didn't want her hair covering the P or the A of her Puma shirt, although his name may be called soon, so maybe that would be for the best.

'I like your shirt.'

'That's nice for you.'

'It makes your tits look lovely.'

'Piss off.'

Brian sat back and read the walls. A nurse came in a few minutes later with a clipboard. 'Brian Hill?'

'Yes.'

'This way please.'

Brian had been staring at Puma Shirt for too long. He stood up with one hand in his trouser pocket to disguise his enthusiasm. He stopped and faced the girl. 'Maybe I'll see you around campus some time.'

'Maybe you won't.'

Brian hurried after the nurse. He was pleased with himself for meeting an attractive young lady on his first day at college and blinkered enough to believe that he had made a good impression.

The nurse stopped. She gestured Brian, with raised eyebrows and a wave of her clipboard, in the direction of a half-glazed door. He knocked and a man's deep voice boomed 'enter'. Brian was sure he had seen two figures through the frosted glass and this was confirmed as he slowly opened the door. He stared in disbelief. His feet rooted. Shoes nailed to the floor.

He saw a fat-faced balding man of around 50. He had a large face like the man in the moon with a few chins. He wore a very old suit, which shone with the gloss of age. If there were such an instrument as a suit horn, it would have been needed to help squeeze this over-sized man into his under-sized clothes. It may also have come in handy to force the doctor into the small space behind his inadequate desk. A few stray hairs had matted together and stuck to his bald scalp with a thin film of sweat. Was this the homosexual elderly doctor that Brian had feared? He had the right face according to all Brian's unsubstantiated opinions on what constituted an aging gay man. His nose was extremely large, red and covered in black-heads, while his lips were of the bloated kind that appear to have been pulled inside out by a corkscrew.

The doctor was bad enough, but, worse still, he had an assistant. A young man, early twenties, sat in the corner. A similar glossy suit, too big, probably from a charity shop as it looked older than the man wearing it. The man's sharp shoulders followed the same creases that the wire coat-hanger had filled in the shop for many months.

'Do sit down young man. I haven't got all day,' the doctor thundered.

Brian sat. He did not want to get his penis out for this man and his assistant to examine.

'Now my boy. Hope you don't mind.' The second sentence was rhetorical. He would proceed regardless. 'My man here is a trainee. Taken him under my wing. He'll be sitting in. Learning the ropes. That sort of thing. Won't say a word. Just ignore him. Now then. What's the problem?'

Chapter 3

Tom's gift

Same day, October 4, 1983: Tom Hill had just started the same sociology degree as his brother Brian, also at Southside University. They had both arrived on campus the day before and each had a room in Dickens Court, block F, floor three, Tom in room five and Brian next door in room four. Eight boys shared a kitchen on floor three and this room was also their living area. Tom and Brian had arrived ahead of their floor-mates and grabbed all the best cupboard space.

While Brian was seeing the doctor, Tom walked the half mile into Southside town centre to buy his brother a birthday present. It was mostly downhill into town as the university sat on the brow of a hill, a prominent position it shared with the town's historic church, which boasted the thirteenth tallest spire in England.

His walk took him through the car park where it seemed every estate car in the country had its boot open and young men and women were pulling out guitars and record players. The odd student even had a television, but not many. Tom scanned the faces wondering if any of these new arrivals would be living on his floor. A tall aggressive teenager with a shaven head climbed out of a van featuring the logo Grundy Electrical Contractors on the side. He stood on the bag of a spotty shy boy, who made an apology and grabbed the grey rucksack. Tom wondered why the cowering youngster was making the apology and not the aggressive bald boy. He would later discover that both boys were to be his floor-mates and would not like each other at all.

Tom left them behind and crossed the bridge over the railway into Thief Lane. It was a busy line with Southside, a popular town for London commuters. Tom passed the football ground. Southside Wanderers had been in the Fourth Division as long as their 2,000 loyal fans could remember. He turned into North Street and crossed the road-bridge over the River Earwash, made famous five years previously when a boating accident had led to the gruesome death of a man who was not aware how little clearance there was between his boat and the bridge.

Beyond the river was the main shopping centre, the product of a recent re-development very similar to many taking place across the home counties to provide glass-covered weather-proof shopping featuring most of the popular high-street chains.

He walked around C&A for half an hour struggling to find something that looked more expensive than his £5 budget. Not much of that time was spent looking at possible gifts. The problem with C&A, or any other clothes shop, for a person like Tom, was the abundance of mirrors. He was incredibly vain. Every time he saw his own reflection out of the corner of his eye, he stopped to take a lingering look of admiration. He was proud of his square jaw and five o'clock shadow, mature features for a boy of only 18. Tom was six feet, a shade taller than his older brother. His black hair was close cropped and never needed brushing. He wore a leather jacket, covered in zips and tassels, white jeans and a pair of brown plastic shoes. He preferred plastic because it was consistent with his vegetarian views. He liked the leather jacket though so the welfare of animals took a back-seat when he made that selection. He had strong views, but little inconsistencies were not unusual.

He was born in August 1965, at the opposite end of the same academic year his brother was born. This meant they had gone through school together, always in the same class, usually as firm friends but there were odd times when accumulated tension led to volatile arguments, but nothing that wasn't forgotten by the next day. Now they were looking forward to helping each other get through their degree course with as little effort as possible. Even the choice of subject had been made with the intention of minimising workload. They had been assured that social sciences were a soft option and the easiest way to become a graduate. They both believed that employers would be far less interested in the content of their courses than the letters after their names.

Tom left C&A empty-handed. He had no idea what to buy his brother and was easily distracted. On this particular occasion, as on many others, by an attractive young lady who stood out partly because of her prominent pink socks, but partly also because of her bottom. She was a short girl but well proportioned and Tom could not take his eyes of her wiggle. She took her wiggle into a shop called Third World Collective. Tom thought that as good a shop as any to find a present and followed.

The girl with pink socks would also feature strongly in Tom's life during his first year at college, but not in the way he may have hoped upon first seeing her. As he entered, the girl came straight back out. He had to be cool so he let her go. Tom was also a virgin, although he initially told Brian one fumbled moment of passion had been full sex when in fact there had been no meaningful follow-up to early signs of promise. Brian had forced a retraction after a lengthy conversation the following morning.

Tom also had a tired old packet of condoms in his back pocket which he had bought from the same pub toilet vending machine as his brother on the same night two years ago. He still had the full set of three though as he did not like waste of any kind. Wasting food was his main pet hate but any natural resources should be consumed with care, including rubber.

It was a small shop but crammed full of stock. The shelves were overflowing with ethnic curiosities. Metallic oriental music floated between carved demons and onyx ashtrays. There was a subtle smell of incense, maybe lavender, floating in the air, but nothing leapt out as the perfect gift for a 19-year-old. Tom was growing impatient though and thought he'd better get something rather than go home with nothing looking like he didn't care.

Tom picked out a T-shirt with an abstract mosaic design involving orange, turquoise and purple drums. He didn't think Brian would like it much but it looked more expensive than the £4 price tag. The attendant placed the shirt in a recycled brown paper bag and Tom headed back up the hill to Dickens Court.

On his way home he passed The Red Lion, which looked like a pub which could be a hit with young Southsiders. Tom remembered the pub from his childhood. It had always been popular with bikers back then due to its large car park, but there were a number of neon signs now and the traditional look had been replaced with a trendy new image. Tom and Brian were both born in Southside but left after primary school. A lot had changed.

Chapter 4

Absent father

Norman Hill was a wealthy man. He ran a thriving globally successful business, which occupied his total attention from the first minute he woke to the last minute at night and often as he tried, in vane, to sleep. He had two sons, Brian and Tom, but he had not seen them for seven years.

The last time he saw them was at Janet Hill's funeral. She had been his wife and their mother, but she had been killed in a car crash at the age of only 38. Until her death Norman had devoted his total attention to Janet and the boys in much the same way as he now did with his business. He could not cope with losing her. It threw him emotionally off balance to such an extent that he could not share his grief with his own sons. He put them into boarding school while he collected his thoughts and considered his future.

As the time apart from his sons grew longer, it became harder and harder to get back together and be the father he wanted to be. Time is supposed to be a great healer, but Norman never got over Janet's death. He felt cheated. She was only 38. She was the kindest, most considerate person he had ever met. She deserved to die in her sleep of old age with her grand-children weeping around her bed.

Norman met Janet at Queen Street County Primary School on the northern edge of Southside. He was five years old but a steady boy who mixed well, so when Janet, also five years old, started school, the teacher asked Norman to look after her for the day. He was delighted to have been given the responsibility by his teacher and helped Janet with her painting, learning the alphabet and sums. He even played with her at lunchtime out on the swings. For the next 33 years, they were inseparable, married at 21 in the church on the top of the hill next to the university.

Tom and Brian were born within a year of each other and the family business was growing steadily. Norman taught his boys how to play football and climb trees while Janet spent all her time driving them back and forth from friends' houses and clubs to make sure they grew up as confident and happy, well-rounded young men.

It was on her way to collect the boys from football training that she was hit by a white parcel delivery van. The driver was in a hurry to make deadlines and attempted an overtaking manoeuvre which asked too much of his van. He never made his deadline as the impact claimed his life as well as that of Janet Hill.

Brian and Tom's love of football was one of the reasons Janet had been behind the wheel of her car at the wrong time. Norman firmly believed that he placed no blame of any kind upon his sons. He told them that on the day he took them to boarding school. He knew it was nothing to do with them, but he still took them to boarding school and he still asked a friend to care for them over Christmas until the next term started. Work had become hectic. He could not get away. He was travelling the world chasing bigger and better contracts.

What use was he to his sons anyway? He should have collected them from football training. On the morning of the crash he told Janet he would make the pick-up.

'Who's picking up the boys from football?' Janet asked over breakfast.

'I'm meeting a new supplier this afternoon but should be done in time,' Norman replied.

'Doesn't matter. I can do it.'

'I'm sure I'll be done. And I'd like to catch the end of training and watch them play.'

'Okay.'

'I'll give you a buzz if I'm running late.'

Norman remembered every word. It was the last conversation he had had with Janet. The new supplier had been held up and Norman called Janet to ask her to collect the boys.

Now seven years had passed and Norman was still collecting his thoughts and considering his future. The pain of losing Janet was as strong as ever, almost as if no time had passed. He couldn't look at another woman and his social life, beyond business networking, was non-existent. He had not seen his boys grow up. He was one of the richest men in Southside now but it was utterly meaningless without Janet.

Yet he had the gift of two wonderful sons. He could not understand how he had let the time slip by. They would be young men now and he knew they would no longer be away at boarding school, but back in Southside at the university. It was time to put things right. But seven years of collecting his thoughts had not been long enough to find any answers.

He did not know what to say or what he could or should do. Taking a back seat at work was his first move. He could then walk up to the university as often as he liked to meet the boys. What happened after the first meeting would depend on how things went.

Chapter 5

Beer

Same day, October 4, 1983: 'Another?'

'Yes please Tom,' Andrew replied with false enthusiasm, despite still having most of his first pint of lager. It was not only his first of the night, but the first of his life. He had been persuaded by Brian to drink lager, but was struggling. He hated the taste. There were benefits though, the glass gave him a reason to pull one of his hands out of his pockets. He never knew what to do with his hands. He felt most comfortable when they were in his pockets, otherwise he felt awkward, and Brian had noticed his nervous demeanour.

Andrew's obvious discomfort was amusing for Brian. Like his brother, Brian was warming to Andrew seeing him as a harmless distraction, somebody he could have a bit of fun with, in much the same way as an attentive pet dog.

Tom, on the other hand, had been careful to put Andrew at ease, bringing him into the conversation. He had listened with interest to Andrew's stories of fishing in the canal and when Brian started asking Andrew what treatment he used to control his acne, Tom tried to switch the conversation to something which Brian may find uncomfortable.

'What did the doctor say about your scrotum Brian?'

It was successful in saving Andrew's blushes but had no impact on Brian. He cared little about who knew of his defective testicle, although getting it out for the doctor had been a trying ordeal.

'Well, you know what doctors are like. Unless you tell them you're dying, they say it will clear up on its own after a few days. So I said I was in great pain, losing sleep and sick with worry. Then I told him about my bollock.'

Brian then faced Andrew to fill in what Tom already knew about the wiggly growth on his left testicle, before continuing. 'He told me to strip off below the waste and lie down behind the curtain.'

The three teenagers were sat at a table in the Red Lion, which Tom had expected to be full of students. The trendy exterior was not matched by a similar interior. Inside the Red Lion, there had been no new décor for decades. The landlord had upgraded the outside to pull in the youngsters and kept his prices as low as he could. As long as he had the edge on prices over the other town centre pubs, he knew he would keep the student trade.

The ceiling had been painted white many years ago, but was now covered with a thick yellow film of nicotine. The green tartan carpet was a sticky grey in the places which had seen the most traffic, including the route to the toilet and around the pool table. There were a few pictures on the walls, mostly featuring cartoon beagles playing pub games, darts, snooker and dominoes.

'He then pulled the curtain back and asked me to stand up. Don't know why he asked me to lie down really 'cos I was already standing up. He took my ball bag in his sweaty old-man hand and prodded around.' Brian winced with discomfort just telling the tale. Tom's anguished expression showed he was sharing his brother's suffering, while Andrew found it hard to concentrate on what they were saying as the room had started to spin around his head.

'He then asked if it hurt. It was uncomfortable but not painful. I wasn't going to be fobbed off though, so I said it did and threw in a few oohs and aahs to convince him I needed treatment. Then his scrawny assistant had a go and he was very clumsy. I didn't have to fake the pain for him.'

'And?'

'Well, straight off he said he knew what it was and I ought to see a consultant at the hospital. He said I may need a small operation to put things right, but it was nothing to worry about.'

'That doesn't sound too bad?'

'But it went downhill from there. He then said, "just to be thorough, I'll check your prostate gland." He put me back on the couch, pushed me on my side with my back to him and put one leg across the other so my knees were on the couch, slightly bent. The whole ordeal was slightly bent. I couldn't see what they were doing but I heard him pulling on some surgical gloves and squelching around in a pot of lubricant.'

Brian took a gulp of his beer.

'Then up it went.'

'His finger?'

'His finger. Up my bum.

Tom pursed his lips and crossed his legs.

Brian finished his beer.

'He then started prodding forward and said, "does that hurt?" Does that hurt?' Brian repeated in a more animated tone, an octave higher than the previous sentence.

'I resisted the temptation to say what I was thinking and just whimpered a little saying it hurt a bit. He then asked if I would mind the trainee taking a look. "It would be invaluable to his studies." Can you believe that?'

'Did you let him?'

'No I bloody didn't!'

Tom finished his beer. 'Shall we try the pub outside the football ground?'

Brian nodded.

'Andrew. How about you? Wanderers' Rest?'

'I haven't finished this one yet.' Andrew had half a pint left and hadn't touched it for a while, but the spinning had stopped.

Brian grabbed Andrew's glass and drank the lot in about five seconds. 'You ready now Leopard?'

'Yes. Sorry. Ready when you are.'

Tom didn't mind his brother drinking the beer. He could see the alcohol was having an effect on Andrew, but in some respects for the good. The soft echo at the end of his sentences had gone.

The three boys walked 400 yards through steady rain to the Wanderers' Rest, Brian at all times trying to avoid the puddles. He had a hole in one of his Dr Marten shoes. This pub was even more dowdy than the previous one. It was one large room with a high ceiling and there was a narrow shelf running around at picture rail height. Every inch of this shelf was filled with models of lions, mostly porcelain, some soft toys and some wooden sculptures. The owners of the pub liked lions. There were pictures on the walls, also featuring lions with brass wall lights above each one.

The boys had been expecting football fans to be the main customers but it was mostly smartly dressed women aged between 50 and 80. The barman told them it was an unofficial meeting of Southside West Women's Institute. They were plotting the replacement of the current president.

Brian lined up three more pints of lager.

Tom returned to Brian's illness. 'So what did the doctor say was wrong?'

'Something called varicocele. Kind of like varicose veins of the scrotum.'

Andrew had not been contributing much to the conversation and thought he ought to say something. 'Oh dear Brian.'

'Oh dear indeed,' replied Brian. 'Too much blood near your balls apparently cuts your sperm count. I should be shagging left, right and centre while I'm still firing blanks.'

Tom smiled appreciatively while Andrew hoped neither of them would ask him about shagging.

'Have you got a girlfriend Leopard?' Brian asked.

Much to Andrew's relief, before he answered, a very hairy and wet dog settled down next to the boys. Brian was not happy. Cleanliness was very important to him and he looked with disgust towards the owner who Brian felt should have the dog tethered at his feet or, better still, at home. The dog then stood up and shook itself vigorously sending a fine spray all over the boys. Brian reached quickly for his glass to cover his beer and prevent any of the spray getting in his glass.

'Not happy. Let's move tables.'

'Fine. It's your birthday.' Tom wasn't bothered by the dog, but didn't mind moving to keep his brother happy. Andrew's head was spinning again and he wasn't sure which table he was sitting at.

Brian settled into the new seat and took off his left shoe to dry his sock. He was going to have to clean all his clothes thanks to the wet dog, which was particularly annoying in the case of his new shirt as his brother had only given it to him three hours previously.

'On the subject of shagging, I met an attractive young lady in the doctor's waiting room today.'

'Yeah?'

'I was trying to read a magazine, but she kept talking to me.'

'Get anywhere?'

'Oh yeah. Nothing definite, but she said, "see you around some time."'

'Sounds promising,' Tom had to admit.

'Students Union for last orders,' Brian suggested.

'Sounds good. How about you Andrew?' Andrew still had half his beer left. Tom reached for it this time and drank it in about five seconds. 'Let's go.'

Andrew struggled to his feet and followed the brothers.

As they passed the ladies from the women's institute and approached the exit, Brian whispered to them both, 'here, watch this.'

The exit was a heavy door with clear glass panels. Tom and Andrew went out first followed by Brian, who stopped with his back to the closed door and kicked it loudly. The ladies of the women's institute turned as one to see Brian drop his pants and press his buttocks against the glass.

They didn't wait to see the reaction and splashed down the dark street laughing, dim orange street light dancing with shafts of rain in the gutters. They chased over the railway bridge and fell through the doors of the Students' Union building and headed for the bar.

They chose seats by the wall so the boys could sit in a row side by side. They could see the whole bar and, more importantly, all the women. It was Freshers' Week and all the new students had a list of welcome meetings, parties and special get-togethers. Tonight was the Freshers' Disco and the boys were pleased to see so many girls, although there were disappointingly more boys.

Most of the courses available at Southside University were science based rather than the arts and this meant there was a ratio of about three male students to every female student. In social circles, this gave the women a greater sense of worth than they enjoyed in the wider world. The result was a clumping effect. Where one girl stood, a gathering of boys formed a circle around her. None of the boys spoke much to each other, but competed for the attention of the girl. The number of girls was so far short of the number of boys that some who would normally find it difficult gaining the attention of boys, could be seen with their own circle of attentive suitors.

The three Dickens Court boys watched and waited. Tom and Brian were both good footballers and picked out a large poster inviting players to sign on at the Freshers' Bazaar. The posters for all the clubs and societies covered all the walls in much the same way as they did in the boys' own kitchen. A good time was promised as various groups urged the new students to 'come along and sign up'. The boys later discovered why the clubs tried so hard to attract the new students. Their share of union funding depended on the number of their members.

'Chips anyone?' Tom asked.

'No thanks,' Brian preferred to spend his money on beer.

'No thanks.' Andrew was struggling to keep his tea down.

Tom joined the queue for chips at the canteen around the back of the snooker tables. There were more club posters on the wall to catch students as they waited in the line. A short red-haired girl, dyed red, not ginger, reached in front of Tom.

'Excuse me. Could I just reach that poster,' she asked with a soft voice and a warm smile.

'I'm sorry,' Tom stepped aside.

Some club posters had the contact details of the secretary repeated along the bottom so you could tear off the number. The pretty red-haired girl wanted the contact details for the Greenpeace Society. She wore bright-coloured loose fitting clothes, espadrille cotton shoes with no socks and a distinctive Greenpeace enamel badge, which featured a white dove.

'I've got a Greenpeace badge just like that.'

'Got this one at Glastonbury this year,' she replied with enthusiasm and warmth.

'Aah. I was there. That's where I got mine. Which bands did you see?'

'Yes please.' The woman serving food asked Tom loudly. He was distracted and almost forgot how hungry he was.

Tom bought his chips and shared them with his new friend.

The conversation flowed easily and when she asked Tom back for a coffee in Bronte Court, he quickly filled in Brian and Andrew and left them together.

Andrew was not only struggling to keep his tea down, but the room would not keep still and now his new friend was gone leaving him alone with Brian, who made Andrew very nervous.

Puma Shirt stood at the bar. Brian pointed her out to Andrew. He had a few beers inside him and had started to believe his own version of how he met the girl. Whilst waiting to order more drinks, and without thinking, as usual, he reached down and squeezed her bottom. It was a mistake. She turned sharply and pushed him to the floor.

She snarled at him through clenched teeth and her eyes narrowed. 'I told you to piss off this morning. What's your problem?'

Brian looked up at Andrew. 'See? She loves me.'

It was all too much for Andrew and he reached for his mouth as it filled with vomit, but the pressure was too great and he couldn't hold it. In much the same way as a finger held over the end of a garden hose, Andrew sprayed everyone within ten feet with an unpleasant mixture of partly digested fish-fingers and chips, which Tom had cooked for him, and the best part of three pints of lager.

Chapter 6

Second year students

The next day: 'I enjoyed our night out.' Short pause. 'I did.' Andrew was first in the kitchen for lunch followed by Tom, who noticed straight away that the soft echo had returned now the alcohol effects had worn off.

'How did you get on with Brian?'

'Haven't you seen him?

'No.'

Andrew was embarrassed about being sick in the union bar and even more embarrassed about being sick twice on the way home and a fourth time in his bed. If these disappointing feelings about himself had not been so all-consuming, he would have had the wit to turn the conversation around and ask Tom how he got on with the red-haired girl.

'Brian was pushed to the floor by a girl and I was sick over them both … I was,' Andrew said coyly, looking away from Tom in shame as he finished his sentence.

Before Tom could respond, the door burst open and Brian marched in with a copy of The Sun under his arm. 'Tom. Big man. Womaniser. How did you get on with Greenpeace Badge?' Brian wasted no time getting to the point.

'Good thanks.'

'Intimate?

'Yes. Intimate.'

'How intimate?'

'Just about as intimate as it gets.'

'You stallion.' Brian patted Tom on the back, but now with mixed feelings. He was pleased for his brother, but slightly jealous that Tom had lost his virginity before him, and on the first night at college, while he had been pushed to the floor by the only girl he had met.

'So. You seeing her again?

'Probably, but only as friends I expect. She has a boyfriend back home but they have an "understanding", although the degree of understanding seemed much less when we both woke up sober.'

'Fair enough. You got off lightly then.' Brian was reminded of another joke and turned to Andrew, who had been listening with huge admiration for Tom. 'What's the difference between a woman and a toilet?'

Andrew didn't know, but this time was aware that he had been asked a joke and waited for the punchline.

'A toilet doesn't follow you around when you've finished using it.' Andrew smiled politely.

The door flew open again and in marched Hugh Grundy from room number eight. He had an assured swagger, partly because he was a second year and partly because he was six feet two with rippling muscles, but while he had muscle to spare, he was lacking in charm.

Andrew turned almost as if in slow motion and his jaw dropped. Fortunately his plate of beans didn't. This was the aggressive student who scowled at him the day before and stood on his bag. He looked even more fierce in the confined space of the shared kitchen. He had a tattoo of a lizard above his left ear, clearly visible as he shaved his head every week. His eyes were unusually far apart, which added to the angry look, as did his thick black eyebrows which sloped inwards. He wore black jeans, blood red Dr Marten boots and a black leather jacket similar to Tom's. Despite his predatory looks and lack of charm, he was extremely sharp witted and coasted through his sociology degree.

Following Hugh into the kitchen was Colin Dean from room three, another second year student. He threw his books on the coffee table and slouched in one of the easy chairs. He wore a T-shirt with a pointing finger on it and the slogan 'I'm with stupid'. He had an arrogant sneer, his jeans were ripped at the knees, old age, not fashion, and his wispy blonde hair fell around his sloping shoulders.

Colin's books sat on the table alongside a very full ashtray and a pile of leaflets advertising clubs and societies. Colin, of moderate build and height, kicked the leaflets on the floor to make space for his muddy feet, then lit a cigarette. He didn't use the ashtray. He couldn't reach it. His ash fell straight onto the cord carpet. Andrew picked up the leaflets and ate his beans in one of the soft chairs, Tom was also eating and Brian read The Sun in the corner.

'My name is Colin Dean, but you can call me … Colin Dean,' the newcomer announced to the whole room. 'Are you all first years?' Without waiting for an answer, he assumed they were and continued. 'Shagged anyone yet?' Again it was rhetorical. 'Not many girls here. You have to get in quick before they're snapped up. Most of the good-looking girls are in the languages department, but half of them have boyfriends back home. Mind you, after Christmas is another good time to grab yourself a chick. The ones with boyfriends back home see them at Christmas and dump them. They've been saving themselves all term only to go home and find their boyfriends have found someone else. They come back after Christmas desperate to take revenge and jump into bed with the first to take an interest, so don't miss out there.'

'Are you a second year Colin?' asked Andrew, who had hung onto his every word, while Brian had continued to read The Sun and Tom had stared out of the window over Colin's shoulder. Brian wasn't really interested while Tom didn't like arrogant people and was going out of his way to show he wasn't interested.

Having finished his cup of tea, Andrew sat with his hands in his pockets while Colin told him how to get through the first year without doing any work.

'I've met everyone on the floor except the person in room one. What's he like?' Colin loudly asked Andrew, or anyone else who was listening.

Tom and Hugh could add nothing. 'I've not met him either,' replied Andrew apologetically.

'Me neither,' added Brian, taking a passing interest, having also met all the boys except for room one.

Chapter 7

Silver birch and cherry trees

A week later: From the university car park, Norman Hill could see down across the whole campus and the town of Southside beyond. It was a red brick university, built in the 1960s, along with many similar institutions across the country. Blocks of lecture halls sat alongside high-rise administration buildings with silver birch and cherry trees lining wide walkways.

Norman had been dwelling on what to say to Brian and Tom for days, since first making the decision to face his sons. He had been putting off this difficult meeting for seven years but was now determined to take a chance. He left the car park and passed the sports hall. The majority of students were very casual in appearance and even the teaching staff had a relaxed dress code. Norman felt out of place in his smart pin-striped suit, but nobody seemed to even notice him, perhaps making the assumption that anyone who wore such smart clothes must be closely linked to the chancellor's office or be a manager in a non-academic department.

He followed a line of apple trees with Bronte Court on his left and Lawrence Court on his right. The wide footpath opened into a small grassed area, the size of a bowling green, with Dickens Court on the far side. There was a row of benches around the outside edge of the lawned section. Norman sat for a moment to gather his thoughts. He was comfortable addressing a crowd in the most hostile of situations and had coped with awkward meetings between individuals. But nothing compared to this. His heart was racing. His mouth was dry.

After 20 difficult minutes waiting, he saw the Dickens Court main entrance open and two young men walked out together. Across the grass, he saw a tall dark haired boy and a well-built young man, scruffy fair hair, deep in conversation. It was Brian and Tom. They did not see Norman. He should have stood up and gone over to meet them, but he couldn't. He just followed them with his eyes, which welled with tears of pride.

They were handsome young men. They laughed and joked. They were happy. They were very happy. He couldn't spoil that. It could wait. They didn't need to meet him just yet. Best let them get settled. They turned the corner and were gone.

Norman felt elation and frustration at the same time. He had seen two young men buzzing with the joys of youth, but he had lacked the courage to make contact, even questioned whether it was the right way forward. But it was. One step at a time. He would come back another time.

Chapter 8

Pink Socks

Another week later: Andrew Leopard sat on the second row in Lecture Hall B between a young Oriental man with round glasses and a heavy looking red-haired girl with freckles and a persistent sniff, so persistent that it happened almost every other breath. She also gave off an unpleasant smell which Andrew thought must be body odour. During his sixth form studies Andrew sat with a boy who considered deodorant to be unnatural. Andrew recognised the same smell from the sniffing girl.

Andrew had made no new friends yet from his economics group, but didn't mind too much as Tom Hill was also doing some elements of economics on his course and they had agreed to share text books. It saved money and gave Andrew the chance to spend more time with his new friend from Dickens Court. Andrew believed that the more time he spent with somebody as assured and 'cool' as Tom, the greater chance he had of succeeding himself, both academically and socially. Tom had already slept with one girl and had been selected for the football team, along with his brother Brian, who, although more flippant towards Andrew than Tom, at least afforded Andrew a greater status than his own father. Yes, he made fun of him, but as an equal, rather than a costly, time-consuming burden. Brian also shared the cost of, and use of, the economics text books, while all three had been sharing the cost of food and sharing the cooking.

The lecture hall was packed with around 80 students for an hour of introductory economics. The hall was gently tiered and the desks were narrow, one continuous stretch for each row, fixed to the floor. There was a blackboard, but it was rarely used, the teaching staff preferring felt tip marker pens on a white board or an overhead projector.

A man in his fifties with a single tuft of grey hair behind each ear and a wispy white beard addressed his attentive audience with a mumbled voice that, even from the second row, Andrew struggled to hear. His first line was something along the lines of 'can you all hear me at the back?', Andrew thought, but couldn't be certain and besides, if he was talking to those at the back, Andrew did not need to respond.

The words were hard to follow, but Andrew was sure he caught the feeling behind them. The professor would rather be pursuing his research than lecturing a bunch of under-graduates whom he held in contempt as beer drinking time wasters living off the state. It was a general feeling shared by many people, as Andrew was later to discover on nights out away from campus while mixing with the working folk of Southside.

Professor Mumbles adjusted his multi-coloured sleeveless v-neck jumper, pulled up his dark brown corduroy trousers and continued. 'Supply, mumble, market forces, mumble, demand?' he asked. Andrew knew it was a question because the professor raised his eyebrows and looked out at the students expectantly.

Sniffer raised her hand. Andrew instantly tensed. The whole room faced the girl right next to him to hear her answer. Andrew had a bright red double headed spot just above his left eyebrow. He could feel the 80 pairs of eyes straying from Sniffer to his own eyebrow. They didn't. But that's how he felt. 'Equilibrium, sir,' Sniffer replied confidently.

'Perhaps, mumble, but then again…'

Andrew's concentration was further broken as Sniffer lowered her arm again squeezing out another pulse of 'natural' odour. Andrew was now certain that she did not use deodorant. While all the students' faces had been turned, almost in Andrew's direction, he had noticed, beyond Sniffer, a more attractive girl. He had seen her a number of times. They only did economics together so Andrew assumed she must be on a similar course with the emphasis on a related but different discipline within the social sciences.

He had only caught fleeting glimpses of her before today but could see her more clearly now. Andrew considered her quite stunning. While she was listening to

Sniffer's answer, her gaze had strayed slightly and Andrew made eye contact with her for a fraction of a second. It was the briefest eye contact, but gave Andrew great encouragement. It was a big enough boost to sustain him for a few days. He would need no more than that. He certainly didn't want to meet her until the spot above his eyebrow had cleared.

Andrew had excellent A-level grades in economics and much of the degree level first year content repeated the A-level syllabus. As such, he was not too worried about trying to follow Professor Mumbles. Instead his attention switched to the attractive girl in the front row about five seats beyond Sniffer.

She was either slouching in her seat or very short. She had strawberry blonde shoulder-length hair tied back with an emerald green ribbon. She had a satin black shawl over her shoulders. Andrew could see no more.

The professor appeared to be winding up with some concluding remarks. He turned off the overhead projector before telling the students which chapter of the set book he would like them to read before the next lecture, gathered his papers and left. A gentle hum of conversation filled the room and the students started shuffling out.

Andrew stayed seated as the room emptied. He took the opportunity to watch the attractive girl stand up and leave. She was short, possibly around five feet, knee-length linen skirt and black pixie boots. She may have been short but had curves in all the right places. As she walked away, Andrew noticed her striking bright pink socks and shapely bottom, with a wiggle which he would have to tell Tom about as soon as he next saw him.

She was the kind of girl Andrew had often dreamed of meeting but never thought he would. But she was one of the

80 people in his economics group. Maybe he would get the chance to meet her. He dared to dream. Perhaps Tom could tell him how he could go about meeting her.

Chapter 9

A film of ash

Two weeks later, November 5, 1983: Andrew Leopard prepared lunch for himself, Tom Hill and Brian Hill. Toast with chicken paste followed by toast and marmalade.

'Andrew. There is nothing I can say that I haven't already said. You have to talk to her,' Tom was running out of ideas to help Andrew meet Pink Socks. Three weeks had passed since Andrew first saw her across the lecture room and he still didn't even know her name. The three boys had become so used to calling her Pink Socks that if they ever discovered her real name, she would continue to be known as Pink Socks.

Andrew had progressed no further than the fleeting eye contact he had enjoyed so briefly and although the large spot he had above his eyebrow on that occasion had gone, another had grown on his chin. He was waiting until he had a clear face, but the stress of possibly meeting his dream girl was giving him more spots.

The conversation ended as Ian Mellor and Roger Evans entered the kitchen. Ian, from room six, had been nicknamed Wanker by Hugh Grundy and the name had stuck. Unfortunately for Ian, he had forgotten to lock the shower room door during his first week at college and Hugh had barged in on him. Hugh was also responsible for Roger Evans picking up the name Crypt. In his case, this was due to a lack of charisma. Roger wore 'sensible' clothes, rarely spoke, had a constant neutral expression on his face and when he came in the kitchen, he prepared his own food, ate it, washed his pots and left. He didn't trust the other students so he kept his food and pots in his own room.

Andrew finished preparing lunch but there was no room on the table. Nobody else was using it but it was covered in mess accumulated during the first month of term. Dickens Court, block F, floor three had become more dirty as each day passed. A peppering of cigarette ash covered every surface, gathering like snow-drifts in all the corners.

A cleaning lady came three times a week but the amount of work was beyond her job description. She did the basics and left the rest for the students. She mopped the kitchen floor, vacuumed the carpet in the corner of the kitchen and in the boys' bedrooms before bleaching the toilets and showers. The boys had to empty their own bins, wash their own pots and keep all the surfaces clean and clear, but they didn't.

Hugh Grundy and Colin Dean were next to arrive and before Andrew could make space to eat on the table, Hugh ran his arm over the whole surface and swept everything onto the floor near the bin before placing his books in the middle.

'Am I the only one that tidies up in here?' Hugh barked, spilled tomato sauce dripping down the sleeve of his leather jacket.

'Cheers mate.' Brian sat down to eat followed by Tom and Andrew.

Among the rubbish was a sports bag. The unwashed contents had been emptied and nobody had claimed the dirty laundry. It must have been left by one of the floor-mates' friends, but nobody had been back to look for it. Tomato stains had now been added to a pair of used underpants, which had been on the floor for nearly two weeks.

'Come on Tom. You play football. These must be your knickers.' Hugh picked them up and dropped them on the table next to Andrew's plate.

'No. I told you. Too small.'

'Got to be you then Brian. Another footballer.' Hugh pressed.

Brian finished his first piece of toast. 'No.'

'How about you Crypt?' No response. He didn't like being called Crypt.

'Wanker?'

Ian Mellor had given up trying to protest his innocence over the shower incident and did respond to the nickname, although he hated it. At least he was being included. 'Not me. I don't do sport.'

'We all know what sport you like,' Colin Dean joined in, before lighting another cigarette.

Andrew finished his lunch and sat on one of the soft chairs in the corner next to Colin. Hugh grabbed the dirty underpants and pushed them over Andrew's head. 'Well done Leopard. You've finally got inside someone's knickers,' Hugh taunted.

Andrew reached up to take the underpants off his head.

'No you don't Leopard. You can wear them to your lectures,' Hugh demanded, smiling in Colin's direction.

Andrew's lip quivered a little and he put his hands back in his pockets. Brian finished his lunch, stood up, brushed past Hugh and pulled the knickers off Andrew's head. 'Give him a break Hugh.'

'Don't get heavy. I was only fooling around,' Hugh shrugged.

Brian returned to The Sun for another look at the page three girl. All the lecturers on Brian's course had said reading a daily newspaper would benefit their studies. Brian's interpretation of their advice had not been what they intended. The breasts were very much to Brian's taste, not too big, not too small and slightly inward curving above the nipple giving them a profile similar to an Olympic ski jump.

'I do like ski-jumpies,' Brian told all the floor three boys.

'Let's have a look,' Colin asked.

Brian held up the paper and the boys all took a good look.

'Nice,' Hugh liked them.

'Yes Brian. Ski-jumpies,' Tom approved.

Andrew had been looking out of the window hoping nobody would ask his opinion.

'Leopard. Marks out of ten,' Colin knew he would be embarrassed.

'Err …' he tried to think of a new subject before he was pushed further. 'Err … It's a nice déjà vu from our kitchen … it is.'

'A nice what?' Colin sneered. This was more fun than he had hoped. Embarrassing Andrew on a sexual matter would have been fun, but his obvious misunderstanding of simple French would be even more entertaining.

'A nice déjà vu,' Andrew repeated slowly and nervously, sensing he had blundered.

Tom quickly rescued his friend. 'Yes Andrew. Lovely view. Who's coming to the bonfire on Southside Common tonight? There's a fair as well. Always gets a big crowd.'

Brian, Andrew, Colin and Hugh were keen to go. Ian Mellor said he had too much work but they all knew what he'd rather be doing. Truth was he didn't have enough money for the fair. Roger Evans assumed he wasn't included in the invite, packed his pots in a box and left the room. Tom had invited Colin and Hugh because he didn't like to leave anybody out and, even though they were sometimes hard work, they added a bit of spice to the conversation.

Tom grabbed his books and left for his statistics lecture. He took the steps two at a time as he passed between the administration building and the library. The autumn leaves had collected in the gutter. It was a crisp dry sunny day, a welcome change after a few days of rain. His walk took him past the civil engineering block. There was a shorter route but the civil engineering block was made of reflective glass panels on the ground floor. He slowed down for this stage of his journey. Vanity couldn't be hurried.

As he strolled past his favourite building with warm sun on the back of his neck, his attention was drawn to the ground. The shadow of a bird danced around his feet. He smiled inwardly and turned to see the bird. There was no bird. He scanned the sky but could not see where it had gone.

The lecture had already started. Tom found a seat at the back but his late arrival had been spotted by the professor, who paused just long enough for his contempt to be registered by Tom.

Chapter 10

Penny for the Guy

Same day, November 5, 1983: Andrew Leopard looked around at the flickering orange faces of the assembled Southsiders as the Guy sank into the flames. His eyes settled on one face, a very familiar face. It was Pink Socks. He became short of breath and his heart beat fast. Tom had repeatedly told him to just walk up and talk to her. 'Just take an interest in whatever she has to say. It will flow from there,' was the standard advice. Tom and Brian Hill both saw Andrew's discomfort and followed his eyes to Pink Socks, giving him a look that said 'grasp the nettle'.

'But she is so pretty … she is.'

'That doesn't stop you talking to her,' Tom encouraged.

'Get in there before she shags someone else.' Brian was impatient and less understanding of Andrew's self doubt.

'He does have a point,' Tom had to admit.

'You have a point too Andrew, but if you don't take your hands out of your pockets and talk to the girl, you'll never get a chance to use it,'

'She probably has a boyfriend at home.' Andrew was finding excuses.

'Maybe she hasn't,' Tom said, at the same time patting his shy friend on the back and gently pressing him in the direction of Pink Socks.

Brian beckoned Tom over and took him to one side. Andrew pushed his hands deep into his pockets while the brothers talked quietly to each other. Moments later they both approached Andrew, each grabbed an arm and cradled him between them. He struggled, feet running against fresh air as they carried him through the crowd.

'Penny for the Guy,' Brian asked Pink Socks.

'Any loose change will do,' added Tom.

Andrew's scared eyes looked up.

She addressed Andrew with a soft Birmingham accent and a kind smile. 'I have five pence. Will that do?'

The brothers turned to Andrew for his answer. Pink Socks waited for an answer, the smile still warm. Andrew's mind raced. He could not think of anything and the pause was growing to an awkward length.

'I … I think I have change,' he stammered. He fumbled in his pocket for coppers and handed them over. Her friends called. She made her excuses and left.

'That wasn't so bad.' Tom told Andrew. 'At least you've made contact now, so you have an excuse to talk to her next time you see her.'

'Maybe you can progress to asking her name next time.' Sarcasm from Brian.

'I think I have change.' Andrew repeated his words. 'She must think I'm an idiot now … she must.'

'Even idiots have girlfriends,' Brian advised. 'Not all Labour voters are single.'

Tom couldn't let that go. 'Not all Tory voters are single.'

Tom tried to find something positive to add. 'She probably thought you were being ironic.

'She hates me.' Andrew was miserable.

The boys were taken along by the flow of the crowd. Southside Common was still a bit muddy from rain earlier in the week. They dodged the mud and stuck to the trail of straw, which the council had put down for footpaths. Tom's attention was caught by one of the fairground stalls offering a wide selection of useless gifts as prizes for hooking a plastic duck. It was easy to hook the ducks and Tom presumed the prizes cost less than the fee to take part. An elderly grey-haired lady with her hands in a money pouch around her waist beamed in Tom's direction revealing an incomplete set of teeth.

'Fancy your chances my lad? Hook one duck and you win anything on the bottom shelf.'

'Maybe I'll try later.' He broke away from her stare before she could push him further. 'Do you remember when we cheated on a stall like this as kids?' Tom asked Brian with a smile of nostalgia. 'We were only about eight years old,' Brian nodded. Tom addressed his memories to Andrew. 'The stall was so busy that the attendant was run off her feet. As quickly as she collected ducks, she handed out prizes and, in the same movement, gathered payment. She left winners briefly to consider what prize they wanted and went back to them. When they finally made their choice, she grabbed the prize and handed it over.'

'Yes.' Andrew listened carefully, his brush with Pinks Socks forgotten for a minute, but only a minute.

'We had no money but she was so busy, we just told her what prize we had chosen, moved around a bit, told her our choice again, and just collected prizes without ever paying. She didn't notice we hadn't paid until we had a pencil sharpener each, four T-Rex badges, a furry pig and three sticks of rock. She was too busy to chase us.'

Andrew was impressed.

Brian had been checking out the ladies, but paused, unusually, to watch a toddler struggle with a toffee apple. She or he, Brian couldn't tell, had only been able to lick the treat and had got toffee all around its mouth, chin and cheeks. The mother had seen the mess and reached for her handkerchief, which she licked and wiped the child's face. As the toddler strained to avoid the mother's attention, the toffee apple was held at arms length. The family dog, which had been following the apple with interest from the start, took its chance, grabbed it and swallowed it after only crunching twice. The child's startled face turned in disbelief as it realised what had happened. The tears came with loud sobs and screwed up eyes.

'Brian,' Tom shouted. 'She was too busy to chase us.'

'Yes. I remember.'

They moved on. It was a popular event. Very well attended and, much to the liking of Tom and Brian, there was an equal number of men and women, unlike the distorted, unreal situation on campus.

'We should come into town more often,' Brian suggested.

'Might be worth it,' Tom agreed.

Brian noticed a trendy looking girl struggling with a cigarette machine. She had a thin face, matching thin mouth with black lipstick and black clothes from top to bottom. Brian had heard such girls described as 'Goths' or New Romantics. She was tall, only an inch or so less than Brian, with crew cut black hair. Although a mild night for November, the girl wore a heavy black coat, which hid details that Brian usually preferred to check in advance. She was still struggling with the vending machine and Brian could see no friends rushing to help her. He thought a 'cool' thump on the machine would break the ice. It broke more than the ice.

The machine's four legs had been on soft ground and the application of force from Brian's fist pushed one of the legs deeper into the mud. The machine fell back and the glass front shattered from the impact with a concrete bollard. As the device clattered to the ground, a large rocket exploded overhead thankfully drowning the sound and giving the three boys the chance to make a quick exit. They ran to the video game tent where Colin and Hugh had been trying a scam on the fruit machines.

The second year friends had been using a system which they had purchased from a final-year mechanical engineering student, whose thesis had been on the workings of gaming machines. They had broken even. It was the latest in a long line of ideas they had tried in the pursuit of easy money, a study which they devoted more time to than any of their academic options at the university.

The nearest pub to Southside Common was the Horse And Groom on London Road. Brian shouted over the noise of the video games, 'meet you in the Horse And Groom.' The boys rushed off.

The three boys followed a wide path to the edge of the common, which led to tennis courts and a crazy golf course. A path between these two facilities led to London Road, but it was only wide enough for two. The three boys had been walking side by side in relative quiet to get their breath back but Andrew noticed the path was about to narrow.

He could see that one of them would be on their own, front or back, while the other two continued side by side. To avoid being left out, he struck up a conversation with Tom as they approached the narrow section of the path. His plan worked. Brian fell in line behind them and the brothers had not noticed Andrew's trick, although Tom did find it a little strange that his friend suddenly started checking on his general health and talking about the weather.

'Bollocks. I was in there.' Brian drank half his pint of beer in one go. It had taken 10 minutes to get served. The Horse And Groom was packed with bonfire night revellers, mostly on the way home from Southside Common, although one or two drinkers looked as if they had never made it as far as the bonfire and spent all night in the pub.

The pub was much smarter than the other places they had visited in town. There were high ceilings with ornate mouldings, gold coloured light fittings with heavy velvet curtains over bay windows. The boys found some standing space alongside a copy of Michaelangelo's David statue. Tom was upbeat as usual and having tried to raised Andrew's spirits after their brush with Pink Socks, now needed to build his brother up.

'But Brian, just think, if you see her again, you will have plenty to talk about.'

Andrew, who had never seen anyone dressed all in black, including lipstick, tried to be supportive. 'She did look a bit weird.'

'True, but I wasn't interested in talking to her or borrowing her clothes. I wanted to squeeze her tits.'

Tom felt that his brother needed to change his focus. 'You do need to do a certain amount of talking in the initial stages. Some blokes even do a bit of talking after the deed.'

'Now that is weird.' Brian's focus was unchanged.

The room was packed and as Tom reached for the David statue to steady himself, he slightly bumped a woman who nearly spilled her drink. She was followed by an aggressive man of about 20 stone, who glared at Tom. No words needed. The warning was noted.

The boys moved to a clearer space near a passage, which led to the toilets. It was a better spot as they were alongside a group of three girls. The young lady closest to Tom was either tanned or of mixed race with bright friendly eyes, long eye lashes and large orange and green gaudy ear-rings, which matched nothing she wore.

She had one plump friend and another in a bright red polo-necked jumper. The plump friend didn't like the gaudy ear-rings, which had been a gift from the girl in the polo-necked jumper, and she had been trying to say so without offending either of her friends.

'Don't get me wrong. I love the ear-rings, but I don't think orange works with your skin tone.'

'It so does. And the green is the same as your eyes.' Polo-Neck was getting defensive.

'I like them and the colours are lush, but maybe they were wrong for this outfit.' Gaudy Ear-rings was trying to be diplomatic.

'Okay.' Plump Friend was being assertive. 'Let's ask a complete stranger.'

'Fine,' said Polo-Neck, who was definitely not fine.

'Fair enough,' said Gaudy Ear-rings, who turned around to face Tom Hill and immediately forgot what she was supposed to be asking. She had seen this young man earlier across the other side of the bar and pointed him out to her friends as the sort of man she would like to be stuck with on a desert island. The three girls had all been picking one man, one outfit and one music album to take to a desert island.

'Hi. How's it going?' Tom asked, wondering why she had turned towards him.

'Good thanks.'

After a pause, Polo-Neck intervened. 'Stop staring at him and ask him.'

'Ask me what?' asked Tom.

'Yes. Okay. Err …' She couldn't think of the best way to ask. 'If you were buying your girlfriend a gift.'

'I don't have a girlfriend,' Tom interrupted.

Her smile widened as she continued. 'If you had a girlfriend and you were buying her some ear-rings, would you choose the ones I am wearing?'

'Hmm. Tough one.' Tom narrowed his eyes and rubbed his chin in thought. He had overheard their conversation and tried to answer in a way that kept them all happy. 'It would depend who they were for.' He paused to register if he were on the right track. Okay so far. 'If they were for you, the orange might not match your skin tone.' Plump Friend was nodding approval. 'But the green matches your eyes.' Polo-Neck nodded. 'But perhaps the green and orange together would not be right for your outfit, so I'm not sure.'

All three girls were happy with that but Gaudy Ear-rings thought Tom had shown greater perception than might have been expected. 'You heard our conversation didn't you?' She asked smiling.

'Yes. Okay. I did. But honestly, they're nice,' he lied. He thought they were tacky, but he loved her smile. It was a bit cheeky and challenging. Tom liked girls with spirit.

Brian took the opportunity to strike up a conversation with Polo-Neck while Andrew looked sheepishly at Plump Friend. He had squeezed a spot that morning on his cheek and he couldn't tell if she was looking at his eyes or the blemish. He held his glass a bit higher to cover the spot, then realised he was holding a half pint glass while his confident friends had pint glasses. He lowered the glass and held his hand over his cheek in a way which he hoped looked natural. 'Have you been up to the bonfire?' he asked.

'Yes. It was very good,' Plump Friend replied politely, but Andrew came back with nothing and the girl started to look around the room before edging towards her friends and joining in their conversations instead. Andrew put his free hand in his pocket and looked down at his shoes.

'Oy. Leopard. Why did you run off?' shouted Hugh Grundy over the heads. He was pushing his way through followed by Colin Dean, both carrying pints of snakebite, half lager, half cider. Hugh spilled a few people's drinks with his impatient advance, but made no attempt to apologise. Andrew explained how Brian had knocked over the cigarette machine.

'Nice one Brian.' Hugh slapped his floor-mate on the back with the same force that Brian had used on the vending machine, but on this occasion it launched Brian's beer all over Polo-Neck, who squealed first as a result of the soaking and second as an apologetic Brian clumsily tried to mop up the beer with his dirty hanky. She pushed him away. This was becoming a habit, Brian thought.

The girls left quickly, although Gaudy had been reluctant to stay with her friends. She had enjoyed meeting Tom and wanted to see him again. Unfortunately she hadn't even told him her name. She had told him which insurance company she worked for in town. He seemed bright, maybe he would contact her there if she had made a good impression.

Tom was angry with Hugh. He had met a girl he liked and who he thought liked him, but he hadn't even got her name, let alone her phone number. 'What a dickhead Hugh.' Tom said forcefully.

If he had been joking Hugh would have let it go. Hugh couldn't tell if Tom was being serious or not, but responded as if he had been. 'Nobody calls me a dickhead.'

'Dickhead.'

'Do you want to take this outside?' Hugh still wasn't sure.

'Ready when you are Dickhead.'

Hugh wasn't sure what to do now. He was more bark than bite and he wasn't much bigger than Tom. Besides, he quite liked Tom and didn't want to fall out so he backed off. 'I'll let you off this once, but watch your step. Nobody messes with Hugh Grundy.'

'Union bar for last orders,' Brian ended the exchange.

'Yes. Let's go.' Tom was ready.

'We'll catch you up,' Colin thought it safe to join in now.

The three boys left.

It was a long walk across town and the union building was shut by the time they got there.

'Coffee Bar,' suggested Brian.

'Sure thing Brian,' replied Tom, but Andrew wasn't keen. He had seen Pink Socks in the Coffee Bar a couple of times and he felt he had had enough humiliation for one night. He made his excuses and headed back to Dickens Court.

The brothers walked beyond the union building, round the bio-chemistry block, along the edge of the staff car park and into the Coffee Bar, which occupied what had once been a store room underneath the lecture halls. It had been converted to a coffee bar after pressure from the student council to provide an alternative place for students to socialise other that the bar in the union building. It was run by students for students and its relaxed rules on closing time had made it the place to go when the union bar shut for a bit of a wind down. They also made toasted sandwiches, which were very popular. A lot of students who hadn't been drinking often went there at the end of a long study session and the atmosphere was more casual than the union bar.

There was a low ceiling and it was not a large room. There were a few bar stools around the outside edge alongside a wide continuous shelf. Above that were murals of iconic actors and pop stars, which had been painted by students in the art department. Lou Reed was alongside Annie Lennox, followed by Charlie Chaplin and James Dean. As Tom and Brian arrived the juke-box was playing Do You Really Want To Hurt Me by Culture Club.

The place was always full in the run-up to midnight and it was standing room only. Tom ordered two hot chocolates and a cheese toastie to share. The boys edged over to the corner under Charlie Chaplin.

'I liked that girl.' Tom was still disappointed to have not collected a phone number from Gaudy Ear-rings in the Horse And Groom.

'Actually I quite liked Polo-Neck. I liked her enough to talk to her face without looking down at her breasts.'

'That's progress Brian.'

He smiled inwardly, pleased with himself for briefly changing his focus away from sex. But it didn't last long. He saw a poster on the notice-board advertising a Greenpeace meeting. 'Was Greenpeace Badge a good shag?'

'Is there anything in your head apart from shagging?' Tom knew there wasn't but thought he needed to make a point.

Brian thought for a moment. 'Football?' More of a question than an answer. 'Did you use one of the condoms we bought two years ago?' If it had been a question the answer was 'no'. Brian had gone straight back to sex.

'I did. And yes. It was good, but brief.' Now Tom paused in reflection. 'Too brief. It can't have been that special for her.' The thought seemed to have only now come to him and there was a bit of guilt creeping into his mind. 'Thinking about it, I have to say I probably used her. She could have been anybody. I just wanted to lose my virginity, so yes, I used her and it's not a good feeling.'

Brian nodded his understanding, but thought to himself that he would be unlikely to feel the same way.

'Having said that, I also felt relieved knowing that virginity was no longer an issue, so next time it won't cloud my judgement and I can make the girl's feelings a higher priority.'

Brian again nodded understanding but knew he would never be as thoughtful as his brother and believed that Tom would not be as considerate as his ideals told him to be. Brian thought Tom was deluding himself.

The juke-box song finished and the hum of conversation filled the Coffee Bar. As Andrew had expected, Pink Socks arrived. Brian noticed her first and pointed her out to Tom. 'There's Pink Socks. I wonder why Andrew can't speak to her.'

'He has no self belief and can't imagine why an attractive young lady would ever want to speak to him.' Tom had a good look at Pink Socks, who was wearing yellow socks today, he had noticed up at the bonfire. 'Mind you. She is a babe. I saw her in town on the first day of term.'

'You taking an interest?' Brian smiled.

'No. No,' Tom replied instantly. 'Wouldn't dream of it. That would destroy Andrew and besides, I like Gaudy Ear-rings.'

'Stop looking at her then.'

'I'm not. I was just wondering how we could help Andrew. If he forgot his spots for five minutes and smiled a bit more often, he'd be fine.' The juke-box struck up again with Billie Jean by Michael Jackson.

Chapter 11

I think I'm in love

Nine days later, November 14, 1983: Andrew Leopard was a sad 18 year old. He woke to find a new yellow head had appeared on a spot he had squeezed three days before. He thought he had seen the last of this particular spot and was looking forward to relatively clear skin and a chance to get to know Pink Socks, but that was out of the question now. It was over a week since he spoke briefly with her at the bonfire, but he had not followed that up yet.

He washed his face and had another go at squeezing the spot, but this turned out to be a mistake. Yellow must have been the colour of the scab as nothing came out when he pressed, but he did make the blemish look worse. His already low morale dipped further. He would have to avoid people for a few more days before he could face anybody with confidence, not that he ever faced anybody with confidence. Andrew was feeling quite sorry for himself.

He dressed and gathered his books for his economics lecture knowing there was a chance that his new bigger spot could be seen by Pink Socks. He crept quietly along the corridor and past the kitchen door. He scurried across campus with his head down and found a seat at the back of the lecture hall. There she was in the opposite corner of the room. He felt a glow of warmth just seeing her from a distance.

Professor Mumbles wound up his summary of diminishing marginal utility and Andrew was straight out, back across campus, quietly past the closed kitchen door and into his room. He settled in the soft chair and reflected, almost tearfully, on his life.

Was he a happy student? Did he like Southside University? Did he like his floor-mates on Dickens Court and would he ever make any progress with Pink Socks? He told himself he was in love, then asked himself what did that mean? If it means you picture yourself alongside somebody every time you do something and imagine how they would react to all your thoughts, then yes, he was in love. But you're supposed to be happy when you are in love. Andrew wasn't happy, but she was in his head all the time. He must be in love.

He fantasised. How nice it would be to hold her hand, to put his arm around her shoulder and sit next to her in lectures. His life would be fantastic if he could enjoy these simple pleasures. His father would be so proud of him if he took Pink Socks home for a weekend to meet his parents. He thought what Brian and Tom Hill would want from a girl. He knew Brian thought only of sex, but Tom would put a girl first. He would enjoy every moment he spent with a girl, whatever they were doing together, but he would still have sex with her. Andrew's thoughts about Pink Socks had never even progressed that far. It would be more than enough to walk side by side through the park.

The whole university experience was not what he had expected. The people seemed so aggressive, so driven by sex in every aspect of life and completely lacking in academic interest, which was supposed to be why they were at university in the first place. He had mentioned the name of a sociologist the day before at lunch and Hugh Grundy had replied 'who the hell is he?' while Brian had looked up thoughtfully, shook his head and returned to page three of his newspaper.

He was rarely happy at college, struggled to keep a smile on his face and when he came up against problems, he found himself wondering what advice his mother would have given him. He felt out of place. His father had always told him 'a place for everything and everything in its place,' but he had no place. He wanted so desperately to break free from his father's control, but now found himself missing the structure that he offered.

He wanted to think for himself, make decisions and make things happen, but he couldn't do it. He knew he carried no respect on floor three. He was an object of fun. They would think differently if he bought Pink Socks back for lunch, but that was never going to happen. A knock at the door broke his train of thought.

'Lunch,' Brian shouted.

It was time to take his big spot into the kitchen and hope that nobody picked on him. He opened the door just enough to push through and sit at the table.

'How hungry are you?' Brian asked.

'Not very.'

Brian placed two fish-fingers on Andrew's plate, six on his own and four on Tom's.

'Just a minute,' shouted Tom.

Brian put one of his fish-fingers on Tom's plate.

'Have you had your hair cut?' Tom asked Andrew.

'No.'

'Looks different.'

Brian continued to read his paper even while they ate. Looking up for a moment, he addressed, the whole room, which was full. All seven boys were there. Just the boy from room one missing. Still nobody had seen him. 'What do you think of this new chap in charge of the Labour Party?'

'Neil Kinnock?' asked Tom.

'Yes,' answered Ian Mellor, who was Welsh. 'He is excellent. He is Welsh.'

'Shut it Wanker.' Hugh joined in. 'The only good thing to come out of Wales is the M4.'

'He's a tosser.' Colin Dean's contribution did nothing to raise the intellectual level of the conversation.

'Is that all you have to add?' asked Tom.

'He's a Welsh tosser.' Colin laughed at his own joke. 'What do you think Crypt?'

Roger Evans didn't react, other than to pack his food in a cardboard box and leave the room.

'All the opinion polls have moved in Labour's direction since he took over,' Brian was conservative with a small 'c' but strongly believed that a Labour government would be a disaster. 'Doesn't matter who's in charge anyway. They'll still argue with each other and never get in.'

Being the older brother Brian had already voted at one general election and had helped Margaret Thatcher return to power.

Tom disagreed with his brother. He was looking forward to voting Labour, whoever was in charge. 'They might be alright. You never know. At least they would think about the poor.'

That set Brian off. 'So how are they going to help the poor if they have no money because they have taxed the rich so much that they leave the country?'

Tom had to respond to that. 'You're missing the point. It's not all about money. People and attitudes are what matter, not balance sheets. The "loadsa money" culture created by Maggie has damaged the moral fabric of the country. '

'We've got more money.'

'Doesn't matter. We're spiritually poor.'

'Good intentions don't put a roof over your head.'

'But we're happier with what we've got.'

'Yes. And what we've got is more money.' The brothers would never agree.

'I'd rather have the money.' Hugh was with Brian.

'I'll take the money.' So was Colin.

'He's Welsh. I'm voting for him.' Ian would have voted for him, whichever party he belonged to.

Andrew finished his second fish-finger delighted that the conversation had drawn attention away from his spot. He had no firm political views and sat listening as Tom and Brian continued rubbishing each other's ideas until they agreed to disagree.

'There are more important things in life,' Colin said to break the quiet that followed the heated exchange. 'Tonight is student night at The Skin Shop.' That was the only nightclub in Southside and Monday night was student night with all drinks for 50p. 'Who's coming?' There were nods of approval from Tom, Brian, Hugh and Ian. 'How about you Leopard?'

'I'll have to say no. I'm a bit short of money … I am.' Andrew had enough money and wanted to go with them, but didn't want to be seen out and about until his new spot had died down a bit. He had never been to a nightclub and the thought of going to one did not appeal, but he didn't want Hugh, Ian or Colin taking his place as Tom's friend, or even Brian's friend. As crude as Brian was, you knew where you were with him and he had looked after Andrew a few times when Hugh and Colin had been unkind.

'Andrew, I saw Pink Socks this morning,' Tom said casually.

He instantly had Andrew's attention.

'Have you seen her today?' Tom asked.

'Yes. In economics.'

'How close were you?'

'She was on the far side of the lecture hall. I don't think she saw me.'

'Well I saw her close up. In the library.'

Andrew waited expectantly.

'She had an enormous spot on her nose.'

'Really?' said Andrew with disbelief and half a smile.

'You see. You're so busy worrying about your face that you haven't even noticed that she is human too. She has spots. She has worries.' Tom could see he was making some progress.

'She probably even farts Andrew.' Brian was less helpful.

Andrew didn't respond to Brian, but thought to himself that even his crude suggestion did add something to Tom's excellent point. A large spot on a girl's nose would not normally be considered sexy or alluring, but, for Andrew, it was the first thing that gave him a feeling of affinity with the girl that he loved.

Chapter 12

The Skin Shop

Same day, November 14, 1983: It was a crisp autumn day. The sun came out every now and then and gusts of wind carried leaves past Norman Hill as he sat on the bench across the grass from Dickens Court. He had made a number of visits to the university and sat on that same bench every time, catching the odd glimpse of his sons Tom and Brian but never making any contact. However much time passed, his thoughts were unchanged. The pain of losing his wife Janet was just as strong. The wish to see his boys was just as strong, but nothing changed. He watched from a distance.

He watched the leaves blow past all afternoon. The orange lights that lined the path turned themselves on as darkness fell. There was a gentle shower but Norman stayed where he was, waiting for Tom and Brian. It was late evening before they came out of the halls of residence laughing and joking with a crowd of friends.

Norman was not impressed with the boys that were with his sons tonight. He had seen them going in and out of Dickens Court but never with his boys. The tall bald student looked and sounded aggressive and his fair haired friend was a creep. A third student didn't look too bad, but he wasn't the serious boy that he had seen with his sons on a few previous occasions.

The boys turned the corner and headed for town. As they passed the union building, Hugh Grundy gestured his arm towards the building. 'Quick one here first?'

'No point. It's 50p a pint at the club,' Brian preferred to keep the costs down.

They crossed the railway bridge and headed down Thief Lane. As they passed the football ground Hugh waved his arm towards the Wanderer's Rest. 'Quick one in here?'

'50p a pint.' Brian kept walking. As they rounded the corner into North Street and the Red Lion came into view, Brian turned to Hugh. 'No. 50p a pint.' They carried on walking through the shopping centre. Colin Dean led the way. He liked to think of himself as the senior member of the group, the one with all the local knowledge.

Tom, Brian and Ian Mellor had not been to The Skin Shop and Colin had proudly told them they would be going up John's Passage. Second on the left after the shopping centre was John's Passage where the club was well hidden from the main shopping streets. The entrance to The Skin Shop looked very similar to the garage doors which lined the opposite side of the street. They wouldn't have found it without Colin's help, although the queue was about 20 people deep and that would have been as good as a sign over the door. Two large bouncers in dinner jackets also showed them they had found the nightclub.

They were all very cold by now, the cloakroom was an extra 50p and none of the boys wanted to pay the same as the cost of a pint of beer to hang their coats up.

A large number of clubbers tonight were from Southside University. The pull of cheap beer saw to that. There were also students from the law school, technical college and sixth forms of all three of the town's schools. There were also a few 'townies'. That was the phrase the students used for the general public in Southside. The townies had phrases they used for the students, but they were not nearly as polite. Students were unpopular with a lot of the permanent residents of the town, who considered them lazy, scruffy, free-loading louts; a needless drain on the public purse.

Having spent most of their government grants on beer, many of those students would go on to share the views of the townies, but, for now, felt unfairly castigated.

The Skin Shop had very soft lighting and all the walls were black. There were three separate bars on three levels with the top level having a balcony overlooking the dance floor of the middle section, which featured chart music. The basement had a second dance floor with Punk music.

Hugh liked Punk but the boys stuck together and headed for the top bar so they could drink beer and watch girls from the balcony. There were a lot of loud girls in red v-neck jumpers with a number of equally loud boys wearing the same garment. It was Southside University Hockey Club doing a bit of team building. It was a mixed club with male and female teams, both were out together. They weren't as loud as the football club could be, Brian and Tom were looking forward to their club night out, which would be more rowdy than the hockey players, but still well short of the rugby club, which set the benchmark for drunken debauchery.

Colin bullied Ian into buying the first round. 'You can get the first round Wanker because you're Welsh.' He was Welsh and couldn't think of a quick comeback, so he accepted it, like he accepted most things, and bought the drinks in the hope that it would be the last time he got his wallet out that evening. Pints of snakebite for Colin and Hugh with pints of lager for Ian and the Hill brothers.

Ten minutes later, Hugh tried to bully Tom into buying a round but failed miserably and, in order to save face, made Colin get the drinks instead. After another 20 minutes, Hugh didn't want to risk putting pressure on Tom again and went up to the bar himself. The brothers went for a game of pool and Colin went to the gents, while Hugh and Ian grabbed a table.

'Seen any girls you like Wanker?' Hugh asked.

'Do you have to call me Wanker?

'No, but it rolls off the tongue easily. Besides, I caught you at it in the shower.'

'You heard some noises. You don't know what I was doing.'

'Pant, pant. What else could it be?'

'Rubbing my hair dry with a towel.'

'The water was still running.'

'Rubbing mud off my knees.'

'Doubt it. I tell you what, I'll stop calling you Wanker if you admit that you were. And I won't tell the others.'

Ian was tempted by that offer but was unsure if he could trust Hugh. 'How do I know I can trust you?'

'I'm a decent bloke. You have my word. It's Ian from now on if you just admit it.'

Ian thought for a moment. It was probably worth a gamble.

'Okay. You caught me wanking. Anyway. Is that so bad? Everybody does it.'

Hugh could not help laughing. 'I knew it. I was only guessing in the first place but I knew I was right.' He was still laughing as Colin arrived back at the table closely followed by Brian and Tom.

'What's so funny?' asked Colin.

'Wanker just admitted that I caught him wanking.' Hugh told everybody, still laughing.

'You git. You promised me.' Ian wasn't happy.

'Well yes. There's a lesson there. You shouldn't trust me Wanker.'

'My round then.' Brian went for more drinks, with Tom's help. At the bar Tom spotted Greenpeace Badge. She was with a young man. Tom had seen her a few times during the first few weeks of term and had, as she had suggested, become friends. Greenpeace Badge introduced Tom to her boyfriend and Brian left them to it.

'Where's Wanker?' Brian asked on his return.

'Went off in a strop,' Hugh said, still smiling. 'And Tom?'

'Busy meeting his chick's boyfriend.' Brian struggled to conceal a hint of jealousy.

'I'd better drink his beer then.' Hugh grabbed the spare pint and downed it in one, which turned out to be a mistake. In order to save some cash for the nightclub trip, he hadn't eaten since breakfast. He had also played poker with some other second years for the whole of the previous night. The combined effect of snakebite, no food and no sleep topped off with a hastily drunk pint of lager, was enough to push Hugh past his limit, which, given his size, took quite some doing. He raced to the toilets and made the cubicle just in time to vomit straight down the pan. Colin raced after him to check on his best friend leaving Brian on his own, having started the evening with four floor-mates by his side.

In the circumstances, he went for a wander and checked out the alternative dance-floor in the basement. It was almost like a members-only section and he felt as if he were being watched by everybody in the room as he strolled in with his pint of beer. The only black he had on was his Dr Marten shoes, but he hadn't polished them since he bought them, so they were more of a dirty grey.

Brian was the only person in the room who wasn't wearing predominantly black and most of the others, male and female, had a large amount of black make-up to add to the sombre look. Very few people smiled. It would have been un-cool. Brian strolled around sipping at his pint and smiling warmly at the Goths, occasionally throwing in the odd dance move as he worked his way around the basement.

As he turned towards the exit, he saw a familiar face. It was Black Lips, the girl he had almost met at the cigarette machine he smashed to the ground up at the bonfire on Southside Common. He always carried a lighter in case he met a girl who smoked. Black Lips reached for her cigarettes and Brian rushed over.

'Can I light that for you?'

She recognised him immediately. 'Thanks.' She leant towards him half smiling without opening her lips, which gripped the cigarette. Her face glowed from the light of the flickering flame. As the tip burned red, her eyes turned to Brian's. 'You're not going to break anything are you?'

'Only your heart if you let me,' Brian joked with a big cheeky smile, but, half wondering if it was too much, added, 'sorry. Only joking. I'm on my best behaviour.'

She didn't reply, but they held eye contact for a while, both still smiling before she asked, 'what's your name?'

'Brian Hill. And yours?'

'Lisa Wentworth-Simpson.'

Brian moved his lips in response but nothing came out. He couldn't think of a reply that recognised that she had an unusual name, which was a little inconsistent with her rebellious appearance, while at the same time hiding the obvious amusement that he felt, also due to the inconsistency between her name and her appearance.

She helped him out. 'I don't look like a Wentworth-Simpson do I?'

Brian raised his eyebrows in agreement.

'Just pretend I said Lisa Evans or Lisa Jones and continue.' She was toying with him, but quite liked him. On previous occasions she had been irritated by the response she got to her upmarket name, but black clothes and heavy make-up can't hide your background. She worked for a large insurance company, which was one of the main employers in Southside. Her family didn't own the company but it did lease the premises to them. A significant portion of the town centre had been owned by the Wentworth-Simpson family since before the First World War.

Brian still had no follow-up comment, but felt that he was being warmly received so invited her to dance. She gladly accepted. The Goths were all very cool and didn't move much on the dance floor. It wasn't the done thing. Brian didn't care what the done thing was and he had fun bouncing all over the place. Lisa was very amused but slightly embarrassed as she was among Goth friends.

'Do you want to go for some chips?' she asked. It would get her away from the judging gaze of her friends while at the same time continuing her encounter with what she considered a very amusing, carefree, fun-loving young man.

'Excellent idea,' said Brian, who thought it would be a good chance to get Black Lips a little closer to his bedroom and away from her weirdo friends.

They got chips round the corner from John's Passage and walked up to the bandstand on the edge of Southside Common near the crazy golf. It was a popular place for young couples to meet but they were the only visitors. Monday night was not a busy night out for anyone other than the students taking advantage of the cheap beer at The Skin Shop.

'Do you still live with your parents?' Brian asked, remembering his brother's advice that he must take a genuine interest in girls he met. He was also remembering to look at her face and not her body.

'I have very little to do with my parents,' Lisa replied. 'We get on very well, but we see things differently.' She paused, starting to feel uneasy about the subject. She did live with them and loved them very much, but preferred not to be seen as part of a wealthy family. She wanted to be seen as an individual with pioneering ideas who had something to say that was worth listening to, fresh and relevant. 'Actually, I prefer not to talk about my parents, if you don't mind. How about you? Do you live with your parents?'

Brian was equally uncomfortable talking about his parents. Brian and Lisa were very different in many ways, but, strangely, their shared reluctance to talk about their parents, seemed to be the first thing that gave them a real affinity with each other beyond the obvious physical attraction.

'No.' Brian replied with a fixed gaze, focussed in the distance, but on nothing particular. She waited for a more thorough answer. He was looking for the right words. He wanted to be honest without giving too much away. 'I have very little to do with my parents. Well, nothing at all really. Circumstances out of my control. I have a modest trust fund which takes care of my education and basic living. It's paid direct into my bank account and that's it.'

She reached for his hand. It wasn't sexual, but Brian happily took it. Despite his sordid instincts, he unexpectedly found himself appreciating the warmth of Lisa's genuine concern, but added, 'Actually, I also prefer not to talk about my parents. Do you mind?'

'Not at all.' And she didn't. He felt the same way about his parents as she did about her own. It made her feel much better about her own stance. But she had no idea that, although he appeared to be taking a very similar position to her, it was for entirely different reasons.

She put her arm around his shoulder and gave him an encouraging peck on the cheek. The conversation flowed and Brian took her back to his room for a coffee.

By this time, Andrew Leopard had been in bed asleep for two hours having spent all evening thinking about Pink Socks, worrying about his spot and worrying even more about whether his friends Tom and Brian were enjoying their night out with Colin, Hugh and Ian. His peace was shattered as Hugh smashed his fist on Andrew's door. Andrew didn't just wake up quickly, he physically jumped. His heart was racing. Hugh's fist continued to bang loudly on his door as he shouted, 'my key won't work. What's wrong with this door? I want to go to bed.'

Andrew dared not open the door, or even turn on the light. He didn't want Hugh to know he was definitely in bed asleep, but he couldn't think what he wanted at this time of night. His heart continued pounding. Then there was a thud and a high pitched yelp, which didn't sound like Hugh. But it was. Hugh had fallen over in a drunken heap and banged his head on the painted concrete block wall. He was a large young man, who liked to be seen as a thug, but he was not good with pain and yelped like a girl.

Colin stepped over his flaccid body and took the key out of his hand. 'Wrong room mate.' He went down the corridor and opened Hugh's door. Andrew half heard Colin struggling to drag his friend along the corridor. His heart rate slowed down a little as he realised the danger had passed, then as he was almost asleep again, he heard a girl's voice followed by Brian's voice. He couldn't hear anybody else and he couldn't tell what they were saying, but they were laughing a lot. He eventually fell back into a deep sleep with dreamy images filling his head of himself and Pink Socks arriving back from The Skin Shop laughing and joking as they walked past Brian's closed door.

Chapter 13

Don't tell Hugh

Two days later, November 16, 1983: Andrew Leopard and Tom and Brian Hill gathered their books after a sociology tutorial, a small discussion group intended to compliment ideas learned in lectures. The three boys had added nothing to the debate, which dealt with Malthus and his theory of natural corrections in world population. They had all been thinking about the trip to The Skin Shop two nights earlier; Andrew because he thought he had missed out, Tom because he had enjoyed spending time with Greenpeace Badge and Brian because he wasn't sure whether he wanted to see Lisa Wentworth-Simpson again.

It was a Wednesday and that meant no lectures in the afternoon, which was set aside for sporting pursuits. Tom and Brian were playing an away football fixture at Westside University and Andrew was going into town to do the food shopping. They had very little food between them and agreed to visit the refectory for lunch.

It was a large dining hall the size of a tennis court, where students and teaching staff mixed comfortably. The food was partially subsidised and very basic, but was still a treat on the budget of most students. Tom and Brian considered it a reasonable treat considering they needed plenty of energy for their game. The match against Westside University was the local derby and a crunch game in the regional section of the national university cup competition.

They sat in a corner by the window, Tom and Andrew happy but Brian disgusted at the mess on the table, which he thought should have been cleaned up by the canteen staff. 'It wouldn't take much to wipe the table,' he said frowning.

'It's so busy, we're lucky to get a table. Besides, if they had enough staff to wipe all the tables straight away, we would have to pay more and couldn't afford to eat here,' Tom replied.

'It's only a few crumbs … it is,' added Andrew.

Brian used his paper napkin to wipe the area immediately around his plate. Tom changed the subject to stop his complaining.

'You still haven't told us how you got on with Black Lips.'

Brian had been holding back the details, because there hadn't been as much to tell as he had hoped. 'Okay. There's not much to tell. We rolled around a bit but the clothes stayed on.'

'And what's wrong with that? Sounds like an excellent start to me.' Tom was disappointed by his brother's lack of patience.

'That's just it. I didn't want it to be a start. You know me. I just wanted a shag.'

Andrew, who still hadn't progressed as far as getting Pink Socks' real name, offered his support. 'That's excellent progress … it is. When are you seeing her again?'

‘Well, that’s the thing. I’ve invited her to the Drag Disco on Friday, but I don’t want a steady girlfriend. I came to college to have fun, not to build a steady relationship. A quick shag’s alright, but that’s it.’

Andrew couldn’t understand Brian’s attitude. What Brian didn’t want was exactly what Andrew did want.

Tom did understand, but thought differently. ‘I think you’re a wally. She looked quite nice, and, from what you’ve said about her, she seems very good company. I’m looking forward to meeting her on Friday. Have you got your dress ready yet?’

‘Pretty much. I’ll get it sorted after football.’

‘I got a dress in a charity shop … I did,’ Andrew added.

Four hours later, Andrew was in great pain. Not from trying his dress on, but from doing the shopping. He carried six heavy carrier bags packed with groceries half a mile from the supermarket in the shopping centre and it felt as if they were pulling his arms off. He struggled up the stairs, along the corridor and into the kitchen, where, much to his disappointment he found Hugh.

‘What have you bought me Leopard?’ Hugh demanded with menace.

‘There’s nothing for you … nothing,’ Andrew replied nervously.

‘No problem. I’ve just eaten.’ The menace went all of a sudden and Hugh seemed almost pleasant.

Roger Evans came in and made a sandwich.

‘How’s it going Crypt?’ Hugh’s tone was still pleasant, even if his choice of words wasn’t.

Roger didn’t reply or look round or even flinch for the slightest moment in his food preparation.

Hugh tried again to trigger a reaction. 'You seen the student from room number one yet Crypt?'

Again no response. Roger finished eating, returned his pots to his cardboard box and left the room.

Andrew had been grateful that Roger had distracted Hugh's attention from him and had busied himself putting the new supplies away. He got up to leave.

'That's quite a spot you've got there Leopard.' Andrew was almost at the door but stopped, wondering how best to react. Hugh hadn't been aggressive, but again, his choice of words was unkind.

Andrew turned around to face Hugh. 'Yes. Quite a spot, but not as big as it was two days ago … it's not.'

'It doesn't look too bad. Is that the reason you have been staying in your room so much this week?' Hugh was guessing but had a fair idea that he was right.

'I haven't. I've been working hard … I have.'

'Well Andrew. I don't believe you. I think you've been hiding.' Hugh could see Andrew felt awkward.

Andrew did feel awkward; partly because it was the first time Hugh had addressed him by his first name, he was a terrible liar and just wanted to get back to his room fast. 'I have to go … I do.'

'See you later Andrew,' Hugh replied, still in an uncharacteristic soft tone.

Andrew felt relieved and reached for the door handle, pulled it open and set off to his room. Two steps later and before the kitchen door had fully shut behind him, Hugh shouted 'Andrew'.

He stopped and swallowed with a slight feeling of fear. Hugh being horrible was unpleasant, but Hugh being nice was a new situation which could be hard to handle. He turned back and stuck his head around the door. 'Yes Hugh.'

'I'm just about to make a cup of tea. Would you like one?'

Saying no would be a big insult.

'Thank-you. That's very kind … very kind.'

Hugh prepared two cups of tea, then opened the kitchen door. 'Let's take them to my room Andrew.'

Andrew followed Hugh to room number eight. It was much tidier than he had expected. Hugh may have treated the communal areas of Dickens Court with a total lack of respect, but his room was immaculate. There was a large Chinese-looking piece of fabric covering the largest wall featuring an emerald green lizard on a gold background. Andrew recognised it as the same design tattooed above Hugh's ear. On the opposite wall was a row of black and white pictures, all the same size, probably A4, each showing the face of a punk rocker. They were all as high as the ceiling and equally spaced. Sid Vicious, Hugh Cornwell, Johnny Rotten, Captain Sensible and Joe Strummer were all featured. On the floor, there was a thick Oriental rug, with rich metallic colours, very similar to the lizard embroidery on the wall.

For a moment, Andrew forgot his fear, mesmerised by the room, full of surprises that he would never have expected from a thug like Hugh.

'Have a seat Andrew.' Hugh waved his arm towards the soft chair by the wardrobe. 'Biscuit?' He held a tin towards Andrew, who was feeling more relaxed than he could have hoped.

'Thanks. You have a nice room … you have.' Not relaxed enough to lose the echo.

'You're very kind.' Hugh replied gently. 'I enjoyed my first year here at Southside. The courses were fairly easy after A-levels. How are you finding it?'

'Not so bad thanks. Probably a bit easier than A-levels … a bit easier.'

'I think they make the first year easier so students can adjust more easily to a new way of life away from home.' Hugh had gained Andrew's trust.

'You might be right … you might.'

Hugh offered Andrew another biscuit. 'Are you adjusting well? Missing anyone at home?'

Andrew was not adjusting as well as he had hoped. He missed his mother and, despite the issues he had with his father, had missed him too, much to his disgust. He was almost angry with himself for missing someone who firmly believed that he would 'never amount to anything'. Hugh seemed to understand what Andrew was feeling. Maybe he would have some good advice. He took another bite of his digestive.

'Yes. I miss people … I do.'

'Go on,' Hugh encouraged him.

But Andrew thought he should save such thoughts for Tom, who he held in the highest regard and trusted totally, unlike Hugh. He changed direction quickly. 'Yes. I miss people, but I am starting to adjust … I am.'

Hugh thought he had been close to some sensitive secrets but followed the change of direction. 'And is there anybody special here at university? Anybody who helps fills the gaps left by those back home?'

Andrew didn't want to tell Hugh how much of a rock Tom had been, but thought he could safely mention Pink Socks. Hugh seemed to be nicer than he had expected and maybe he could help. 'There is a girl I'm very fond of … I am.'

Hugh's eyes lit up. He was getting somewhere now. 'And what's her name?' he asked casually, reaching for another biscuit.

'Well. I don't know. I haven't asked her yet … I haven't.'

Hugh disguised his amusement and pushed for more details. 'If you don't even know her name, how can you be so fond of her?'

'She's beautiful and has a kind smile. You can see how considerate she is by the way she talks to her friends and she laughs a lot … she does.'

'It sounds to me like you are more than fond of … what was her name again?'

'Pink Socks.'

'Pink Socks?'

'She had pink socks on the first time I saw her and that's what I call her … I do.'

'So. As I was saying. It sounds to me like you are more than "fond" of Pink Socks."

Andrew hadn't even told Tom yet that he loved Pink Socks, but he felt he could tell Hugh.

'Please don't tell anyone, but, yes, you're right. More than fond. I love her. I love Pink Socks.'

Hugh was now struggling to hide his amusement and a smile crept across his face. 'Marvellous. You're in love. I do think you should ask her what her name is though.' The sincerity was slipping.

Andrew started to feel he had made a mistake and got up to leave. 'Thanks for the tea. I must start cooking. Tom and Brian will be back soon. You won't tell anyone will you … will you?'

Hugh's sneer returned as he assured Andrew his secret was safe and ushered him out of room eight.

Andrew prepared sausages, which he grilled, mash, made from powdered potato, and spaghetti from a tin. As he was trying to squash the lumps of powder in the mash, the door flew open and the Hill brothers marched in triumphantly chanting football songs having narrowly beaten Westside University to qualify for the knockout stages of the national cup competition.

Andrew felt a warm rush of camaraderie as both Tom and Brian kissed him on the cheek and lifted him off the ground as if they were raising the national cup. As they sat down to eat, Brian talked Andrew through his winning goal. Ian Mellor came in for his tea and Brian talked him through his winning goal. Roger Evans came in and Brian did the same again, but this time with no response at all. Hugh and Colin came in next and Brian started to talk them through his winning goal before Hugh stopped him.

The kitchen was full, except the student from room one, who still hadn't been seen by anybody. Hugh had a large audience as he betrayed Andrew's trust. 'Brian. You are not the only one with good news. Friend Andrew here has something to share with us all.'

Andrew had been feeling good, but suddenly he was emotionally deflated. He knew what was coming and he wanted to be anywhere but the kitchen on floor three of Dickens Court, block F.

'Tell us Andrew.' Hugh was beaming triumphantly.

'What is it?' Brian was curious.

'Yes. What is it?' Colin knew already and couldn't wait to see Andrew's embarrassment.

Tom could see his friend was mortified. 'Just eat your tea Andrew. You don't have to tell anybody anything.'

A short silence followed with everybody watching Andrew.

Hugh, who was loving the pain he could see in Andrew's face, ended the silence. 'Andrew told me he loves Pink Socks. Pink Socks! Can you believe that? He doesn't even know her name, but he loves her.'

Andrew put his hands in his pockets and looked down at his feet. He felt like crying, but that would be humiliation on a new level.

Colin Dean started singing. 'He wants to kiss her. He wants to marry her. He thinks he loves her.'

It was too much for Andrew. He ran out of the kitchen and locked himself in his room and lay on his bed with his head in his hands. He had only felt this bad once before and he could hear his father's words repeating over and over in his head.

'You didn't pack the pump. You stupid boy. What were you thinking? No wonder you haven't got any friends. You'll never amount to anything.'

'Andrew told me he loves Pink Socks. Pink Socks. Can you believe that? He doesn't even know her name, but he loves her.'

'You stupid boy. No wonder you haven't got any friends. You'll never amount to anything.'

Maybe his father was right. He couldn't even ask the girl her name. And how pathetic must he be to have made the same mistake twice. After confiding in his father he had promised himself not to make the same mistake again. Why did he tell Hugh? He's the nastiest person he knew. How could he have been so stupid?

In the kitchen Hugh and Colin had not stopped laughing and Ian Mellor was still smiling. Brian was slightly amused but saw an opportunity to have a couple of extra sausages. Roger Evans carried on as if nothing had happened, put his pots in a cardboard box and left the room. Tom, however, was disgusted.

'Hugh. You're a twat. Why don't you give the boy a break? You can see he's struggling. The last thing he needs is somebody pointing out his weaknesses.' Tom didn't raise his voice but hoped his words might have some impact on Hugh.

They didn't. It was water off a duck's back and Hugh was still smiling. 'You're right Tom, but come on. He doesn't even know her name yet. He's got to grow some balls. If it don't kill you, it makes you stronger. Maybe I've done him a favour.'

Tom shook his head and left the room. He knocked gently on Andrew's door. No answer. He knocked a little harder.

'Who is it?'

'Tom.' A moment later the key turned and the door slowly opened. Tom went in closing the door behind him and settled down in the soft chair. Andrew sat up on the bed.

For a couple of minutes, they said nothing. Tom thought it best to leave Andrew to his thoughts first. When he was ready to talk, Tom would listen.

Eventually Andrew looked at Tom. 'I'm sorry. I don't know why I told Hugh. I wanted to tell you first … I did.'

The last thing Tom wanted was an apology. He was worried about his friend and wanted to build his confidence back up. 'You've nothing to be sorry for.' He paused before adding, 'do you love her?'.

Andrew raised his eyebrows in a manner which gave his answer greater meaning. 'Yes. Yes I think I do.' He stopped to gather his thoughts before adding, 'I know I don't know her name and have only said one sentence to her, but I've seen her with other people. She's special and yes, I love her … I do.'

Tom took in what Andrew was saying. He had to give him good advice. 'There's nothing wrong with that and if it's a genuine feeling, you shouldn't care what Hugh has to say. But you mustn't trust him. Some thoughts are best kept to yourself.'

'You're right. I know you're right and it's not the first time I've made that mistake … it's not.' Andrew was feeling as low as he had ever felt and once the subject had been introduced, he couldn't stop talking. He told Tom all about the caravan trip to Wales and his father's cruel words.

Tom listened with sympathy before telling Andrew about his own parents.

After hearing Tom's story, Andrew decided his parents were not so bad after all. 'You should spend the Christmas holiday with my family … Brian too.'

'Don't say it if you don't mean it. I might just hold you to that.' Tom had no plans for Christmas and Andrew's offer was the most sensible he had so far. Greenpeace Badge had offered, but with the complication of the boyfriend, Tom wasn't keen.

'Right. I'm off now. Got to sort out my dress for Friday.' The Drag Disco was a very popular annual event at Southside University and if you didn't dress up you couldn't get in. 'But one last thing before I go. This stuff about Wales and your father.'

'Yes,' said Andrew expectantly.

'Don't tell Hugh.'

Chapter 14

The Drag Disco

Three days later, November 19, 1983: It was Saturday, which for Tom and Brian Hill was another football day, but this time against local teams, rather than other colleges. It had been a good win for Southside University but Tom had played a very mediocre game. He was in a thoughtful mood ahead of The Drag Disco and sat alone in his room with no lights watching his small black and white television.

He wasn't a fan of game shows and turned it off leaving the room almost dark. His curtains were still open and the soft amber glow of the footpath lights three floors down filled his small study room. He knelt on his bed and looked out of the window with his head resting on his hands and his elbows resting on the windowsill. Looking down at the cherry and silver birch trees with the wide paths and grassed area in front of Dickens Court, there was clean snow reflecting the orange light. Winter arrived two days before and steady snowfall had left a crisp thin layer across the whole of Southside.

Tom enjoyed moments of peace when he could collect his thoughts and reflect on the big questions in life like why we are here and what happens when we die or why is there so much pain in the world? He never had any clear answers, but firmly believed that you make your own luck and when you're gone you're gone. He had shared these thoughts most recently with Greenpeace Badge, who thought very differently. She told him everything happened for a reason and would often say to him 'if it isn't meant to be, it isn't meant to be'.

Andrew Leopard knocked on Tom's door half expecting Tom to be out, as there was no light at the foot of his door. Tom pulled it open and flicked on the lights before looking Andrew up and down. He wore a knee length red dress, a blonde wig and black fishnet stockings.

'What do you think?' Andrew asked. He needed approval. The large spot he had earlier in the week was now almost faded away and the bright clothes and make-up drew attention away from the few spots he still had, so Andrew was feeling relatively good, despite being dressed as a woman.

'The dress fits well, but your breasts are at different heights and you only appear to have one hip.'

'What about my lipstick?'

'Bright and smudged but effective.'

'I think I've laddered my stockings … I do.'

'Wouldn't worry. It's fashionable.' Tom hadn't started dressing for The Drag Disco, but his gear was all prepared.

The Drag Disco was such a popular event that it had to be held in the Main Hall, the venue used when bands played at the college or for exams at the end of the academic year. It had its own bar in a separate adjoining room. It was getting close to the end of the first term and many of the students were starting to run up heavy overdrafts at the bank. Grants were paid at the start of each term. As a result, Andrew, Tom and Brian had agreed to go out a bit later than normal and start the evening drinking cans from the supermarket in their study rooms.

As Tom slipped into an extremely short green dress he had picked up at a jumble sale, Andrew opened a couple of cans and sat looking at his beer through the small opening in the top of the can. He had spent most of the afternoon, as usual, thinking about Pink Socks and had reached the conclusion that Tom would not have had the same problems he was having. And not just because he was better looking, but because he knew what to say and do and when to say and do the right thing. In short, if Andrew were Tom, he and Pink Socks would now be a couple. If he could think like Tom, he could make the next step. With this in mind, he had decided to try and be more like Tom.

He watched Tom apply his lipstick in the mirror above the sink in the corner.

'Tom!'

'Yes Andrew.'

'I think I need a new approach … I do.'

'To what?'

'Pink Socks,' he said assertively before expanding. 'Well. Not just Pink Socks. Everything really.'

'Sounds like a good plan.'

'If you fancied Pink Socks, you would have done something about it and she would be your girlfriend by now.'

'Not necessarily. But, yes, I would have done something.'

'My mother always tells me that the right girl is out there waiting to meet me and I'll know she is the one when I meet her … I will.'

'So your mother believes in fate? Whatever is going to happen will happen and there's nothing you can do about it?'

'Pretty much. Yes.'

'So if Pink Socks is the right girl for you, you just have to wait and it will happen?'

'Yes.'

'Do you really believe she's right?'

Andrew thought for a moment. He had never doubted that she was right. 'I'm sure she's right, but if I thought like you, it would help move things along a bit faster.'

'So does that mean I was destined to meet Greenpeace Badge?'

'I think it does. Yes. After all, you didn't approach her, she reached past you to look at a poster and you acted in your usual way, which led to a close bond. If she had reached past me to the poster, nothing would have happened. So what do you do differently to me? How can I be more like you?'

Tom rubbed his chin in thought. He had no patience for people who sat back and waited for things to happen to them. He liked Andrew a lot and wanted him to be happy but felt very strongly that Andrew would never be happy unless he took control of his own life and made things happen. Andrew was now asking Tom how he could give fate a little push. That was tough to answer when you don't believe in fate at all.

After a great deal of chin rubbing and considered thought, Tom came up with a plan. He finished his second can of beer, adjusted his false breasts and sat next to Andrew.

'So. As I understand it, you want me to teach you my approach to life?'

'If you could, that would be fantastic … it would.'

'Okay, here's what you must do.' Andrew listened carefully in the firm belief that his wise and gifted friend would help him get close to Pink Socks. 'I want you to do three tasks this evening and then I'll tell you what they mean.'

'I'm happy with that.'

'You can't ask me what the tasks mean until the end of the evening.'

Andrew nodded.

'You just do them without question.'

Andrew nodded again.

'Agreed.'

'Yes. Agreed.'

'Right. First thing you must do is walk across campus to the football pitch and pretend to score a penalty before kissing each post.'

'In my dress and stilettos through the snow?'

'Yes. And on the way back, after every ten steps, you must stand on one leg and bark like a dog.'

Andrew screwed his face up in horror. 'You're joking right?'

'No. It doesn't matter if you score the penalty. It's an imaginary ball. Kiss the posts and come back.'

'Barking on one foot every tenth step?'

'Yes. Every tenth step. And when we go out tonight, for the whole evening, if anybody drops the word disco into the conversation, you must say to them "do you come here often?" again standing on one leg.'

Andrew now looked utterly bewildered but nodded slowly and set off to the football pitch.

Fifteen minutes later, Brian, next door to Tom, was on his third can of lager and was struggling with his suspender belt when he thought he heard a dog bark outside. He had been listening to Bohemian Rhapsody by Queen and turned the music down before looking out of the window. He had never seen a dog on campus.

There was no dog, but Brian was very alarmed to see where the noise was coming from. Andrew Leopard, wearing a red dress, blonde wig, bright red lipstick and stiletto heels was making very slow progress towards Dickens Court. He must have thought he was being followed because he stopped every few steps and looked all around before barking like a dog with one foot off the ground.

Things then got even more surreal as Brian looked beyond Andrew to see what appeared to be a Chicago gangster fast approaching his timid friend. The gangster had a violin case, presumably a machine gun, under his arm and wore a fat white tie over a black shirt with a brown pin-striped suit. Brian expected trouble but the gangster stopped to talk to Andrew and the two walked together towards Dickens Court.

Brian returned to his suspender belt. He was a little nervous. It was nearly a week since he had rolled around on the bed with Black Lips and was already regretting inviting her to The Drag Disco. He had been very drunk at The Skin Shop and a few weak cans of cheap lager had not been enough to prepare him for her visit. He had thought about the possibility of a long-term relationship all week. To Brian a fortnight would mean long-term and he had concluded that he couldn't afford it. Beer, football, one-night stands. He had to focus on his priorities.

There was a knock at the door. Brian shouted 'come in', but when the gangster pushed open the door and pointed the violin case straight at him as he struggled with his lingerie, he fell back in a heap on the floor spilling beer all over his dress.

'You're obviously pleased to see me,' said Lisa Wentworth-Simpson, her stick-on moustache twitching as her black lips moved.

'Ooh … you gave me a fright. What an excellent costume.'

'Looks like you need a bit of help with your underwear,' said Lisa, reaching for Brian's thighs.

Tom and Andrew let themselves in. Andrew had already introduced himself To Lisa. Tom didn't wait for an introduction.

'You must be Lisa. I'm Brian's brother Tom. Excellent outfit.'

'Why thank-you. And that's a very nice green dress you're wearing,' She then grimaced a little. 'Although it doesn't match your lippy and you've got more on your face than your lips.' She then turned back to Brian. 'I think I'd better do your lipstick.'

She carefully did his lips, which completed the outfit. 'Beautiful. You're quite the disco diva.'

Andrew stood on one leg and quietly asked Lisa if she came here often.

'Sorry Andrew?' she asked.

'Nothing … no. Nothing.'

'Louder next time,' Tom urged Andrew.

They collected Hugh Grundy, Colin Dean and Ian Mellor in the kitchen and headed for the Main Hall. The six boys and Lisa stood at the bar in their dresses and gangster outfit studying the room for people they knew. There were plenty. It was packed and a lot of students had gone to a lot of trouble dressing up.

Andrew bought the drinks for Tom, Brian and Lisa. A tall bearded barman handed Andrew his change.

'While it lasts, we have special disco punch for 50p a glass.'

'Do you come here often?' replied Andrew.

The barman looked at Andrew with disgust. 'You gay or something?'

Tom overheard and rescued Andrew. 'Sorry mate. He's a Danish exchange student. Gets mixed up.'

The barman smiled at Tom understanding the error and spoke very slowly to Andrew one word at a time. 'I'm … sorry … Have … a … good … evening.'

They edged away from the bar. 'Thanks Tom.'

'No problem. Right. Here's the third task for tonight.'

Andrew leant towards Tom. The music was quite loud. 'If anybody says the word "original" tonight, and that's unlikely, you must say to them "are you a lesbian?" Okay?'

'I can't see that happening. So, okay.' Andrew was bemused by his tasks, but prepared to go along with them in his pursuit of Pink Socks, even though the barman nearly punched him.

'Can you see Pink Socks here?'

Andrew had a good look around to check. He had already checked the whole room for her three times. 'No.'

'Good. You need to practise talking to girls. Do you recognise anybody else from your economics and politics course?'

'There's a couple of girls over by the fire exit, but I've never spoken to them in class.'

'Follow me.' Tom headed for the two girls with Andrew reluctantly following.

'Hi. How's it going?' Tom asked the girls with a friendly smile.

'Good thanks.'

'You look like economics and politics students.'

'How do you know?' said the taller of the two coal miners.

'Complete guess,' said Tom, 'but the miners' strikes in the 70s were a big issue in the world of economics and politics, so it would be a good choice of outfit.'

The taller miner had been taken in by Tom, but the other girl recognised Andrew and faced him. 'Hold on a minute. You're on our course aren't you?'

Andrew was feeling the effects of the canned lager, which gave him a small boost in confidence. 'Yes. I've seen you … I have.'

'You never talk to anyone. We thought you didn't like us.'

Tom again rescued Andrew. 'Oh not at all. He's very friendly … just extremely studious.'

The taller miner wasn't convinced. 'We certainly didn't expect to see you at The Drag Disco.'

Andrew raised his left leg and replied. 'Do you come here often?'

'Ooh … that's original,' said the tall miner.

'Are you a lesbian?' Andrew said reluctantly.

'Charming. We were right. You're not very friendly.' The girls hurried off.

'I think I offended them … I did.'

'Who cares? It was funny.' Tom couldn't hide his amusement and laughed, slapping Andrew on the back, which jolted the lower of his two breasts further down towards his tummy.

Tom and Andrew returned to the others to find Hugh, Colin and Ian taking much more interest in Lisa than Brian.

Hugh tried his luck first. 'Are you Brian's bird or can you dance with me?'

'Well … actually … '

'How about a dance with me?' Colin butted in before she could finish answering Hugh.

'I don't think … '

'Let's hit the dance floor baby.' Ian also dived in before she had chance to answer.

Brian returned after a lengthy conversation with another player from the football team, who had taken part in the same game earlier but still had to listen to Brian talking him through another goal, which he assured him was even better than his winner against Westside earlier in the week.

'Would you like to dance?' Lisa asked Brian, anxious to get away from the unwanted attention of his friends.

'Sure.' They headed for the dance floor, Brian still holding his beer. He wiggled his hips a bit, but not with any great enthusiasm. He didn't want to spill his beer.

'Your friends all asked me to dance with them,' she told him.

'Bastards,' he replied with feeling, not because he was worried he may lose Lisa, but because his friends had tried to take her from behind his back. It would have suited him if she had danced with one of them.

Lisa, on the other hand, had built up her hopes during the week that Brian could be a good long-term prospect. She had been looking forward to The Drag Disco and taken the previous day off work to prepare her outfit.

'I enjoyed our time together on Monday,' she whispered in his ear.

'Me too,' he replied trying a little harder to sound sincere.

'I quite like you.' It was her first compliment.

'You're pretty special yourself.' Brian played along. 'I'm out of breath. Let's sit down.'

They returned to the others. Andrew was looking unhappy after offending his fellow politics students. Lisa, being very kind-hearted, saw his discomfort. 'You don't look too happy. What's wrong?'

Lisa was spoken for so Andrew felt comfortable talking to her. 'I can't talk to girls and when I do, they call me unfriendly and walk away.'

'You don't seem unfriendly to me. Let's sit down and you can tell me more.' She guided him to the seats and Brian was relieved to be able to share a beer with his floor-mates, with Lisa safely in the hands of the one person Brian knew would never ask her for a dance.

'You shagged her yet?' asked Hugh.

'Of course ... she's only human,' Brian replied defensively.

Tom had noticed his brother's flippant treatment of his guest and ushered him to one side for a quiet word.

'I know it's none of my business, but it looks like she's fallen for you and you're treating her very badly. It's a shame because she's lovely. Better than you deserve.'

'I know. You're right, but I don't want a steady girlfriend so what do I do?'

'Just be honest and tell her how you feel, but do it soon. Leave it too long and you'll hurt her even more.'

Brian looked past Tom to where Lisa and Andrew were deep in conversation. Andrew was enjoying the attention and Lisa was enjoying the chance to help somebody who seemed to be a genuinely good person.

'Leave it with me Tom. I'll have to wait for the right moment.'

The brothers went back to the others. Hugh and Colin were winding up Ian who had not had much luck with his chat-up line of 'let's hit the dance floor baby', which he had tried four times. To make things even harder for Ian, Hugh had placed one hand on top of his head and rubbed his left cheek with his other hand. This had been a distraction so Colin could place a condom on Ian's right shoulder without him noticing. The lubricant held the condom in place on Ian's blue nylon dress.

Hugh then offered Ian an incentive. 'Ian. Your chat-up line is rubbish, but if it works on that fat girl at the end of the bar, I'll buy you a pint.'

'You're on big man. Just watch and learn.'

Ian strutted towards the chosen girl. 'Let's hit the dance floor baby,' he said with great confidence, but the girl seemed distracted. She was looking at his shoulder. He followed her gaze and saw the condom. His shocked red face turned to see his floor-mates creased up with laughter. It was too much embarrassment. He left.

Two hours later Colin and Hugh headed for the Coffee Bar while Lisa, Andrew, Tom and Brian trudged through the snow back to Dickens Court.

'That was a good disco,' Lisa said, waving her violin case in Brian's direction.

'Do you …' Andrew began.

'It's okay. The game's over,' Tom stopped him.

'So. Can you tell me now?' Andrew asked, with no echo; again due to the volume of alcohol.

'Yes. What's it all about?' asked Lisa, who had been told about the tasks by Andrew.

'So YOU made Andrew bark!' Things fell into place for Brian.

'I'll tell you over coffee. You joining us Lisa?' Tom asked, because he knew Brian wouldn't.

The four of them made themselves comfortable in Andrew's room and helped themselves to his stock of custard creams. Andrew put on his Jim Reeves tape, which played quietly in the background. Tom sat at the desk, Andrew in the soft chair and Brian alongside Lisa on the bed leaning back against the wall. Lisa felt very comfortable, Brian felt very uncomfortable and Andrew wanted to know why he had been standing on one leg for most of the evening.

'Okay Tom. I've completed all the tasks. What was their meaning?'

Tom had everybody's undivided attention and looked Andrew in the eye knowing he would be unhappy with his answer.

'Andrew,' he paused. 'The tasks have no meaning whatsoever. They were utterly pointless and will tell you no more about me, or you, than you already know.'

'Excellent.' Brian laughed.

Lisa raised her eyebrows hoping for a better explanation, while Andrew felt a little cheated.

'So if they were pointless. Why did you make me do them?'

Tom addressed Andrew more firmly. He wanted him to see the point and accept it.

'Life is a random set of opportunities that fall in your path. Nothing happens for a reason that has been pre-planned by anybody. What you do with the opportunities you are given is entirely down to you. If you want something to happen. You have to make it happen. Nobody can do that for you.'

Andrew looked disappointed. Tom was looking for a glint of realisation in Andrew's eyes, but saw nothing, so he continued.

'You are waiting for Pink Socks to come to you because your mum told you it's in the stars. That's a load of bollocks. Total and utter bollocks. If you want to get close to Pink Socks, or whatever her name is, you've got to go to her and ask her out. She might say yes. She might say no. It doesn't matter if you fail. At least you could move on.'

Tom stopped, waiting for a positive reaction.

'Your destiny is in YOUR hands. Nobody else's. Can you see what I am saying?'

Andrew didn't want to give up on his idea that fate would take care of him. The thought that he had no choices in life and all would be taken care of was comforting.

'I can see what you're saying,' Andrew squirmed. It was hard to disagree with his best friend when Tom had been so passionate in his delivery. 'But there must be some greater guiding force.'

That set Tom off again. 'Andrew. We're born. We live. We die. We're not put here for a reason and we go nowhere when we're dead. We are JUST here. Even the Bible says we come into the world with nothing and we take nothing when we go. When you're dead, you're dead, but while you're here, you make the most of the opportunities that fall in your path. All I did tonight was change your path slightly.'

Andrew, Brian and Lisa had slipped into deep thought, tossing the ideas over in their minds. Tom was ready to defend his ideas and his treatment of Andrew, which he believed had been necessary to shock him into doing something about the girl he thought he loved.

As Jim Reeves sang Distant Drums in the background Lisa had a few ideas of her own to share.

'So. Tom. You don't believe in life after death?' she asked.

'Dead is dead is dead.'

'Maybe it's not that simple,' said Lisa.

Tom was always prepared to listen to new ideas. Brian grabbed two more custard creams. Andrew was still shell-shocked.

Lisa continued. 'Well … I heard a theory once, and I think there's something to it, that your soul never dies. Experiments have been done that show animals lose a tiny amount of weight the very instant they die. Some believe that could be the soul leaving the body.'

Brian was sceptical and nodded but with a smile that said he found the idea a bit crazy. Tom considered the theory but had no response. Andrew was imagining himself approaching Pink Socks and had heard very little of what Lisa had said.

She went on. 'Maybe that's why people who have a brush with death have an out-of-body experience. Perhaps they have died, the soul leaves the body, but returns when the person is revived and bought back to life.'

'Could be,' Tom acknowledged. 'So where does the soul go?'

'Who knows? Maybe it enters another body the instant they are born or conceived. Some think the soul enters animals. Maybe it just sits in limbo not realising it has left the body. There could be loads of lost souls floating around not realising they are dead.'

Brian thought this a bit silly. 'I think they would realise they were dead as time passed and they got hungry.'

'But what if time is meaningless when the soul leaves the body. When the soul lived in the body, the body needed the food and the body wore out and died, not the soul. Perhaps time is meaningless for the lost soul as it waits for a new body.'

Tom was following the idea with interest. 'Then a few seconds would be the same as a few years?'

'Yes,' agreed Lisa, pleased that at least Tom had followed the argument, even if Brian looked thoroughly bored and Andrew had fallen asleep.

‘We’d best leave him to it,’ Tom said, covering Andrew with a blanket.

Lisa went to the toilet.

‘You haven’t talked to her yet have you?’ Tom asked while it was just the two of them.

‘Not had chance, but it’s worse than that. She’s asked me to go to dinner with her parents next Saturday and I didn’t say no, which she took as a yes, but I can’t go anyway.’

‘Why not?’

‘Derrr. Football club night out.’ Brian couldn’t believe Tom had forgotten.

Tom couldn’t believe Brian was putting football ahead of Lisa’s feelings.

When she returned, Tom left them to it in the hope that Brian would do the right thing.

Chapter 15

Football club night out

A week later, November 26, 1983: Fifteen players from Southside University Football Club sat on both sides of a long narrow table in the Red Lion. Tom Hill sat between Slogger and Leaps Like A Salmon, while Brian Hill sat opposite Tom, between Who Me and I Got The Last Touch.

‘They took £25m worth of gold bullion this morning from the Brinks Mat warehouse near Heathrow. That’s less than 20 miles from here,’ said Who Me, a player always in trouble with the referee.

'That's enough to buy eight Diego Maradonas,' replied I Got The Last Touch, who often claimed goals following goalmouth scrambles.

Slogger's booming voice briefly overpowered the others. 'Maradona's a girl. Barcelona and all your other top European teams are full of pansies. You only have to breathe on them and they fall over. You have to be tough. It's a man's game and tough tackling wins games.'

The team was split between those who preferred the traditional English style of football and those who preferred the technically superior continental game. Slogger, captain and centreback for the second team, as his name suggested, was in favour of the more physical English game.

Leaps Like A Salmon, who was good in the air, but even better with the ball at his feet, disagreed. 'Bollocks Slogger. Football is a game of chess. It's a thinking man's game and the Italians have got all the right moves. That's why they are world champions for the third time.'

'Brazil have won it three times as well,' shouted Brian. 'Silky skills are the key. If it's not entertaining, it's not worth winning.'

Brian was a very skilful striker and scored a lot of goals, often from hopeless situations, but when trying the almost impossible he sometimes gave the ball away. Tom, on the other hand, was a no-nonsense central midfield player and never gave the ball away, but he rarely scored goals. The two brothers were very different in many ways and Tom was now suspecting that his brother had not done the right thing with Lisa Wentworth-Simpson.

'Another drink Brian?' Tom shouted over the heated discussion.

'Please.'

'Come and help me.'

'What? Carry two drinks?'

'Yes.' Insisted Tom.

Brian slipped away from the table and joined his brother at the bar.

'Have you phoned her yet?' Tom asked. Lisa was probably, at this very minute, singing Brian's praises to her parents and waiting eagerly for a knock at the front door.

'Not yet.' Brian could see the disappointment in his brother's face. 'I meant to, but ...'

'But what?' Tom knew his brother didn't want a regular girlfriend but he didn't want to end things either. Brian had enjoyed another roll on the bed after The Drag Disco, but still not used one of his condoms. He half wanted to take the relationship further, but didn't want to have to put the work in and, for Brian, it was work.

'But I was too busy.'

'No you weren't.' Tom didn't like being fobbed off. 'Whether you see her again or not, at least have the good manners to let her know you can't make it tonight.'

'I will.'

'Now. Or I'll do it for you, and that would definitely bring things to an end.' Tom handed his brother a two pence coin for the payphone.

Brian dialled the number. It was engaged. 'Let's get the beers and I'll try again.' He tried again. Still engaged. 'I promise I'll try again later.'

They returned to the table where the footballers were arranging a game. Losers would have to drink some of their beer, the amount depending on how badly they lost. It ranged from one to four fingers depth on their pint glasses, with the fingers placed horizontally on the outside of the glass. All drinking was to be done using the left hand. Again there were drinking fines if you made a mistake, levied by Slogger, who was elected as drinking chairman for the evening. If a fine of more than four fingers were needed, the offender would be ordered to drop his pants and show his bum, as Brian had done for the ladies of the women's institute two months previously at the Wanderer's Rest. In the first game, the players took turns to name a newspaper in time to rhythmic clapping and table thumping.

Thump, thump, clap. 'The Guardian.' Tom.

Thump, thump, clap. 'Daily Telegraph.' Leaps Like A Salmon.

Thump, thump, clap. 'Daily Mail.' I Got The Last Touch.

Thump, thump, clap. 'Southside Gazette.' Brian.

Thump, thump, clap. 'The Sun.' Who Me.

'That's not a newspaper,' shouted Slogger. 'It's a comic. Two fingers.' Who Me disagreed but kept his thoughts to himself. If he questioned the chairman, his fine would probably be doubled for showing a lack of respect for the leader. The players jeered loudly as Who Me drank his beer.

'Two more fingers Who Me. You used your right hand,' Slogger added quickly followed by more jeers as Who Me drank more beer.

Brian had a mouthful of his beer, but was seen by the chairman.

'I didn't give you permission to drink Brian,' Slogger blasted with authority.

'Sorry Mr Chairman.'

'Two fingers.'

Who Me lost the last game so he started the next round and chose phrases to describe women's breasts.

Thump, thump, clap. 'Tits.' Who Me.

Thump, thump, clap. 'Knockers.' Goal Hanger.

Thump, thump, clap. 'Boobs.' The Hard Man, first team captain.

Thump, thump, clap. '… err.'

Slogger thought it a serious crime to lose after only three people on the subject of breasts. 'Four fingers.' Loud laughter.

'Four fingers?' High pitched protest.

'Your whole pint.' Slogger wasn't prepared to have his authority questioned.

Erections came next.

'Hard on.'

'Wood.' Tom.

'Stiffy.'

'Ramrod.'

'Boner.' Brian.

' … err … ' Who Me couldn't think straight. He had been punished too often. He had an empty glass and anticipated the loud cries for punishment. He climbed on his chair, turned around, undid his belt and dropped his pants to whistles, cheers and loud applause.

The footballers went through another three games, countless beers and a number of exposed bottoms before Who Me fell asleep as singing took over from games. When a song about sexual activity with a variety of animals came to an end, Who Me woke up and reached for his beer. It wasn't there. He had finished it and the barmaid had taken his empty glass, but in his drunken state, he thought his pint had been taken.

'Where's my drink?'

'What was it?' asked Slogger.

'A pint.'

'A pint of what?' asked Tom.

'Lager probably. Who cares anyway. I can drink anything.'

'Anything?' asked Brian, doubting Who Me's bold claim.

'Anything Brian.'

'I bet you can't.'

'I bet I can.' Who Me's drunken bravado was about to be tested.

The noise level had dropped as all the players listened to Brian and Who Me. 'Five quid says your full of shit.' Brian offered the bet.

'Your on.' The boys shook hands vigorously.

Brian finished his pint and invited a few of the players into the toilets. They returned five minutes later with Brian's pint glass full of urine. Brian placed the glass of warm yellow liquid in front of Who Me.

'There you go,' said Brian proudly.

But Who Me didn't look as surprised as Brian had hoped. He lifted the glass in front of his face, took a long look at the contents, then downed it in one, slamming the empty glass back on the table.

For a brief moment, the footballers were silent in disbelief, but then gave Who Me the loudest cheer of the night.

Who Me held his hand out towards Brian. 'Five quid mate.'

Brian didn't have that much left and thought quickly. 'Double or quits?'

Who Me was feeling invincible and shook Brian's hand vigorously. 'You're on, but I feel bad taking your money.'

Brian picked up Who Me's empty glass and disappeared to the toilets again. Ten minutes later he returned with a pint of what he described as 'toilet punch'. As soon as Who Me saw Brian's disgusting cocktail, he vomited the pint of urine, among other things, all over Slogger and I Got The Last Touch, who had been proudly thumping him on the back.

This was too much for the landlord who ushered the footballers quickly off his property. All 15 boys made it back to the university, but they were too late for last orders at the union bar and headed for the Coffee Bar.

The other customers were not pleased to see the footballers, who bullied the staff into turning up the juke-box. They all sang loudly along to Come On Eileen by Dexy's Midnight Runners.

Who Me saw his girlfriend standing in the corner and rushed over. They kissed passionately for a moment before Who Me helped himself to her cheese toastie. Tom wondered if she could taste what her boyfriend had been drinking earlier in the evening.

The footballers were singing Pinball Wizard by The Who as Andrew Leopard walked through the door after an evening in front of the television with Ian Mellor. He was looking for Brian after taking a number of phone calls in the Dickens Court kitchen from a very angry Lisa.

He quickly found the footballers, but had trouble being heard.

'Brian.' Even shouting, Andrew's voice didn't carry well.

'Brian.' He tried again.

After six tries, Brian saw him and turned with a smile and clasped Andrew's cheeks in his hands. 'Andrew, my little love muscle. How are you?'

'I have a message for you … I have.'

'Pardon.'

Andrew shouted. 'Lisa phoned.'

'Shit.' Andrew now had Brian's full attention. 'What did she say?'

'She wanted to know where you were.'

'What did you tell her?' Brian asked urgently.

'I said I didn't know, but she kept ringing back and I told her you were in town … I did.'

'Bollocks. At least you didn't tell her we would be in the Coffee Bar.'

Andrew didn't reply but the pained expression on his face told Brian that Lisa knew he was in the Coffee Bar. 'Shit. I'd better get out of here.'

Too late. Lisa was striding towards Brian with menace.

'Bastard.' She shouted with venom.

Brian thought to himself that she was quite right to be angry. He had spent the evening drinking with his football friends while she had spent the evening with her parents waiting for Brian to turn up for dinner. He hadn't tried to call her again. He still had Tom's two pence coin in his pocket. The noise level in the Coffee Bar had dropped as the customers had all turned to see what was happening.

'Why didn't you at least phone me? It was humiliating waiting for you with my mum and dad after I had foolishly told them how nice you were.'

Brian had no answers. He could see she had been crying and he knew she had a difficult relationship with her parents, so this couldn't have helped.

'I tried to call but you were engaged.' Brian looked around at the coffee drinkers. Their expressions were condemning. Lisa had their support. Even some of the footballers appeared to be on her side.

'Bollocks you tried. I can't have been engaged all week.' Lisa was even more wound up by Brian's lame excuses. The anger was overpowering and she launched a fist towards Brian's face.

The strike was unexpected and the impact, which later gave Brian a black eye of a similar shade to Lisa's black lips, pushed him off balance and he fell to the ground. Lisa turned and left to gentle applause from the majority of girls in the room and even a few of the men.

Brian picked himself off the floor and the conversation slowly returned to normal in the Coffee Bar. Through his half-closed eye, Brian saw Tom looking at him in judgement. The look was enough. No words were needed.

'Sorry Brian.' Andrew needed forgiveness.

'Oh don't worry Andrew. It's not your fault. I'm the plank.' He gently massaged his swollen eye, but was still looking at the door fearing further attacks, when Pink Socks came in with her friends. 'Look who's here Andrew.' His smile returned knowing that the attention would be switched away from him now.

Andrew watched her buy a drinking chocolate but tried not to look over too often, so as not to appear like a stalker. Good advice from Tom, who joined his brother and Andrew. Next to walk through the door was Colin Dean followed by Hugh Grundy. They had also enjoyed a night on the town despite being heavily overdrawn at the bank.

'Now's your chance,' Tom said, placing a friendly hand on Andrew's shoulder.

'Leopard's chance for what?' asked Hugh, who joined his floor-mates.

'To meet Pink Socks,' said Brian foolishly, as Hugh and Colin didn't know what she looked like and it would have probably been best kept that way.

Hugh looked around for a girl with Pink Socks, but the Coffee Bar was too busy to get a clear look at anybody's feet. It wasn't hard to pick her out though as Andrew checked she was still there every couple of minutes.

'Aahh … very nice. Out of your league though. Be okay for me,' Hugh teased Andrew.

'I would,' said Colin.

'You going to speak to her then Leopard?' Hugh said with a cocky smile.

Andrew had waited all term to meet Pink Socks. He certainly wasn't going to do it with Hugh and Colin in the background waiting to laugh if he failed. 'Now's not a good time. It'll wait … it will.'

'Don't mind if I have a go do you?' It was rhetorical. Hugh and Colin headed for Pink Socks, while Andrew simmered with quiet rage. His spots were under control at the moment and, before Hugh and Colin had come in, he had been close to making his first move. His mood went downhill as he watched with despair. Pinks Socks was happy to chat with Colin and Hugh and was even laughing with them. What could she possibly see in them?

'They don't care about Pinks Socks,' he said with undisguised anger. 'They're only talking to her because they know I love her … I do.'

'No law against it though,' Brian pointed out, his eye throbbing.

'He's right. You had two months to do what they have done in two minutes and she's happy talking to them.' That was as close as Tom would get to telling his friend 'told you so'.

Andrew watched Hugh and Colin laughing and joking with Pink Socks, all the time fearing that they would become her friend, or more, or tell her about Andrew's feelings for her. That would be a disaster. He anxiously watched for fifteen minutes before Pink Socks left with her friends.

Hugh and Colin returned grinning with self importance.

'Karen Fisher,' said Hugh, waiting for Andrew's reaction, which was a horrified blank expression. 'That's her name Leopard. Pink Socks is Karen Fisher. First year Economics and Psychology. She was fascinated by my theories on unrequited love.'

'You didn't tell her about Andrew did you?' asked Tom.

'Maybe. Maybe not.' Hugh loved seeing the pain in Andrew's eyes and the disgust from Tom and Brian. Hugh and Colin smiled at each other and left. The others followed moments later, dejected, after what should have been a very upbeat night out.

Chapter 16

Festivities on floor three

Two and a half weeks later, December 13, 1983: Andrew Leopard knocked on Tom Hill's door. He had an idea and wanted to share it with his best friend. Andrew sat in the soft chair while Tom carried on shaving at the sink in the corner. The radio was quietly playing Islands In The Stream by Dolly Parton and Kenny Rogers. Andrew noticed a new Arsenal team line-up on the wall next to the Altered Images poster.

'I've had an idea.'

Tom grunted for Andrew to carry on. He was doing his neck and needed to keep his skin taught to avoid cuts.

'Now we know Pink Socks' name, I can leave her a Christmas card in the department pigeon holes and put a kiss on it. Then I might be on her mind when next term starts … I might.'

Tom couldn't help noticing that Andrew had started his sentence saying 'we know' instead of 'I know', as if the pursuit of Pink Socks were a team effort, but he didn't pick him up on it. He finished his neck and rinsed. 'Good idea.' He didn't think it was a good idea, but anything was better than doing nothing. 'Oh and I meant to say, yes please to your kind offer. I had a chat with Brian and we'd love to spend Christmas with your family.'

Andrew was taken by surprise. He had offered, but never expected Tom and Brian to accept. An urgent phone call would be needed to his parents.

'And I also meant to say. Are you okay for the Christmas dinner shopping just after lunch?'

'Yes. Fine.' The boys on Dickens Court, block F, floor three were all planning a trip to town ahead of their shared Christmas dinner. It was one of many Christmas dinners. Every course, club, group, society and department at Southside University was planning a party. Almost every floor of every block in the halls of residence had its own Christmas dinner planned.

Four hours later Andrew, Tom, Brian, Hugh Grundy, Colin Dean and Ian Mellor crunched through the deep snow, there had been more heavy snow showers, in the direction of town. Roger Evans had been invited to join them, but had been 'too busy'. They had also knocked at room one but got no answer from the resident who was now known as The Invisible Man, another Hugh nickname.

Despite the covering of snow, it was a crisp, dry and bright day with a gentle breeze and even a few patches of blue sky. The sun came out every now and then dazzling the boys as it reflected off the snow.

Between the students' union, the last building on the bottom side of campus, and the railway bridge, there was a large grassed area either side of the path. The path was heavily used as the railway bridge was the only link on the bottom side of campus between the university and the town. Many students, full of festive spirit, surrounded by deep snow needed only the slightest catalyst to trigger a snowball fight.

Who Me had woken up the morning after the football club night out with a very bad headache and a disgusting taste in his mouth. He couldn't eat anything all day as images of Brian's 'toilet punch' had ruined his appetite. So when he saw Brian walking towards him a couple of weeks later through deep snow, he couldn't help himself reaching down and rolling a large snowball. Brian was too busy talking to see Who Me approaching and as they passed each other, Who Me pushed the snow in Brian's face and ran up the hill towards the union building.

Brian reacted fast and scooped up a snowball, which he hurled at his running team-mate. It missed Who Me, but struck the left leg of Hugh, who had stopped to tie his shoelace. His reply bounced off Colin's shoulder onto Ian's ear. In the melee that followed, a few stray snowballs hit a number of innocent passers by, some shook their heads in disgust at the juvenile behaviour of their fellow students, but others joined in. A crowd attracts a crowd and the numbers grew.

As Hugh set off after Brian, Colin stuck his foot out and the big man fell in the snow face down. Ian, taking a chance, pushed Hugh's face deeper in the snow. He jumped up quickly to face Colin and Ian. At the same time Tom crouched down behind him on all fours. Colin gently pushed Hugh in the chest and he fell back in the snow over Tom.

Five minutes later, they were too cold and wet to care who had hit who and they crossed the railway bridge. They were halfway along Thief Lane when Hugh said 'Karen Fisher', with a cruel smile spreading across his wide face.

'Pink Socks?' Asked Brian.

'Yes,' said Hugh, pointing along the road. Fifty yards ahead of them was Pink Socks with her friends returning from town loaded with carrier bags, probably full of supplies for their Christmas dinner.

Andrew tucked in behind Tom, hoping she wouldn't see him. As they approached, Tom asked Hugh, 'did you tell her about Andrew?'

'Yes, but I didn't mention his name or point him out.' Hugh saw no reason why he couldn't tell them now. He had already enjoyed two weeks of Andrew squirming in fear of what he might have told Pink Socks.

'So she thinks one of your friends likes her but she doesn't know which one?' Tom continued.

'That sounds about right, although I didn't say it was one of my friends. I just said "somebody I knew". '

Both groups kept walking as they met, but exchanged greetings.

Colin nodded towards Pink Socks. 'Karen.'

She smiled back.

'Merry Christmas Karen,' Hugh was more vocal.

'Merry Christmas Stu.' Brian and Tom smiled. She couldn't even remember Hugh's name.

They had almost passed now, but Brian noticed that it wasn't Hugh or Colin that she looked at as they passed. It was Tom. They held eye contact for a moment. She smiled and Tom quickly looked away. The shared look had only been noticed by Brian. He said nothing and thought very little of it. His brother was a good looking young man and lots of girls gave him a second look.

Hugh felt uncomfortable having been called Stu, but as the boys turned into North Street, it was Brian who started to feel uncomfortable. Up ahead on the other side of the road, also coming towards them, was Lisa Wentworth-Simpson and her friends. A few yards ahead of the boys, a large delivery van was parked half on the road, half on the path. When the van hid the boys from Lisa and her friends, Brian stopped. 'I'll catch you up in the supermarket.' It was just over a fortnight since Lisa had given him a black eye, which had now mostly faded, but he didn't want her to see him. It would be awkward.

A few seconds later the boys crossed the road and Lisa saw them. She stopped. 'How's it going Tom?' she asked.

'Good thanks. We're shopping for our Christmas dinner. How about you?'

'Just been for lunch. Going back to work now. Your brother not with you?'

'Ahh … Lisa. Yes. Brian. I'm so sorry. He can be such an idiot.'

Lisa turned to Andrew. 'And how are you? Looking a bit happier today.'

'Good thanks. Brian is a pratt … he is.'

'You're a sweety. You all have a good Christmas.' They headed back to work.

Brian had been watching from a distance through the cab windows of the delivery van.

A dark haired man, a good six inches taller than Brian and probably about ten stone heavier had been unloading televisions but noticed Brian peering through the cab of his van. 'What's your game boy?' he snarled.

Brian jumped. He had been worried about what Lisa might do to him but this tall driver was a bigger and more immediate threat. 'Just hiding.'

The driver didn't like that. 'Are you trying to be clever?'

Brian's normal answer would have been, 'unlike you, I don't have to try', but given the difference in size and this man's natural aggression he thought such an answer would be unwise. 'Hiding from my girlfriend on the other side of the road.'

The driver's anger went. He was happy with that. He had a boys-stick-together way of thinking. 'Oh right. That's okay then. I thought you was going to rob my van.'

'No. Not at all. Merry Christmas.' Brian hurried after his friends.

Further back along North Street, Norman Hill had been watching Brian watching Lisa. He had spent the morning on the bench across the grass outside the entrance to Dickens Court , block F, and had later followed his boys and their friends into town. His urge to speak with his boys had not gone, but watching them from a distance had become a comfortable compromise. As long as they were happy, he would leave them alone, but if things started to go wrong, he would have the opportunity to help them get back on their feet.

Brian found his friends arguing in the supermarket over which turkey to buy.

'Chicken is the same thing but cheaper,' Colin insisted.

'There's only one quid in it.' Ian wanted real turkey.

'I don't care as long as it's fresh.' Tom didn't think a frozen bird would defrost fast enough. They were eating later the same day.

'Frozen chicken and we'll stick it in the bath for an hour.' Brian couldn't afford fresh. He grabbed the bird out of the freezer compartment and placed it in the trolley. They argued over every item on their list and it was two more hours before they got back to Dickens Court and put the frozen chicken in the bath.

Another three hours later, Colin set six places at the table and Hugh unscrewed the cap on a very cheap bottle of Bulgarian wine. They were litre bottles and there were four between them. Tom and Brian put the finishing touches to the Christmas tree. It wasn't a Norway spruce. It was a Leylandii conifer in a plastic pot, which Colin and Hugh had stolen from outside the front door of a bungalow on the way back from their previous week's drunken night on the town. All their decorations were scraps picked up from other parts of campus and town. The tree lights were all amber, taken from road-works near the shopping centre. The overall effect was like a collage, but surprisingly homely.

Ian brought in his tape player and put on a tape he had put together featuring Adam And The Ants along with the Stray Cats and Blondie. An unusual collection but a change from his usual Tom Jones and Bonnie Tyler stuff.

'I think the chicken's ready,' announced Brian.

As they served up, Roger Evans came in to prepare his tea.

'Still time to change your mind Crypt,' Hugh kindly offered.

No reaction.

They all sat down to pull their discount crackers. They wore paper hats and complained about the cheap pressed plastic toys. Brian's cracker contained a set of false red lips. Andrew's had a simple magic trick which they couldn't work out and Colin's had a plastic strip which told you what mood you were in depending on how much it twisted when you touched it.

The food was awful. The chicken hadn't defrosted fully so the middle wasn't cooked even though the outside was brown and crispy. The potatoes had almost turned to mash before they were put in the roasting dish after being boiled too long, the 'real' gravy that Colin had made was extremely oily and the plastic bag containing the giblets had not been removed from the chicken before it went into the cooker. It had been frozen solid and the boys were unaware that it existed, so even if the bird had been defrosted, they wouldn't have taken out the giblet bag.

The wine, which seemed a bargain while they were in the supermarket had a nasty kick which hit you just after swallowing, but it was strong and went down fast, which was good because the more wine they drank, the better the food tasted.

'You make any money yesterday?' Brian asked Colin. Hugh and Colin had been into town the day before proudly boasting that they would come home with much more money than they went out with, although Brian suspected that if the new money-making scheme had been a success, they would have been told by now.

'We broke even,' replied Colin defensively, without looking up.

'What was the plan,' Tom asked.

They had failed to make the intended killing, so Colin saw no reason why he shouldn't tell them what they had been doing. It was a very high risk scheme. At one point they had been £100 down and were very relieved to end the day where they started. 'We were in the bookies.'

'Gambling?' laughed Brian. 'I thought it was supposed to be a clever idea.'

'Let him finish.' Hugh defended his friend.

'We set a target of ten pounds. Then we bet enough money on the favourite in the first race to hit the target. If it had won, we would have left the betting shop.'

'Did it win?' Brian.

'No.' Colin didn't like his ideas being rubbished. 'It didn't have to though for our scheme to still work. On the next race we bet, again on the favourite, enough money to cover our losses and still hit the ten pound target.'

'Did that win?' Brian couldn't help laughing as Colin squirmed.

'No, but.'

Tom was also laughing.

'Let him finish,' Hugh repeated. He could see Colin was getting wound up.

'No, but again, it didn't have to for the scheme to work. We just kept betting on favourites with enough money to cover the accumulating losses and still hit the target.'

'How many bets?' Brian asked.

'A few,' said Hugh.

'How many?' Brian.

'Six,' Colin admitted quietly.

Tom , Brian, Ian and Andrew couldn't help laughing. Even Hugh had to smile. He always went along with Colin's scams, but Colin was the 'brains'.

'So how come you only broke even?' Brian wondered how they finally got a win but didn't hit the target.

'We lost so much that we could only bet enough to cover the losses. We were over a hundred quid down.' Hugh filled in the details Colin had missed.

Colin was not used to being laughed at. His ego was hurt and, with half a litre of strong Bulgarian wine inside him, he lashed out at the weakest target.

'What you laughing at Leopard?' Colin shouted.

Andrew had been sharing the joke and laughed along, a little, but was the least deserving of Colin's rage. Andrew had also got through about half a litre of wine, and, unlike beer, it had not left the room spinning around his head, although it had had another effect on Andrew. The echo had gone, same as the beer effect, but with the wine, he was a little braver and surprisingly angry. He didn't think it was fair that Colin had singled him out.

'It is a bit funny Colin, but we all laughed. Not just me.' Andrew defended himself.

The music finished and Hugh replaced it with a Stranglers tape, which he played at full volume. He didn't want the argument stopping him hearing his favourite tunes.

They shouted over Rattus Norvegicus. Goodbye Toulouse played as Colin squared up to Andrew. He needed to save face and Andrew's uncharacteristically confident reply was not what he had expected, so he raised the stakes. 'Nobody laughs at me Leopard. Especially someone who can't ask a girl her name after two months trying.'

The two boys were now face to face, stood up, and Colin had edged inside Andrew's personal space.

Andrew had no comeback this time, so Colin pressed home his advantage, feeling that the normal hierarchy was about to be restored. 'You're too late anyway. Karen is my chick now.'

Andrew stopped backing off, his unusual bravery was turning to more anger.

Colin knew how Andrew felt about Pink Socks and had only gone up to meet her to upset him.

Andrew knew Colin had passed Pink Socks on the way into town and they didn't talk to each other. It didn't add up. 'That can't be true. You never spoke to her today.'

'We exchanged greetings. I nodded. She smiled.'

'But you didn't speak. You're making it all up.' Andrew was not only very angry, he felt cheated and was close to tears, but held them back. 'She doesn't like you.'

Colin could see Andrew was holding back the tears and went for the kill. 'We don't need to talk. She said nothing the other day in her room when I was shagging her.'

Colin expected Andrew to run off to his bedroom or sob quietly in the corner.

Andrew wanted to run off to his bedroom or sob quietly in the corner, but the half litre of Bulgarian wine was steering him in a different direction. He reached up with both hands and grabbed Colin. His fists clenched and twisted the lapels of Colin's shirt. Andrew pushed him ferociously back and kept pushing until Colin fell back on the Christmas tree.

'You turd Colin,' Andrew shouted over The Stranglers. It was the worse word he could think of.

Colin was on his back with his arms and legs flapping in the air like an upturned beetle. None of the others had intervened in the argument. For Brian and Hugh, it was the best entertainment they had had all term, Ian didn't think it was his place to join in and Tom was delighted to see Andrew standing up for himself.

Before Colin could struggle back to his feet and before Hugh could turn the music back down to its normal level, there was a loud thump at the door. 'Turn that music down,' a very cultured voice boomed. 'Some of us are trying to study.' They then heard heavy footsteps stamping down the corridor.

Tom flicked the music off and pulled the door open just in time to see the door to room number one slammed shut. The boys, now in silence, crept along the corridor to room one, which had light spilling out from the crack at floor level. It was the first contact any of them had enjoyed with the occupant of room one, but none of them was brave enough to knock on the door and wish The Invisible Man a merry Christmas.

Chapter 17

Christmas with the Leopards

Twelve days later, December 25, 1983: 'I think I'm ready for a whisky,' Frank Leopard announced to his guests. 'Would you like to join me?'

'Thank-you. Yes,' Tom replied.

Brian also accepted. Maureen Leopard was in the kitchen cooking so Andrew jumped up to get the drinks.

The three boys sat around the sitting room as Andrew's father told them the secrets of his success and how he had progressed up the corporate ladder despite a 'number of clowns' who had foolishly tried to stand in his way. He told them he expected Andrew to follow his father's excellent example but doubted that he had the necessary backbone yet.

'I'm hoping university will toughen the boy up.' He talked about Andrew as if he were in another room. 'Easily distracted. Needs to focus on the job in hand. Where's that whisky? Like I said. Easily distracted. You distilling it yourself boy. Look lively, your friends will die of thirst. Eh boys?' He winked at Tom and Brian.

Brian nodded in agreement to be polite.

Tom looked away. He didn't want to collude with Frank in deriding Andrew.

'Thanks Andrew.' Tom took the whisky.

'Thanks.' Brian took his glass.

Andrew passed Frank a glass of whisky and water. Frank continued to look past Andrew at his guests without breaking from his conversation and waved his finger towards the coffee table so Andrew knew where to place the glass, but didn't thank him, or look at him.

'And I said to him, "if my handshake isn't enough re-assurance, we have no deal." He soon backed down and the rest is history." Frank waited for Tom and Brian's smiles of approval before taking a sip of his drink.

He recoiled in disgust as he took the first mouthful. 'Andrew you idiot. You've just murdered a glass of my finest Scotch malt. You've put warm water in it. How many times have I told you? Run the tap for a while until the water is cold.'

Andrew jumped up and took the glass. 'Sorry. Shall I get some cold water … shall I?'

'Well. The water won't get itself will it?'

It was another of those difficult questions and this time Andrew took it as rhetorical and went for some cold water.

'I'm sorry. Don't know what's the matter with him. Is he like this at college?' Frank addressed both boys.

It was an awkward question, certainly for Tom, as he thought answering the question was in some way agreeing with Frank that Andrew was at fault for putting warm tap water in his father's whisky. Tom thought Andrew had done nothing wrong at all and, in fact, it was Frank at fault, but it would be impolite to say so. Such subtleties were lost on Brian who fell back on humour as an easy way of tackling difficult questions.

'He's just like this at college Mr Leopard,' Brian replied. 'He put warm water in my beer the other day.'

Andrew returned with cold water in a plastic measuring jug.

'You fool. We have a silver jug for the water. What kind of a house will our guests think I provide for you bringing water in a plastic jug. If it's worth doing, it's worth doing properly.'

Andrew hurried off again.

'He's his mother's son. No doubt about that. I've given him everything he's ever needed, the chance to make something of himself. And how does he thank me? He embarrasses me in front of guests.'

Andrew couldn't find the jug and returned. 'Do you know where the jug is … do you?'

'A place for everything and everything in its place. It's in its place boy.'

That was no help. Andrew had tried 'its place' and it wasn't there. He knew asking for further help would trigger an angry response so he asked his mother.

'Have you tried the spare bedroom Andrew? He had a whisky last night when he was working on his train set.' Maureen Leopard suggested.

Andrew ran upstairs, not wishing to keep his father waiting too long. The jug was on the table, next to a model of the Flying Scotsman. He returned with the cold water and again, Frank wagged his finger in the direction of the coffee table, while not breaking from his conversation to thank his son or look at him.

'He won't make that mistake again.' Frank finished another story. 'Have you offered your mother any help Andrew?'

'No,' Andrew said apologetically.

'She's been cooking your meals for 18 years and you can't even help her on Christmas day. Look sharp and get in the kitchen.'

Andrew hurried off.

'That's the trouble with some people these days,' Frank went on. 'Everybody wants something for nothing.' He sat back and took another sip of his whisky.

Maureen had been up early preparing food, wrapping presents and tidying the house. She was proud of her home, a fairly standard three-bedroom suburban semi-detached house in a quiet cul-de-sac, but with a few distinct features she had worked at. The curtains were all home-made and matched the carpets, as did the furniture. Colour co-ordination was important to her and it didn't stop at the front door. She spent hours in the garden manicuring the lawns and hedges. She weeded the borders regularly and planted a wide variety of bedding plants, also in colours chosen to compliment those which featured prominently inside the house.

Her Christmas dinner preparations were complete in time for the Queen's message. She went through to the sitting room. 'Dinner will be ready after the Queen's speech.' She flicked on the television and sat down next to Andrew.

Frank stood up for the National Anthem joined closely by Maureen. Brian and Tom wondered if they were getting up for the food but waited. Andrew stayed seated following the lead of his friends but an angry look from his father soon had him on his feet. As the anthem began, Tom and Brian realised why they were standing and immediately joined them based on the premiss 'when in Rome'. The Queen spoke of technology bringing the world closer together but emphasised the point that we must communicate with greater depth. 'Let us all resolve to communicate as friends in tolerance and understanding.'

Tom thought to himself that Frank wasn't communicating with tolerance and understanding towards his son. In fact he had seen people treat their pets with greater respect than Frank had shown for Andrew, but he said nothing. He was a guest and it would be very rude to question the host's conduct.

With the speech finished, Maureen invited her family and guests through to the dining room, which was actually the same room but at the far end through an arch. It had previously been two separate rooms but the Leopards, along with many other families, had followed the fashion for knocking through to create 'a more fluent living space'.

After stopping to say grace, again the boys adopted the 'when in Rome' policy, they all tucked in to heavily piled plates as Bing Crosby crooned in the background. With healthy appetites taking over from healthy conversation, the dominant sound was of clinking cutlery on China, but Frank broke the peace when he turned to Andrew. 'I must say boy, your acne seems to have improved a great deal.'

Tom was aghast at Frank's thoughtless choice of subject, Maureen felt a twang of sympathy while Brian had to hide a smile. But Andrew felt huge embarrassment and half choked on a sprout before replying with a now very crimson face. 'Thank-you father, but I'm nearly out of tablets.' He took tablets to help restore the balance of hormones, which his doctor thought a probable cause for the spots. 'Perhaps you could pick some up for me when you get your flatulence tablets.'

Excellent reply thought Tom, while Brian could no longer hide his smile. Maureen could not believe Andrew's rudeness, while Andrew realised, only after speaking, how unkind his answer must have sounded in front of guests.

'Oh I'm so sorry.' He quickly tried to repair the damage. 'I haven't told them about your wind. I promise.'

As Brian's smile turned to stifled laughter, Andrew realised he was making matters worse.

Frank was outraged. 'I think you've said enough boy. If that's the way you treat your nearest and dearest, I'm surprised your new friends want to spend Christmas with you.'

Andrew looked down at his food and nothing more was said until Bing Crosby finished. The silence was awkward, but again it was Frank who brought it to an end. 'The record isn't going to turn itself over is it Andrew?'

'No it's not father.'

'Less of your cheek boy and look sharp.'

Andrew went through the arch to the sitting room and turned over the vinyl on the record player.

After Christmas pudding, Maureen poured brandy for Frank, Tom and Brian. She didn't think to offer Andrew one. He had never had one in the past and, even though he was the same age as his guests, it never crossed her mind to ask him.

Andrew wondered why he was never offered brandy, but he hated the stuff anyway so didn't wonder for long. He had been given wine, along with the guests, but a much nicer vintage than the Bulgarian plonk they had enjoyed at college. Again, for Andrew, the room was not spinning but he felt a shade braver, which was about to land him with a problem.

The brandy and wine left Frank in reflective mood. He had three boys in their late teens at his dinner table. He thought back to his days as a teenager. He had not been to college. He left school after O-levels and did his national service. Very different to university, but some things probably never changed. 'So boys. Had any luck with the ladies at college?'

Brian replied first. 'Oh yes Mr Leopard. I have a girlfriend called Lisa. She works for an insurance company in Southside.'

'Good lad. Been together long?'

'Couple of months. Taking it steady. You know.'

Tom was not as good a liar as Brian, so he stuck to the truth when Frank turned to him and raised his eyebrows. 'Oh nobody for me Mr Leopard. I'm concentrating on my studies and playing football.'

Frank turned to his son. 'Well boy. You don't play football, so you can focus on chasing the women, but I don't suppose you have a girlfriend have you?'

Andrew was tired of being put down and wanted his father to be impressed for once, so the wine did his talking for him. 'Well actually I do. A nice young lady called Karen Fisher. She's in some of my classes and we've been seeing each other since the first week of term.'

Frank was impressed and rocked back on his chair. 'Wow. That's my boy. I always knew you had it in you. You kept it well hidden for a long time, but, good lad. Sounds serious. Is it?'

'We're very fond of each other.'

Brian again had to hide a smile. This had been the most entertaining Christmas he had had for years. Tom was less amused. Andrew hadn't even asked the girl her name yet, so announcing to his parents that they were an item could only end in tears.

Tom was right. Frank was about to give Andrew a new headache.

'Have you got a photograph of her?' Frank asked.

'No. Nothing,' Andrew replied honestly.

'No matter. We can see her for ourselves. We are coming to visit you at the end of January. I have a conference near Southside. Didn't your mother tell you?'

Chapter 18

Road-works

A week later, January 3, 1984: Brian and Tom Hill sat with Colin Dean and Hugh Grundy in the soft chairs in the carpeted corner of their Dickens Court kitchen. The second years had arrived back from the Christmas break in the morning, while the brothers had just got back after a very long and slow journey in Frank Leopard's Volvo estate. Andrew Leopard was re-organising his room to accommodate his Christmas gifts.

'Did you see Karen Fisher over the break Colin?' Tom asked.

'No. I dumped her just before the end of term,' Colin lied.

'Bet you never got in her pants anyway.' Brian was more to the point.

'Yes I did.' Colin was defensive.

'Bollocks you did.' Hugh was never one to help his friend out of a corner. 'You never touched her. You made it all up just to spite Leopard and he gave you a slap … ha, ha.'

Ian Mellor marched into the kitchen wearing a new pair of black leather gloves, saving Colin the trouble of finding a witty reply.

'Have a good Christmas Wanker?' Brian asked with a friendly smile.

'Thanks. Yes. Had a week in Tenerife.'

'Alright for some,' Colin said with a little jealousy.

'I had a week in Elevenerife,' boasted Hugh, who always liked to go one better.

'Sounds good Wanker.' Tom was pleased to see Ian happy.

'New gloves Wanker?' asked Brian.

'Yes. Christmas present.' Ian pulled up a chair to join his floor-mates. 'How about you? Where did you go?'

'Stayed with Andrew,' replied Brian.

'I bet that was a laugh a minute … it was.' Hugh joked. 'Are his mum and dad just like him?'

'No. Completely different most of the time,' Brian said. 'But on the drive back, Andrew and his dad were just the same. They wouldn't stop complaining about road-works. Every other sentence was about digging up the road and how we should improve our rail network. They must have said the word "road-works" about 100 times.'

'Quid each,' said Hugh, placing two 50p coins in the ashtray.

'What for?' asked Colin.

'A quid each and when Leopard comes in, the first to make him say "road-works" gets the five quid.'

Brian placed a one pound note in the ashtray. 'I'm in.'

Tom followed along with Colin and Ian. It was the start of a new term and that meant another instalment of their grant money.

Five minutes later Andrew strolled in and placed a few items in his cupboard before he noticed the silence. He looked around and five of his floor-mates were watching him. It was unusual that they should notice him at all, but, strangely, they were all smiling at him as well. He felt uneasy.

'Did you have a good break Andrew?' Colin asked warmly.

Much the same as Hugh, Colin never used Andrew's first name, so the uneasy feeling grew, especially as the last time he saw Colin was at his feet having pushed him into the Christmas tree in a drunken rage. Before he could answer, Hugh jumped in with another question.

'You're looking tired Leopard. Did you have a good journey back?' Hugh knew Andrew wouldn't trust him if he used his first name again.

But again, he faced a new question before he could answer.

'How long did it take you to get back?' Ian Mellor.

'The train system is far too expensive. What do you think Andrew?' Brian asked.

'Busy traffic today.' Tom

Andrew eased his hands out of his pockets. He had never been so popular and it was a good feeling. He joined the others in the corner with his head held high. 'I had a great Christmas thanks. Got back this afternoon. My dad drove us over. It was a nightmare. There were so many …'

'Andrew,' shouted Brian, cutting his friend short before he gave Tom the victory.

'What Brian? Are you okay?' Andrew was worried.

'I really like your shoes.' It was the first thing that came into Brian's head.

'Bastard Brian,' Tom said quietly to his brother.

The other three breathed a sigh of relief, thankful that Brian's quick thinking had kept the bet alive.

Andrew was feeling so confident that he volunteered his next comment. 'You should have seen all the road-works …' Andrew stopped mid sentence as the five boys all groaned together. Nobody could claim a win for that and they all reached into the ashtray and took their money back.

Andrew's brief moment in the spotlight ended as quickly as it started. Nobody looked at him now. His friends returned to talking among themselves. Andrew slipped his hands back in his pockets.

Roger Evans shuffled into the room with his cardboard box to prepare cheese on toast. The hush returned as the other six boys checked out his new set of clothes. A new pair of grey trousers, a new pair of brown shoes and a new v-necked jumper in a new pastel shade of blue. Pretty much the same outfit as before Christmas but new. He finished his food preparations, placed his food and pots back in the box and left.

Ian broke the hush. 'I'm going to have to go for a lie down. I think I'm suffering jet lag.' It was a good way of reminding his friends he had been to Tenerife.

'Jet lag?' blurted Hugh. 'We're in the same time zone.'

'Yes. The plane was delayed for five hours,' explained Ian.

Ian was confused. He could not understand why his comment had sparked such laughter. 'What's so funny?'

'Wanker. That's not jet lag.' Hugh enjoyed pointing out Ian's error. 'That's just a delay.'

Ian left the room.

'That's almost as bad as Leopard's déjà vu faux pas,' Hugh added.

Andrew pushed his hands deeper into his pockets and before Hugh could turn his attention to Andrew, Tom changed the subject. 'Would you like a cup of tea Andrew?'

'Yes please Tom,' said a relieved Andrew.

'Brian?'

'Please.'

Tom put the kettle on and pulled three cups out of the cupboard before pulling open the fridge. 'We're out of milk. I'll just nip to the shop.'

'No. I'll go Tom.' Andrew preferred to buy the milk than be left with Hugh and Colin.

As he walked across campus to the on-site Spar shop, Andrew thought about Pink Socks. He had less than a month before his parents' visit to progress from smiling at her from a distance to making her his steady girlfriend. At least his spots were under control. He thought the best opportunity would be after the next economics lecture. He would approach her when it finished and ask how her Christmas had been.

The campus Spar was called a 'supermarket', but it's limited stock, compact size and high prices made it more of a corner shop, handy for the odd bottle of milk but you'd never do your weekly shopping there. Andrew was not the only student caught short of supplies at the start of the new term and the Spar was packed. He hurried through to the fridge section and there was only one bottle of milk left. As he reached for it, another student also put their hand out.

Andrew turned to see who his competition was for the last bottle. It was Pink Socks. 'I'm sorry … I am,' he mumbled. 'You were first. You have it.'

'No. I'm sure it was you. You have it,' she smiled. 'Don't I know you?'

'Sort of.'

'Yes I do. You're in my economics group, aren't you?'

Andrew quickly remembered what he had planned to say. 'How was your Christmas?'

Pink Socks thought it a strange answer to her question but let it go. 'Very good thank-you. And you?'

'Very good thank-you.' Andrew was stuck now. He hadn't thought what question to ask her next. After a few seconds he handed her the milk and hurried away. Before leaving the shop, he realised he hadn't even asked her name. He stopped without turning. Should he go back and ask? Would he seem weird going back to ask her name? Would he appear uninterested if he didn't? He was feeling brave and found her in the queue waiting to pay.

'Yes. I am in your economics group … I am. My name is Andrew Leopard.'

'Pleased to meet you Andrew. I'm Karen Fisher.'

'See you in the next lecture Karen,' Andrew said with fresh vigour. He walked briskly back to Dickens Court with a new spring in his step. He felt a million dollars. He had made the first step. She was lovely. And he had done it faster than he had planned. It was two days until the next economics lecture. He couldn't wait to tell Tom and Brian.

He pushed the kitchen door open and waltzed into the kitchen with a confident swagger, smiling from ear to ear. His posture was so out of character that Tom took a double take. He looked a different person.

Tom could see something had happened. 'Have you seen my friend Andrew Leopard?' he asked Andrew.

'My name is Leopard … Andrew Leopard,' he replied, as if he were James Bond.

'Where's the milk?' Brian hadn't noticed the change in posture.

'There was only one bottle left and I let Pink Socks take it.'

'Pink Socks?' asked Tom with great excitement. 'You both went to buy milk and you let her have the last one.'

'I did. And we had a whole conversation.'

'She's only small. You could have bullied her into letting you have the milk. I'm dying for a cup of tea.' Brian was not as excited.

Tom, on the other hand, was delighted for Andrew, but still thought he could have done better. 'What did she need the milk for?'

'I don't know. I didn't ask.'

'And what did you need the milk for?'

'You know that. A cup of tea.' Andrew wasn't following Tom.

'It's great that you met her finally, but you missed a great opportunity.'

'What?' Andrew's euphoria was starting to fade.

'You could have said to her, "I only need milk for a cup of tea. Why don't you join me and then you can take the rest of the bottle?" You would have still appeared gracious, but you would have taken a bigger step forward.'

'You're a sly bugger,' Brian said.

Andrew wished he were a 'sly bugger'. It had been, as Tom said, a 'great opportunity'.

Chapter 19

Vicky Owen

Nine days later, January 12, 1984: Tom Hill and Andrew Leopard headed into town to pick up the photographs Tom had taken of their Dickens Court Christmas dinner. It was cold and there was steady rain.

It was over a week since Andrew had met Pink Socks in the Spar and since then, he had got no further than saying 'hello Karen' at the end of economics lectures. Time was running out before his parents' visit and he needed Tom's advice. Things had to start moving.

As they approached the railway bridge Andrew turned to his friend. 'I've been to the Spar shop every day this term hoping to bump into her again and she's never there.'

'I hope you're not waiting to use the cup of tea line.'

'Well yes.'

A train approached and passed loudly under the boys. Tom knew Andrew wouldn't be able to hear him if he spoke. 'Just say, "You're a babe. I have a ten inch penis. How about a shag?" And see what happens.'

The train passed and rumbled into the distance.

'Sorry Tom. I missed that.'

Tom repeated himself. 'Just say, "You're available. I have ten rich tea biscuits. Let's share a tea bag." And see what happens.'

Andrew thought his friend was turning loopy. 'And you think that will work?'

'No. Maybe not.' Tom was mentally exhausted on the subject of Pink Socks.

As they passed the football ground, side by side, with Andrew closest to the curb, a large white van raced past, very close to the edge, hitting a puddle and sending water all over Andrew's new grey trousers. Andrew shielded Tom from most of the spray. He was already cold and wet and considered waving a fist at the driver, but didn't, just in case he was an enormous thug who might slam on the breaks and come back to punch him.

As the van drove away, he noticed a slogan on the back, which read 'say it with flowers'. Perhaps that was the way forward. 'How about I send her some flowers?'

'Yes. Good idea.' Tom just wanted Andrew to do something. Anything other than talk about what to do. 'Let's order them now.'

'No. No,' Andrew replied desperately.

'Why not?' Tom was close to losing his patience.

'There has to be an occasion.'

'No there doesn't,' Tom yelled, exasperated.

'She'd think I was stupid if there were no reason for sending them.'

'There is a reason. You fancy her.'

'But I don't want her to know that … I don't.'

'Why do you want to send her flowers then? I thought that was the whole idea.'

'To try and make her like me … I suppose.'

The boys walked into the shopping centre, which gave them welcome relief from the rain. In the photographic shop, they were waiting for the assistant to return with their pictures when a pretty girl stood next to them at the counter. Tom recognised her. He had seen her in the Dickens Court reception area collecting her mail.

She wore conservative clothes, pleated grey skirt and sensible shoes. Her anorak was open and Tom saw a light brown cardigan underneath. She had a plain, but attractive face, very little make-up and shoulder-length dark brown hair held in a pony tail. A carefully trimmed fringe followed the straight line of her eyebrows. Her expression was almost a smile and at around five feet four she looked quietly confident. Appearances can be deceptive though, as Tom was later to find out.

Tom paid for the pictures and the girl was then served.

'Let's go then.' Andrew wondered what Tom was waiting for. He hadn't noticed the girl from Dickens Court. He only had eyes for Pink Socks. Tom, however, had noticed the girl and liked what he saw.

She collected her pictures and swung around to see Tom, recognised him and smiled.

Tom could see she had recognised him, but probably didn't know from where. 'Hi. I think we're neighbours. Well. Sort of neighbours. I've seen you in reception at Dickens Court.'

Her eyes lit up. She knew exactly where she knew him from and was delighted that he had recognised her. 'Yes. I'm in Block B.'

He reached out his hand. 'Tom Hill. Pleased to meet you.'

'Vicky Owen.'

'You heading back now?

'Yes.' She had planned a bit more shopping, but didn't want to miss the chance of walking with her new friend.

'We'll walk with you. Oh I'm sorry. This is Andrew.'

'Hi,' said Andrew, who felt as if he had just become invisible.

'Hi Andrew.'

They set off. Tom and Vicky were in deep conversation. Andrew tagged along behind them. As they left the shopping centre, Vicky put up her umbrella and

Tom squeezed under it with her. There was only room for two.

As they passed the football ground, Andrew noticed Tom and Vicky speed up a little and assumed it was because they didn't want to be with him. He was wrong. It was because Tom remembered the puddle by the edge of the road and had seen a car approaching fast. Andrew eventually put two and two together as the spray drenched him for a second time.

Tom turned round. 'You alright Andrew.'

'Yes. Thank-you.'

'I thought you'd have remembered that.'

Andrew felt a bit stupid as well as invisible. Tom and Vicky returned to their conversation. She had been spending her Christmas money in the sales.

'So what did you get?' Tom asked.

'A nice pair of gold stud ear-rings.'

'Sounds nice.'

'Some new jeans. Reduced.'

'Do they still fit?'

'Reduced in price nutter, not size.' Vicky laughed a little. The joke wasn't very funny, but she'd been watching Tom since the second week of the previous term and whatever he said was amusing and charming. 'I also got a "save the whale" T-shirt from a shop called Third World Collective.' Now she was worried. She thought she may look like a radical lefty and scare Tom off. 'It has a load of Greenpeace stuff. Do you know it?'

Tom knew it well. It was the shop he went in for Brian's birthday present at the start of term. And he had been back since. A few times. He probably even had the same T-shirt. 'I know it. I go there a lot. I'm a member of Greenpeace.'

Wow thought Vicky, who had never been brave enough to join something as subversive as a pressure group. 'How do you become a member?'

'Fill out the form and pay a modest subscription. That's it. You can be as active as you want. They don't mind. The bigger the membership the bigger the voice.'

'I'd like to, but I don't think my father would approve. He thinks you get your name on a secret police file and it stops you getting a good job.'

'I'd rather save the whale than get a high paid job. Besides, the membership is growing so fast that there will come a time when people who aren't on the list will look out of place.'

She loved his defiance and strong opinions. 'You're right. And it's none of my father's business what groups I join.'

They were back at Dickens Court now. It was still raining.

'You'll have to walk the last few yards to your block without my umbrella.'

'No worries. Thanks for sharing. I'll bring you round a membership form if you want.'

'Please. That would be great.'

'What room?'

'Floor two, room six.'

'About eight?'

'Thanks. See you later.'

Chapter 20

Dinner for two

Eight days later, January 20, 1984: The temperature was not much more than freezing, but there was no wind or rain. Norman Hill sat on his favourite bench across the grass from Dickens Court. For seven days in a row, he had watched Tom walk briskly from block F to block B at eight o'clock every night, always on his own and with a smile. The first visit ended at around ten, but the finish time had been progressively later as the week went by. Last night had been around midnight. His walk was always less swift on his return.

Tonight was a little different. He emerged at eight, as usual, but wearing smart clothes. He even wore a tie and he had polished his plastic shoes. He had smart black trousers, with a crisply ironed crease, and a herring bone grey blazer. The walk was quick and the smile was broad. He disappeared into block B.

Tom knocked gently on Vicky's door, then stood back, so she would see his smart clothes from top to bottom as she opened the door.

'Wow Tom. You look good.'

'Thank-you very much. So do you.'

Vicky wore a knee-length dress in a soft lilac shade, fairly high-cut neck and short sleeves. She had sensible burgundy shoes with a bit of a heel, but not too much, and a burgundy ribbon holding her hair in a pony tail.

Tom noticed her arms were lightly freckled and briefly imagined them draped around his shoulders. They had not yet kissed, but there was a strong chemistry and tonight was their first formal date. There was a shared anticipation of romance having spent every night of that week talking together about their hopes and dreams. Their ideas were well matched and when they disagreed it was good natured banter.

Tom had grown fond of her very quickly and was happy to take things slowly. He was looking forward to a more physical relationship, but was in no hurry as he was uncharacteristically finding the idea of a long-term romance attractive.

Vicky pulled on a pink cardigan and locked her door behind her.

Norman, on his bench, had expected Tom to be in block B until after midnight, so he almost missed them as they came out together. Now he knew why Tom had been walking so briskly all week with such a big smile. He swelled with pride as Tom and Vicky linked arms and turned towards town.

Past the railway bridge, they went left instead of heading right into town. A short walk in this direction took them to Royal Avenue. Halfway up this smart street was The Pepper Pot, a tidy restaurant where Tom had a table booked for two. Not your top class place, but on Tom's budget, it was up-market. It was a busy Friday night, so it was a good job Tom had booked. The bow-tied waiter led them to their table in a dimly-lit corner. He reached across the table to light a candle, then handed them their menus.

Vicky's warm smile gave her an air of confidence, which Tom liked, but it was an illusion. She had very little real confidence and struggled with self doubt. She could feel herself falling very quickly for Tom, but he seemed too good to be true and she kept thinking back to her mother's advice after her last failed romance. 'If he seems too good to be true, he probably is.'

During her A-levels, she had been encouraged to apply for Oxford or Cambridge. Her test results were outstanding and the school, along with her parents, had been expecting great things, but she was sidetracked by an older man, a kitchen salesman in his mid twenties. All her friends had been jealous. He was tall, good looking and wealthy.

He drove a brand new car and took her to the finest restaurants. Vicky had fallen in love with him, very quickly, and by the time she discovered he was married with two children, it was hard to walk away. Her studies took a back seat as she settled for being 'the other woman'. As time passed, the dream of Oxford and Cambridge melted away. The test results dropped. It was only a visit from the kitchen salesman's wife, including threats of violence, that prompted her parents to put an end to the romance by moving away.

Vicky had only just scraped into Southside University after a late surge in performance. Being the mistress had left Vicky feeling as if she were second best. Studying at Southside University instead of Oxford or Cambridge had been a huge let down for her parents more than Vicky, and their poorly disguised disappointment also made Vicky feel second best.

She no longer had feelings for the kitchen salesman. She sat in The Pepper Pot, looking at Tom with great desire, all the time thinking, 'If he seems too good to be true, he probably is.' Her mother had also told her to 'keep men waiting. If they love you, they'll wait'. All week Tom had been visiting her and she had wanted to kiss him every night but kept telling herself to keep him waiting.

So she sat opposite Tom with what he thought was a confident smile. Tom's smile was also confident and assured. In his case, it was total unconditional confidence, which came from a firm belief that his honest and considerate approach deserved to be well received. He was a good looking boy and had been told that many times by many people, but he never made light of the advantage it gave him. It created more opportunities for him, but he only took the opportunities if the girls he met appeared to like what they heard as much as what they saw. He thought he had reached that point with Vicky and was happy to spend a whole week's food money on treating her to a special night out.

'So Vicky. What's the naughtiest thing you've ever done?' Tom asked before tucking into his vegetarian lasagne. They had missed out starters. Tom was feeling generous, but he could only afford a main course on a student grant.

'Ooh let me think.' Vicky swallowed a mouthful of sea bass and looked up at the ceiling for inspiration. 'It would probably have to be when I was five.' She faced Tom briefly. 'No.' She looked back up at the ceiling for more inspiration. 'When I was eight. My mum used to bake lovely cakes, but she had a rule of only one piece a day to stop us all getting fat.' Vicky had a sip of her sweet white wine. 'She did a lovely fruit cake one summer and I had eaten my one piece, but wanted more, so when my mum and dad were outside gardening, I put the cake in a carrier bag and hid it in my room. Then I dropped the plate on the floor next to the table where I had found it, let the dog in and ran to tell my parents the dog had jumped up to the table and eaten the cake.'

'You naughty girl.' Tom laughed a little. 'Did you get away with it?'

'No.'

'Why not?'

'My dad had a good look at the broken plate on the floor and saw there were no crumbs and I'm such a bad liar that he worked it out.'

'What did he say?'

'He sat me down and said, 'Spoony is a lovely dog, but he told me he doesn't like fruit cake. The raisins get caught in his teeth. He's more of a sponge cake dog. So if he took the cake, he probably didn't eat it. I'm going to finish cutting the grass now. If Spoony puts the cake back while I'm gone, I won't punish him." And then he left.'

Tom smiled. 'And did the dog return the cake?'

'Yes it did, but only after I'd eaten another piece.'

Vicky and Tom laughed together and both took another sip from their wine, touching glasses in a toast to bad behaviour.

'What about you?' Vicky asked. 'I bet you've done some really bad things.'

Tom rubbed his chin in thought. 'I killed four men.'

'No?' Vicky hoped he was joking.

'No. Only joking. It was just one man.'

She was getting used to his humour. 'Come on. Proper answer.'

He rubbed his chin again. 'I've got one.' He then took another mouthful of lasagne and said nothing. He was being playful.

'Tell me then.'

'Okay. When I was sixteen, our housemaster used to park his car outside our dormitory, two bays along from the space reserved for the headmaster. He was a horrible housemaster. He used to smack us on the back of the head.'

Vicky was intrigued. 'Go on.'

'It was an old Rover and the passenger side back door wouldn't lock for some reason. Me, my brother and a couple of other boys, got up in the middle of the night and got in his car through the back door, took off the handbrake and pushed it back a bit, then forward into the headmaster's space.'

Vicky laughed. 'What happened?'

'Well. He didn't get in any trouble, at first, but we did it every night for two weeks until the headmaster banned him from using the staff car park.'

Vicky laughed again. 'Did you get caught?'

'No, but I think he knew it was us because he hit us on the back of the head even more after that.'

They finished their food and the waiter topped up their glasses before handing them a dessert menu. Vicky chose ice cream, while Tom ordered a coffee. With his plate out of the way Tom edged towards Vicky, resting his elbows on the table and his head in his hands. 'I feel very comfortable when I'm with you,' he said.

Vicky also leant forward. 'That's good. I love being with you.' Vicky wondered if she had given too much away. She held her spoon in her right hand and rested her other hand on the table.

Tom reached for her free hand. She cautiously tried to pull it away, but Tom gripped harder until she accepted his affection and gently squeezed his hand in return. They walked home still holding hands and at the door to block B, Vicky stood on her toes, reached up and kissed Tom. 'Thank-you for a lovely evening Tom. I'll see you tomorrow.'

Tom was happy with that. The evening had gone well. She had kissed him. He had a girlfriend. He walked back to block F with a big smile.

Chapter 21

The Leopards meet Pink Socks

Ten days later, January 30, 1984: Ian Mellor's music box was playing in the kitchen. Hugh Grundy, Colin Dean and Ian were listening to Southern Death Cult. It was early Monday evening and the three boys had nothing to do, except studies, and they only ever opened their books the night before an exam or if an essay were due the next day. To pass the time, Colin was entertaining the others by burning posters on the notice board with his cigarette lighter. The orange flames briefly licked up the wall before fading away to leave a dirty black smear of carbon on the paintwork. The boys sat and admired their work.

The door opened and Andrew Leopard came in followed by Tom and Brian Hill, all wearing orange and purple horizontally striped T-shirts.

'Nice shirts. You off to a fancy dress party?' asked Hugh.

'No.' Tom didn't like the shirts at all. 'Andrew's parents are coming to eat with us tonight and his mum gave us these shirts for Christmas.'

Brian noticed the black marks on the wall. 'Err. Disgusting. Who did that?'

'Colin. I told him not to. He just doesn't listen sometimes.' Hugh thought nothing of betraying his friend's confidence. If anything, it provided entertainment.

Brian didn't like mess. He leant aggressively over Colin, who was sat on one of the soft chairs in the corner, with his face only inches from Colin's, well inside his personal space. 'Clean it up now,' he said firmly.

Colin could see Brian was not joking and knew better than to ignore him but wanted to save face. 'No need to get stressy. I was going to do it anyway.' He squeezed out from under Brian and started cleaning with help from Andrew, who didn't want his parents thinking badly of his college home. Andrew did most of the cleaning while Tom and Brian started cooking. They had insisted on providing the meal for the Leopards in return for the kind hospitality they had been shown over Christmas.

The walls didn't look too bad after a good scrubbing, but Andrew had bigger problems to worry about, problems that had given him sleepless nights for most of January. Firstly he had not got any further than smiling and greeting Pink Socks and secondly he didn't want Colin and Hugh anywhere near the kitchen when his parents visited. They knew all about Andrew and Pink Socks. Hugh would enjoy nothing more than telling Andrew's mother and father how much of a failure he had been.

Ian Mellor had agreed to spend the evening with his friends in Bronte Court and left as soon as the three boys came in wearing their orange and purple shirts, but Hugh and Colin needed a more mercenary approach, which Andrew had been preparing. 'I think there's a free band on in the Union bar tonight,' he stammered.

'You trying to get rid of us Leopard?' snarled Hugh.

'No. I wouldn't dream of doing that … I wouldn't … I wouldn't.'

Tom noticed the double echo. Andrew must be very nervous, so he came to his friend's rescue. 'Yes he is trying to get rid of you. His parents are coming for dinner and he doesn't want them to see your ugly faces. I'll give you a quid for the fruit machine in the union bar.'

'Two quid and I'll think about it,' said Colin, feeling he had a strong hand.

Brian was still angry with him for burning the posters. They had cleared up the black stains, but the kitchen smelled bad. 'A quid is all you're getting.' Brian thrust the note in Colin's hand.

'If we don't win, we might come back,' warned Colin.

'If you come back, I might stick the fire extinguisher up your bum,' warned Brian.

'No need to get heated,' Hugh intervened. 'We're going.'

Less than five minutes later, there was a knock at the door.

Tom pulled it open. 'Come in Mr Leopard.' He shook his hand firmly. 'Mrs Leopard. You're looking well.' Tom gave her a hug.

'Nice shirt,' she replied.

'Thanks,' said Tom.

Brian also hugged Maureen Leopard and shook Frank Leopard's hand.

Maureen then hugged Andrew for a little longer than he felt comfortable with before Frank took his son by the hand. 'Looking good my boy.'

'Thanks. Good journey?'

'Not too bad. Usual road-works, but could have been worse.'

'North Circular okay?'

'Nasty, nasty road.'

'Road-works by the river?'

'Dreadful. Anyway boy. Where is she?'

'She'll be here in a minute … she will.'

Tom opened a bottle of Bulgarian wine and poured a drink for the guests, who sat on the soft chairs in the carpeted corner of the kitchen. As Frank explained to everyone how he had corrected a number of 'brainless fools' at his conference, there was a gentle knock at the door. Greenpeace Badge pushed it open and walked in smiling at the dinner guests.

Andrew rushed over and gave her a peck on the cheek before making the introductions. 'Karen this is my mum and dad, Maureen and Frank … it is.' He then turned to his parents. 'Mum and Dad, this is Karen.'

'Hi Maureen. Pleased to meet you.' She kissed Andrew's mother gently on both cheeks. 'Frank.' She kissed him too.

'Wine Karen?' offered Tom.

'Thanks Tom.'

'Have a seat Karen,' said Frank, looking sternly at Andrew. 'Let the girl sit down boy.'

Andrew jumped up. 'Sorry Karen. Have a seat.'

'So Karen. Andrew tells us you have been together since the beginning of last term,' Frank began.

Greenpeace Badge didn't respond, having briefly forgotten she was supposed to be called Karen. Tom gave her a little nudge.

'Sorry Frank. Miles away. Yes. Where did we meet?' She side-stepped the question. 'You tell them Andrew. It's such a nice story.'

Tom thought it a good time to get everybody sat at the table. 'Dinner's almost ready. Let's sit.' They had borrowed a second table from the girls' floor below and covered them both with a clean bed sheet. The knives and forks were all different and the plates were all different as they were all borrowed from a number of different people. The guests had wine glasses while the boys all drank from mugs.

As they took their seats, Tom suggested quietly to Andrew that he use the Greenpeace poster as the answer for his parents. Once seated, when the noise died down, Andrew and Greenpeace Badge both spoke at the same time. While Andrew was saying 'in the union building', she was saying 'in the Coffee Bar'.

'Come on Andrew. Don't tell me you've forgotten already.' Frank said, immediately assuming that if the two stories didn't match, it was Andrew who had it wrong.

Greenpeace Badge filled in the gaps. 'We met in the union building before having a drink together in the Coffee Bar. Andrew had been queuing for chips.'

Maureen tutted, not happy with Andrew's eating habits.

'And I reached past him to see a Greenpeace poster,' continued Greenpeace Badge. 'We just got talking because Andrew is a member as well.'

Frank wasn't happy with that. 'You never said anything about that. I'm not topping up your grant money so you can give it to loony lefty pressure groups. You'll never get a proper job if your name is muddied by the shame of militancy.'

'But,' started Andrew.

Frank wasn't finished yet though. 'Those unwashed, radical, yoghurt knitters would bring this country to its knees before they saw sense.'

Andrew was about to answer when Tom intervened with a diplomatic stance aimed at stopping Greenpeace Badge from laying into Frank and blowing her cover.

'Mr Leopard. Andrew isn't a member. He borrowed my Greenpeace shirt that night as his laundry was still wet,' said Tom facing Frank, but half turning towards Greenpeace Badge. He went on. 'I, as a member, and I think I speak for most other members, appreciate that the more senior people within our community may treat our group with a little suspicion.' Then, in an effort to divert the conversation, added, 'Do you belong to any groups Mr Leopard?'

'Well yes.' He leaned back as Brian placed a plate of curry in front of him. 'I'm in the Rotary Club. We support a number of charities.'

Maureen sat quietly during the discussion of pressure groups and charity organisations. She let Frank represent them both on matters which required worldly knowledge, but she did remember saying what a nice badge Tom had with a pretty white dove at Christmas. He had told her it was a Greenpeace Badge. But she had thought nothing more than 'what a pretty badge'. She now noticed Karen wearing the same badge.

After swallowing a mouthful of Brian's curry, which looked like vomit, but tasted rather nice, she turned to Karen. 'What a lovely badge. Tom has one just like it.'

The triviality of her comment took the heat out of the conversation and Tom took the opportunity to top up the drinks, opening a second bottle of Bulgarian wine.

Andrew inwardly breathed a sigh of relief. 'Nice curry Brian.'

'Thanks Andrew,' he replied.

Maureen had never had curry before. Dinner in the Leopard household had always been strictly 'meat and two veg', but she surprisingly found herself enjoying the food. 'Yes Brian. Very nice. You must give me the recipe.'

'Thanks Mrs Leopard, but there is no recipe.'

'You clever boy. You can remember it all without one?'

'No. Not really. It's more of a formula than a recipe.'

Maureen was fascinated. 'Please go on.'

'Well Mrs Leopard. The name says it all.'

'And what's it called?

'What's-left-in-the-fridge-at-the-end-of-the-week curry.'

Maureen laughed assuming he was joking.

He didn't laugh and wondered what she had found amusing, but carried on anyway. 'You get a tin of curry paste and mix it with all the leftovers in the fridge.' He put another mouthful in and washed it down with a swig of Bulgarian wine.'

Maureen's interest in curry ended as quickly as it started and she picked through her food trying to identify the different ingredients.

The Leopards were grouped around one end of the table with 'Karen' and the brothers at the other end. Ian Mellor's tape player had Dire Straits playing in the background and Greenpeace Badge took the opportunity for a quiet conversation with Tom, while Brian and Andrew spoke about economics and politics with Frank. There was enough noise in the room for Tom and Greenpeace Badge to speak quietly without the others hearing.

'So how are you getting on with the lovely Vicky?' she asked.

'Very well thanks.'

'You falling in love?'

'Oh no. Not at all. I don't even know what that means.'

'Well that's a relief.'

Tom paused briefly and looked Greenpeace Badge in the eye. 'Why's that a relief Sanita?' Greenpeace Badge's real name was Sanita Harrison. Tom called her Sanita to her face, but Greenpeace Badge when he mentioned her to his friends. 'Sounds to me like you may be a little jealous.'

'Don't be so silly. I'm perfectly happy with my boyfriend. You know that.'

'I know you slept with me so you can't be that happy with your boyfriend. I thought we were working well as friends, but now I'm seeing more and more of Vicky, you don't seem to like her.'

'She's too plain for you.'

'I agree she looks a bit plain, but she adores me. That counts for a lot and she has hidden depths. The more time I spend with her, the more interesting she becomes.'

'Sounds like you're trying to convince yourself as much as me.'

Maureen had noticed 'Karen' deep in conversation with Tom and wondered what they were talking about. Frank hadn't noticed at all and was busy telling Andrew and Brian that the only way to succeed in life was to know the right people and the 'right people' were nearly always Rotarians.

Sanita hadn't finished with Tom. 'I think you're papering over the cracks. A lot of people who look plain are exactly what they appear … plain. Take Andrew for example. His clothes are straight off the dummy in Marks & Spencer, and, I hate to be unkind, but his personality is the same as the shop dummy. There's nothing there. I like him and yes, he has a heart of gold, much the same as Vicky, but I would feel a bit embarrassed taking him home to meet my parents.'

'I know what you're saying, but I think you're wrong. There's more to Vicky than meets the eye and, given enough time, I could fall in love with her.'

Maureen had not stopped watching Tom and 'Karen' and was starting to suspect things were not right when Colin and Hugh walked back in the kitchen.

Andrew panicked and jumped out of his seat. His parents had been fooled so far, but Colin and Hugh would probably give him away. 'Colin, Hugh, this is my mum and dad. Mum and Dad this is Colin and Hugh … it is … it is … that.'

Andrew was almost trembling and started gathering the dinner plates as his father shook Colin and Hugh's hands.

'Frank. The boy forgets I have a name sometimes. And this is Maureen.'

She also shook their hands.

'Coffee anybody?' asked Andrew.

'No sugar Leopard,' said Hugh.

'Same for me,' shouted Colin. They had won on the fruit machines and drunk their profits. They had returned curious to see what Andrew's parents were like.

'Have you been studying in the library?' Frank asked Hugh.

Hugh had to think for a minute what a library had to do with him. 'Ahh yes. That's right. We've been in the library. Stopped for a quick drink on the way home though.' He patted Frank on the back. 'How was Andrew's cooking?'

'Brian cooked. Excellent. Something foreign, but still quite good.'

'So how do you like our kitchen?' Hugh asked.

'Nicer than I feared,' answered Maureen. 'Although it could do with a woman's touch.'

'Our kitchen is just as messy,' said Sanita.

Colin and Hugh both looked at Greenpeace Badge wondering why Tom's old girlfriend was having dinner with Andrew's parents and Maureen's reply confused them even more.

'Oh I can't believe that Karen. I'm sure you're just being kind.'

Colin and Hugh looked at each other and the confused expressions were slowly replaced by wide smiles as they put two and two together and came up with Pink Socks impersonator.

'How are you Karen?' Hugh asked Greenpeace Badge.

'Yes, how are you Karen?' Colin also asked, before she had time to answer Hugh.

Tom didn't give her time to answer either of them and turned to Andrew's parents. 'You haven't seen Andrew's room yet. You take them through Andrew and I'll bring the coffees.'

Sanita reached for Andrew's hand and dragged him out of the kitchen. Frank and Maureen followed. Colin was about to go through the door when Brian grabbed his collar from behind. 'No you don't shit-for-brains.'

'That's not very nice,' said Hugh.

'Okay, so you've worked it out,' said Tom. 'You don't have to spoil it for him. He's getting away with it. Give him a break.'

'What's it worth?' asked Colin with a cheeky smile.

'I won't beat you up,' suggested Brian.

'We'll owe you a favour,' Tom said, directing the offer to Hugh, who he thought would realise that was the best they could hope for.

He was right.

'Fair enough,' said Hugh. 'But it'll need to be a big favour because exposing your scam would have been a lot of fun.'

Tom and Brian carried the coffees into Andrew's bedroom.

Maureen had the one soft chair. Frank sat at Andrew's desk and the boys sat in a row on the bed with Sanita sandwiched between Andrew and Tom.

Andrew was hugely relieved that they had got away from Colin and Hugh and his secret was safely within the walls of his own room now. Frank didn't mind which room he was in as he continued to tell everyone how he had lit up the conference with pioneering insight and sharp wit that none of them had enjoyed at previous meetings.

Sanita was bored of hearing Frank's self-congratulatory stories. She was tired of pretending to be Karen Fisher and she was fed up of hearing about Vicky Owen. She wanted Tom to tell her that she was the only girl for him and Vicky had been a mistake. Sanita had a boyfriend, who Tom knew about, but she would prefer Tom. She only stayed with her boyfriend because she didn't think Tom was interested in a long-term relationship. And now it looked like he was about to settle down. It should have been her and not Vicky Owen. She excused herself to visit the ladies' room.

'Any more of that wine Andrew?' Frank asked.

'Yes. In the kitchen … it is.'

'I'll go,' said Tom.

In the kitchen he grabbed the half empty bottle of wine and headed back to Andrew's room. Outside the closed door he met Sanita on her way back from the ladies. As he reached for the handle, she put her hand on his and stopped him.

'There's something we need to get sorted before going back in,' she said.

'Oh right. Fire away,' said Tom, unaware that his friend was no longer happy as 'just good friends'.

She reached her hands around the back of his head, pulled him towards her and kissed him passionately on the lips, just as Maureen, who also needed the ladies, pulled open the door.

Maureen was aghast and her jaw dropped open in shock. 'I thought there was something going on,' she cried. 'How could you Tom? She's not YOUR girlfriend.'

Tom was doubly shocked. No. It wasn't his girlfriend and he didn't realise she had such feelings for him and finding out at the same time as their scam unfolded left him stuck for words. 'She's NOT my girlfriend Mrs Leopard.' His words didn't help.

Frank was angry now. The boy that was supposed to be his son's friend was kissing his son's girlfriend. What a way to repay his family after hosting them over Christmas. 'Don't just stand there Andrew. Do the right thing. Give him a piece of your mind. He's betrayed you.'

Andrew didn't respond. He was also in shock. The evening was not going to plan and his best friend appeared to have the sort of problem that he could only dream about having, two women fighting over him.

Frank raised his voice now. 'Where's your backbone boy? You're your mother's son alright. If there was anything of me in you, you would take some action here. Spineless. You'll never amount to anything.'

During their Christmas stay at the Leopards, Tom had bitten his tongue when Frank had derided his son based on the 'when in Rome' dictum, but they were no longer in Rome, they were at Southside University and Tom was no longer prepared to hear Frank repeatedly rubbish his own son. He walked back into the room and faced Frank, having regained his composure.

'With all due respect Mr Leopard, you are wrong,' Tom said firmly to Frank.

'You stand there kissing my son's girlfriend and you have the audacity to tell me I'm wrong.'

'She's not Andrew's girlfriend. She's not mine either, but that's another story. She's not even called Karen Fisher. She's Sanita Harrison, a good friend of mine and she pretended to be your son's girlfriend because he wanted so badly to please you. I don't know why. Because you treat him like shit. You treat him like something you have trodden in. It's no wonder he hasn't got the confidence to get his own girlfriend with a father like you. You chip, chip, chip away at him all the time and you're so wrapped up in your own importance that you can't see what you're doing to him. The whole charade tonight was about YOU. Andrew gave you what you wanted, what you expected, and I've no idea why. You DON'T deserve it!'

The room fell silent as they all took in what had happened.

Frank could not believe anybody would show him so little respect, but clearly he had been right. He should never have allowed a loony lefty member of Greenpeace into his home at Christmas. He was probably filling his son's head with radical garbage. 'We're leaving. Come on Maureen. Andrew, this isn't over. Goodbye Brian and goodbye Karen, or whatever your name is.'

They left in a hurry.

After they had gone, Andrew, Brian and Sanita all looked at Tom in disbelief. Tom felt a huge weight off his shoulders having told Frank Leopard what he needed to hear, but at the same time, felt a new weight on his shoulders having discovered that Sanita was jealous of Vicky.

Chapter 22

Walking down the aisle

A week later, February 7, 1984: 'Have we got enough fish-fingers … have we?' asked Andrew Leopard.

'I think so, but get some anyway. They're always good for a cheap meal,' replied Tom Hill.

It was late Tuesday afternoon. Tom and Brian Hill, Andrew and Vicky Owen were doing their weekly food shop in the town-centre supermarket. The three boys were still sharing shopping and cooking while Vicky had joined them after Tom had offered to carry her shopping back to campus. It wasn't a full weekly shop for her. It was just for one special meal, which she was cooking that night for Tom.

They shared one trolley, which Andrew pushed. Vicky used the front while Tom and Brian argued over what to put in the back for the boys. Tom preferred the cheapest items, unless there was a good organic alternative and Brian preferred branded products, a little more expensive, 'but you knew what you were getting'.

As it turned out, the visit to the supermarket presented more complicated choices for Tom than whether to choose organic baked beans or Heinz baked beans. 'We forgot cheese. Back in a minute,' Tom said. Two aisles back, he reached for a small slab of cheese. When he looked up, Sanita Harrison was facing him.

'How's it going Tom? Are you on your own?' she asked.

'You're looking lovely. I'm with Brian, Andrew and Vicky,' he replied, almost apologetically.

'The lovely Vicky!' Sanita no longer needed to hide her thoughts on the subject of Vicky or her own feelings for Tom. It was a week since she had kissed him, but there had only been small-talk between them since then. Sanita had been reluctant to talk about the kiss for fear of rejection. As long as the problem were left dangling, she still had a chance of winning him over. 'What colour ribbon does she have in her hair today?'

Tom was reading between the lines. 'That's a little unkind Sanita.' He was also avoiding the big questions as he still had some doubts about Vicky, but, despite the doubts, he wanted to give the romance every chance of progressing. 'She's making me dinner tonight. I'd better get back. She'll be wondering where I am.' He hurried back to the others.

Tom placed the slab of cheese in the trolley as they rounded the end of the frozen food aisle and headed down the jams and biscuits aisle. It was Andrew's turn to be caught off guard now. Coming in the other direction, flanked by two friends, was Pink Socks pushing her trolley.

Karen Fisher and her two friends were doing their weekly shop. She saw the boys from Dickens Court at the far end of the aisle by the crisp section. She had met Andrew, but not the nice-looking tall dark-haired boy. She didn't know the other boy but had seen the three together in the social sciences department. She hoped the girl with them was just a friend.

Andrew turned to Tom like a rabbit caught in headlights. He said nothing but Tom could see in his startled face that he was pleading for guidance. 'No need to be nervous. You've already met. You have to go past her, so you have no choice but to say something. You have no choice in the matter at all so there is nothing to be nervous about.'

Andrew disagreed and felt almost faint with anxiety. He had a bad spot on his left cheek, but he had greeted her with worse earlier in the term.

Tom tried different advice. 'Just pretend your James Bond.'

Andrew was still unable to speak to his friends, let alone Pink Socks.

Tom could see that unless he gave Andrew some lines to say, he would say no more than 'hello'. 'Right Andrew. You can see from here, her trolley is pretty full, so when we get closer, say to her, "What a lot of shopping. Are you having a party?" Then see what she says and take it from there.'

'Okay. I can do it … I can.' Andrew felt short of breath and his heart was racing, but he was determined to deliver the line. As she came closer, Andrew felt like running, but he didn't, he took a step forward to face Pink Socks. 'Hi Karen. How are you? Wow. What a lot of shopping. Are you having a party?'

Tom was stood next to Andrew and discreetly reached across and patted him proudly on the back as Karen replied.

'Andrew.' She looked down at her shopping. 'There's not that much. You've got more. When's your party? Are we invited?'

Tom inwardly smiled and thought excellent result, but was soon disappointed as Andrew let another opportunity slip away.

'No. No. We're not having a party … we're not.' An awkward pause followed. Tom, Brian and Vicky all hoped Andrew would keep talking, so they waited, but nothing came.

Karen ended the silence. She waved her hand towards her friends in turn. 'This is Emily and Charlotte.' She then looked at Tom, but spoke to Andrew. 'And your friends are?'

'Tom, Brian and Vicky.'

They all greeted each other. With the formalities over and having given way to Andrew for his chance with Pink Socks, Brian thought he was now allowed to wade in. He particularly liked the look of Emily, but had focussed a little too much on her breasts instead of her face, which had not gone unnoticed by Emily. 'Hi Emily. I'm Brian. Andrew's not having a party, but I could rustle up a few snacks for you and me. How about it?'

If he had concentrated on her face she would have said yes, but it was clear to Emily that he had only one thing on his mind so she dismissed him. 'No thanks. Let's go Karen.'

As they edged away, Karen looked back over her shoulder. 'Nice meeting you Tom, Brian, Vicky. See you around,' she said, all the time looking at Tom, something, which Brian spotted again, but said nothing. Andrew was too busy mentally kicking himself to notice who Pink Socks had been looking at.

Vicky had also noticed that Tom had turned the head of another girl and her self confidence was tested. Why was this young man, who seemed too good to be true, with her, when he had so much choice? If she fell in love with him, it would be certain to end in tears. There would always be another girl waiting to grab him when her guard was down. Have a bit of belief in yourself she repeated in her head as they turned down the bread and cake aisle.

Coming in the other direction was Sanita Harrison. This could be awkward thought Tom. 'Hi Sanita. How are you?' Tom said.

'Good thanks Tom. Are you going to introduce me?' Sanita replied curtly, all the time looking at Vicky.

'Yes of course.' He reached his arm towards Vicky. 'This is my girlfriend Vicky Owen.' Then he reached his arm towards Sanita, while facing Vicky. 'This is Sanita Harrison. We are both in the Greenpeace Society.'

Vicky had joined despite fearing what her father may think, but had not been to any meetings. This seemed a good opportunity to meet another member. Sanita looked quite pleasant and Vicky spoke with her about Greenpeace.

Tom was alarmed to see them getting on quite well and was even more alarmed when they walked ahead together still deep in conversation. He was worried that Sanita would sabotage his chances with Vicky, but thankfully they were still all smiles as Sanita turned towards the check-outs, while the boys headed up the beer and wine aisle.

As they walked back along Thief Lane, the winter sun warming their faces, the boys carried bags in both hands while Vicky carried a bottle of wine in each hand. Andrew struggled and fell behind with Vicky for company while Tom and Brian strided ahead. Andrew got on well with Vicky, just as he had done with Lisa Wentworth-Simpson. He was comfortable talking to girls when they were part of a couple. He knew that they knew that he had no hidden sexual agenda. That took the pressure off and he could be natural.

Brian and Tom had opened up a gap of around 20 yards by the time they reached the football ground. 'Did I tell you I got a letter from the hospital this morning?' Brian asked Tom.

'No. What did it say?'

'It was an appointment to see a specialist about my lumpy ball-bag. I only had to wait four months. That must be an NHS record.' Sarcasm from Brian.

'They won't operate though will they?'

'No. I doubt it. They'll probably have a look and then leave it for another four months. Still, I don't mind. It's uncomfortable, but not painful. But I'm sure the operation will be painful, so the longer the wait the better.'

'I'm sure the operation won't be painful, otherwise they would have told you there is nothing to worry about.' Sarcasm from Tom.

'On the subject of ball-bags,' Brian changed the subject. 'Have you boned Vicky yet?' Brian's language lacked subtlety. 'That is, of course, if you intend sticking with her and not going back to Greenpeace Badge.'

'Oh I'm sticking with her. And no, I've not. We're taking it steady. Maybe you should try it. I saw you looking at that girl's tits in the supermarket. Until you did that, she had been checking you out. I think you could have been in there.'

'Maybe. But I don't want to waste time taking it steady and, like you said, she had been checking me out. I'm not offended by that. If looking at her tits was a problem, she was not the girl for me.'

'Fair point.' Tom had to agree.

Three hours later, Tom knocked on Vicky's door ready for their dinner date. She pulled the door open. Tom hugged her and gave her a quick kiss on the lips before handing her a small gift wrapped in tin foil.

'Ooh … thank-you Tom. What is it?'

'Nothing much. I just thought you might like it.' It was the first present Tom had bought for any girl. He hoped it would reassure her that she was special to him.

Vicky had cleared her desk and grabbed an extra chair from the kitchen so they could eat in the peace of her bedroom. She had set two places and lit a scented candle, which she had bought from Third World Collective in town. She wore the same lilac dress she had worn on their first date at The Pepper Pot.

Her eyes burned bright as she pulled away the tin foil from her gift to reveal a deep purple silk scarf. 'You shouldn't have.'

'No. No. I wanted to. I thought it would match your lilac dress.'

She draped it around her neck. 'Thank-you Tom.' She wrapped her arms around him and they kissed. She then rushed off to the kitchen and returned with two wine glasses and a bottle of chilled wine.

'I hope you like moussaka,' she said handing Tom a glass of wine.

'I certainly do.'

'Vegetarian of course.'

She rushed off to the kitchen again. Tom shouted after her. 'Need any help?'

'No thanks,' she shouted from down the corridor.

She set the plates down on her desk and sat with Tom before taking a sip of her own wine.

'Wow. This looks good,' Tom said with enthusiasm.

'Let's hope it tastes as good.'

By the time they started the second bottle of wine and moved onto a dessert of sherry trifle, Vicky had grown tired of light-hearted conversation and, after questioning her own self confidence in the supermarket, wanted a bit of reassurance. The gift had been a good start, but she wanted more.

'Tom,' she said in a way that introduced a more serious tone.

'Yes Vicky,' Tom said in a way that showed he knew she wanted to introduce a more serious tone.

'Have you ever been in love?' A tough question from Vicky.

'Hmm … Let me think … I don't think so. No. Although I'm not altogether sure I know what it means to be in love.' They were gazing into each other's eyes, their faces almost too close for comfortable focussing. Only the flickering candle-light separated them. In the background, Vicky was playing a tape of Fleetwood Mac. 'What do you think love is?' Tom asked.

'That's a difficult question.' Vicky raised one eyebrow in thought. It hid behind her fringe. 'I think it is when somebody becomes so special to you that you can take pleasure from seeing them laugh and smile.' Tom had nodded approval of her answer, so she went on. 'Do you think you will ever fall in love Tom?' An even tougher question from Vicky.

Tom rubbed his chin in thought feeling a small amount of pressure to give the right answer. 'Tough one. Quite possibly, but I would never tell a girl I loved her just to win her over. I would only say it if I meant it.'

Vicky made her question more direct. 'Could you see yourself falling in love with me?' The toughest question yet from Vicky.

Tom definitely felt pressure now, both in what he said and how quick he said it. He liked Vicky very much and hoped they would stick together for quite a while, but he was wary of making any firm commitment and, even acknowledging that he could fall in love at a later stage, was making more of a commitment than he wanted to. He saw his whole life before him like a winding road with surprises around every corner. He liked surprises. They were the spice of life for Tom. Making too big a commitment was like driving down a straight road. You could see too far ahead and there was not enough excitement.

He was not prepared to make any real commitment to Vicky and she sensed this in his delayed response. When he finally replied, it was cagey and guarded. 'We have a special bond. It is growing and I am enjoying every minute of it.'

It was not the reassuring answer she had hoped for, but she hid her disappointment well. She felt she had already fallen in love with Tom, but dared not say so. She didn't want a relationship where the commitment was all one-way. She would not tell Tom she loved him until she had some indication from him that he at least believed it was possible that he could, at some point, fall in love with her.

Tom could see she was disappointed. He reached his hand to her face and caressed her cheek. She squeezed his hand. He placed his free hand around her waist and pulled her towards him. 'You know I'm very fond of you. Let's just see how things go.'

Vicky forced a smile. She felt like crying, but she didn't.

Tom lifted her clear off the floor. She squealed a little, surprise more than protest. He placed her on the bed and lay down beside her. They talked and kissed for a couple of hours before falling asleep, still fully clothed on top of the bed.

At around four in the morning, Tom woke up. He crept out of the room to the toilet and returned without waking Vicky. The thin curtains were not enough to block out all the light from the footpaths and an amber glow softly lit Vicky's face. Tom watched her sleeping peacefully and felt a hint of guilt. He could have said what she had wanted to hear, but he didn't want to lie, just to keep her happy in the short term. Honesty kept things uncomplicated.

Vicky rolled towards Tom and opened her eyes. 'Hey Tom. You okay?'

'Yes thanks. Bit cold though. Shall we get in?'

Vicky wanted to keep him waiting. No sex without commitment she told herself.

Tom could see she wasn't sure. 'Don't worry. We don't have to do anything. We can just keep each other warm.'

She stripped down to her underwear. Tom followed her lead and they cuddled up together in a warm embrace.

Chapter 23

Room number one

The day after: A cold pan of beans sat on the cooker hotplate in the Dickens Court kitchen. It would stay cold until Brian Hill remembered it was on the broken ring. Six pieces of toast were burning under the grill as he stared at the naked girl on page three of his newspaper. It was lunchtime.

Tom Hill was deep in thought staring out of the window at the cherry trees in the courtyard below. The smell of burning toast brought his focus back into the kitchen. 'I think lunch is ready.'

Brian jumped up and pulled the black toast out of the cooker. As he began scraping the black surface off the toast, he looked into the pan of beans and wondered why they weren't bubbling. Dipping his finger into the cold pot, he remembered the ring was broken. He cursed and switched to the other ring. There were only two. 'It'll be a few minutes yet. I had the beans on the wrong ring.'

Brian finished scraping the brittle toast before sitting back down by the coffee table. He watched Tom looking out of the window and guessed that Vicky Owen must be the reason for his vacant stare. 'How did it go with Vicky last night?'

'Ooh … not too bad,' Tom said, almost sighing.

'Did you?' Brian asked with a naughty smile.

'Did I what?' Tom replied.

'Did you?' Brian repeated, this time with a knowing nod and a thrust of the hips.

'We spent the night together for the first time, but no, we didn't.'

'Why not?' Brian couldn't understand why his brother was so patient.

'Well, to be honest Brian, that's what I'm trying to work out.'

Brian nodded for Tom to continue.

'From what she was saying, I think she may be in love with me and I don't know how I feel about that.'

'Did she say she was?'

'No. But reading between the lines, I got the feeling that she was, but didn't want to say.'

'Why not?' Now Brian couldn't understand Vicky. His understanding of girls was extremely limited at the best of times, but this was beyond him.

Tom thought he had read the signals right, but wasn't sure. 'I don't think she wanted to say, because I wasn't very kind about her.'

'What did you say?' Brian was intrigued now.

'Nothing bad, but nothing good either. I think she wanted some kind of indication from me that I felt the same way as her before she was prepared to tell me she loves me. And.' Tom paused for effect. 'I don't think she wants to have sex until I tell HER that I love her.'

'So why don't you just tell her.'

'Because I don't.'

'So?' This was the most confusing of all. Tom just had to say one little fib and he could shag Vicky. What could be more straight-forward.

'I don't love her. I may, eventually, but I'm not prepared to lie.'

'Not even for a shag?'

'Not even for a shag,' Tom confirmed to Brian, and probably to himself as well.

'So what are you going to do then?' Brian thought Tom was wasting his time with Vicky if she was waiting for something that Tom couldn't give her.

'I don't know. I like her a lot and, you never know, I may fall in love, but I'm only 18. I can't see myself with the same girl for ever. There are so many others that I would be missing out on.'

'That's a good point. Might be time to cut and run.'

'No. I don't think so and besides, I could be completely wrong.'

Just as the beans began to bubble, Andrew Leopard walked in the kitchen followed by Hugh Grundy, Colin Dean and Ian Mellor. Next through the door was Roger Evans, who silently made a cheese sandwich and left. Nobody spoke to him. He never replied so people had stopped noticing him at all. He was just part of the furniture like the table or fridge.

Andrew had been waiting all morning to see Tom. He had an idea and needed his opinion. 'I think I'll send Pink Socks some roses on Valentine's Day,' he said, expecting enthusiasm from Tom.

'That's not for another week,' Tom said sharply. He wanted Andrew to move faster. He wanted Vicky to move faster, but he didn't want to push her, so he took his impatience out on Andrew. 'But okay. It's better than nothing. What message do you have in mind?'

Strange question Andrew thought. 'Nothing. It's a Valentine's card. It's supposed to be anonymous … it is.'

'Then you're probably wasting time and money. You're not going to win her over if she doesn't even know the roses are from you. In fact, worse than that, Colin or Hugh will probably dive in and pretend they sent them.'

'Aah … but what if I tell her before anybody else dives in?'

'Sticking your name on the card is the only way to guarantee that and you've not exactly been quick so far in talking to her,' Tom pointed out. 'I need a wee before we eat.' Tom disappeared.

Colin threw his books on the floor in the corner, sat in one of the soft chairs and lit a cigarette. He then leant forward and, using the red-hot tip of his cigarette, burned a row of dots along the rim of the coffee table.

Hugh couldn't find any clean pots. 'Where's your small pan Wanker?'

'I've hidden it,' said Ian.

'Why?' asked Hugh, a little annoyed.

'Because you always use it and never clean it.' Ian was tired of washing his own pots after Hugh and Colin had borrowed them. 'If you promise to wash it when you've finished, I'll lend you it.'

'Fine. I will,' Hugh lied. He had no intention of washing it and was irritated that Ian had made such a fuss.

Brian and Andrew had finished their lunch before Tom returned from the toilet.

'You took your time,' Brian said loudly.

'That's because I have just been in room number one,' Tom proudly announced to the whole room.

Everyone immediately turned round, eagerly waiting to hear more. Anything to do with the mysterious room number one commanded instant attention.

'Go on then,' Brian urged him. 'What's he like?'

The boys gathered around the coffee table.

'The door was slightly open so I knocked and there was no answer, so I pushed it open a little,' Tom said.

'And?' Hugh said at the same time as Colin said, 'go on.'

'There was nobody there, but I took one step in so I could have a good look around.'

There was disappointment because Tom had not seen the student, but they still wanted to know what Tom had seen.

'He's got some strange stuff. I think he might be a post grad research student, possibly something to do with music, because there was some sheet music on his desk. And he must have some money. There were shelves packed with books and pictures all over the walls, not posters with Blu Tac holding them up, but fine art abstract prints, or originals, in fancy gold frames. There was an old tapestry on one wall, probably an antique, with some kind of classical scene on it, nymphs and shepherds dancing by a lake. There were loads of shiny silk cushions on the bed and there was a sculpture of Napoleon. I think it was Napoleon … just his head and shoulders.'

'Sounds like a weirdo,' said Colin.

'Sounds gay,' said Hugh.

'Sounds rich,' said Brian.

'Oh … and one other thing,' added Tom. 'The sculpture of Napoleon had a big black tear under one eye. Just one eye and it looked as if it had been cut out of black cardboard and glued onto the white marble.'

Chapter 24

Focus on the thug

Six days later, February 14, 1984: Hugh Grundy plodded steadily along Thief Lane, past the football ground, on his way back to Southside University after a very unpleasant trip into town. It was a dark day for Hugh in many ways. He was bitterly cold wearing only his usual black jeans and leather jacket. Fashion came before common sense. Besides, he was supposed to be a hard man and that meant you didn't feel the cold. A biting wind battered his wide face with ice-cold drizzle. His shaved head kept no heat in and he was 'too cool' to wear a hat.

It wasn't just the weather that had made it a dark day for Hugh. Nobody had sent him a Valentine card, none of his 'easy-money' schemes had paid off, but worst of all, he had just spent the last of his grant on something he didn't really want, but knew he needed.

After two years of tripping over his feet, Hugh had begrudgingly accepted that he needed glasses, which he now wore. The arm, which rested over his left ear, cut right through the neck of his tattooed lizard and the large deep red frames, which matched his Dr Marten boots, perched on his nose making him, in his opinion, look like a geek, an extremely aggressive geek, but, nevertheless, a geek.

As he got closer and closer to Dickens Court, he started to realise that it was not the wearing of the glasses which made him feel uncomfortable, it was the probable reaction of his floor-mates.

As he crossed the railway bridge, he noticed a small aeroplane, the size of those you see on telly spraying crops, battling with the wind over Southside University. The wind was so strong, the plane appeared to hardly move and it was so low that, now wearing glasses, Hugh could read the large code letters on the body of the plane. He wondered why it was so low. Must be taking photographs he thought. You could take a lot of pictures of houses very quickly. Maybe there was something in that for his next money-making scheme. His mind raced, but all the time, fell back on what his floor-mates would say when he walked in the kitchen wearing his new glasses.

He expected the usual jokes and intended giving somebody a good slapping to make sure he nipped it in the bud, but, even though he was the biggest on the floor, he didn't want to tangle with the Hill brothers. They would put up too much of a fight. And he quite liked them. Tom was a bit self-righteous but fairly friendly and he always did well with the chicks. Brian was better. He was more of a man's man, knew what women were for and always had a laugh and joke. And both the Hill brothers were in the football club so they enjoyed a few beers. No. He didn't want to tangle with them.

No Balls Leopard wouldn't dare say anything and he was harmless anyway. He would probably be too scared to even look at Hugh's new glasses. Wanker would only say something after somebody else had started. He liked to jump on the bandwagon but didn't have the bottle to start anything himself. Maybe he would be the one that needed slapping.

Then there was his best mate Colin Dean. Hugh never helped Colin out so he didn't expect any support from him, but he was a wimp anyway. He talked a good game, but he couldn't even stand up to No Balls Leopard, who had knocked him over during the Christmas party. What an embarrassment that had been. A friend of his knocked over by a spotty boy who was too shy to take his hands out of his pockets. Colin had only ever been a friend of convenience for Hugh. He just happened to be in the next room during Hugh's first year. Hugh would much rather Tom and Brian had started at Southside a year earlier, then Brian would have been his best friend, possibly Tom too. Hugh was soaked as he went through the doors of Dickens Court, block F, and headed up the stairs.

Tom and Brian sat in the corner of their Dickens Court kitchen with a cup of tea. They should have been to a sociology lecture but it was raining and they didn't want to get wet.

'Who do you think it's from then?' Brian asked.

'No idea,' replied Tom. He had received two cards, one signed 'all my love Vicky' and the other, which had a picture of bread on the front, saying 'would you like a roll with me?'.

Brian got no cards, but he hadn't sent any either. Tom had sent Vicky a card. He wrote 'you are my favourite girl in the whole world', which was the kindest thing he could say without going as far as saying 'I love you'.

'Made any progress with Vicky yet?' Brian asked.

'No. Not really. We're still at the sleeping-together-but-no-sex stage, but there was an interesting development last night,' Tom replied.

'Go on.' Brian sat forward with interest.

'We were about to doze off when I said, 'Sweet dreams." She was facing away from me, straight at the wall, and replied softly, "And you Tom". Then about a minute later, even softer, she said, 'I love you Tom."

'Shit … What did you say?'

'I had to think for a second. She wanted an instant "I love you too Vicky", but it didn't come."

'So what did come?'

'Nothing. I said nothing, hoping she thought I hadn't heard her, but a few minutes later, I thought I could hear her crying. I wanted to tell her I loved her, just to make her feel good, but I couldn't do it.'

Andrew Leopard, Ian Mellor and Colin Dean marched into the kitchen.

'Anybody seen Hugh?' Colin asked.

The boys all shrugged their shoulders.

'That's funny. He wasn't at lectures and he's not in his room.'

Before they could settle down the door flew open and Hugh walked purposefully into the middle of the room. He stood straight and tall, a good six feet and three inches including the heels of his boots. He puffed out his chest, almost daring anyone to comment. He might be wearing glasses, but his fists were just as hard. The kitchen was silent apart from a pan of baked beans bubbling on the one good ring of the cooker.

Before anybody spoke, Roger Evans came in with his cardboard box, stopped, looked up at Hugh's glasses and stared rudely. Noticing the tension in the room, he pushed his own glasses back up his nose, turned straight around and left the room.

Brian was trying not to laugh and broke the silence. 'What's wrong Hugh? You look paned.'

Before Hugh could respond, Tom, who was trying to hide a smile added, 'Are you on drugs Hugh? Your eyes looked glazed.'

If Hugh were a cartoon character, he would now have a bright red face and steam racing out of his ears. 'Watch your mouth Hill or there'll be trouble. Is that clear?'

'Clear as glass,' Tom quickly replied, with a friendly smile.

As Hugh had expected, Ian Mellor took the opportunity to join in now the banter had started, with an ill-timed cliché. Hugh darted in his direction and grabbed his lapels, holding him against the wall about a foot off the ground. 'Apologise now or die. What's it to be Wanker?'

Nobody jumped to his rescue. It was good entertainment and Hugh was hurting his pride more than anything.

'I'm sorry. I'm sorry,' Ian wimpered.

Hugh pressed home his advantage. 'Louder Wanker so everyone can hear.'

'I'm sorry Hugh,' Ian shouted.

Hugh let go and he slid back down the wall.

Again there was an awkward moment, which Brian ended with a song. 'Four eyes a jolly good fellow.'

Hugh edged in Brian's direction, but he was ready. He stood and held up both hands, palms flat towards Hugh, like a policeman stopping traffic. 'No need for violence. A bit of banter never hurt anybody.' Hugh backed off a little. 'Actually I think they look quite good. What do you think Tom?'

'Yes Hugh. A good choice of frames. They're very "you".'

After a while the hum of conversation returned and Colin used Ian's pan to prepare Hugh's lunch. He left the dirty pan for Ian to wash.

Andrew sat next to Tom. 'Can I ask you a big favour?'

'You can ask.' Tom replied.

'I've got the roses for Pink Socks in my room. Could you take them to the economics department and put a note in her pigeon hole?'

'Why don't you do it?'

'It's my department. Everybody knows me. They're less likely to know you … they are.'

Tom didn't think it made any difference. His sociology department was in the same building anyway, so some people would know him in the economics department, two floors below. He looked out of the window. It was still raining and he had already missed a lecture to avoid the rain. Mind you, if it hadn't been raining, he would probably have found another excuse to miss the lecture.

'Oh okay.' He gave in. 'You'll owe me a big favour though.'

'Thanks Tom.'

Ten minutes later, Tom was soaked as he walked down the corridor in the economics department looking for the pigeon holes. He found them above a desk and placed the card in the hole marked F for Fisher. He placed the flowers on the desk underneath. As he turned to leave, he saw Pink Socks at the other end of the corridor coming towards him.

He had been briefly introduced in the supermarket and wondered if she would recognise him. She certainly did and having seen him with the flowers, was hoping they were for her. She smiled warmly as she approached with the intention of stopping for a chat. 'Hi Tom. How are you?'

Tom could see she was about to stop. He politely smiled back and walked a little faster, so he didn't have to stop and chat. 'Fine thanks Karen. You okay?'

As he hurried back to Dickens Court through the rain, he cursed his bad luck. Why hadn't Andrew put his name on the card like he had told him to? Now Pink Socks was going to think the flowers were from Tom.

Chapter 25

Southside District Waiting Room

Eleven days later, February 25, 1984: It was getting towards the end of term and most students were running out of money. Visits to the pub had become rare but tonight was a promotion night in the Union Bar with Fosters for 50 pence a pint. Having drawn two each with the top team, Tom and Brian Hill were in a mood to celebrate, especially as Tom had scored a goal, a headed equaliser from a corner. It was only his second of the season, Brian was on 35.

Andrew Leopard, Tom, Brian, Vicky Owen and Hugh Grundy shared a table. Colin Dean and Ian Mellor played snooker.

Hugh was not happy. He had tried his new idea for making money earlier that day and failed after being stopped by the police. He had gone with Colin to the smart tree-lined streets off Royal Avenue where Southside's most wealthy residents lived and climbed the tallest tree armed with Colin's camera. Having clung to the uppermost branches, he had taken what he hoped would pass as aerial photographs of the houses, which he wanted to sell to the owners of the homes.

Unfortunately, one of those residents had spotted him. They thought he was a burglar checking out his next target and called the police. He thought he had done nothing wrong. 'I paid good money to put film in that camera. You make an effort to earn some honest money and there's always someone waiting to knock you down.'

'Why don't you just get a part-time job?' asked Vicky.

'It's not that easy,' Hugh defended himself. 'There's three million unemployed and jobs are scarce.'

'Can't be that hard. Tom's got a job,' Vicky replied proudly.

Tom had successfully applied for bar work three nights a week at The Horse And Groom in London Road. He desperately needed the money. Having a girlfriend was expensive. Only Brian and Vicky had been told the news.

'When do you start?' Andrew asked. He was a little upset that he hadn't been told.

'Next week. Another one Brian, Andrew?' Tom grabbed their empty glasses and went to the bar with Vicky.

It was a popular event and there was a big queue at the bar. It took ten minutes to get served. Tom reached over a couple of heads with drinks for Vicky and Andrew. 'You take these and I'll catch you up.' She headed off. Tom had seen Greenpeace Badge and wanted a quiet word.

'Sanita. How's it going?' he said holding both his and Brian's drinks.

'Good thanks. Very good,' she said with forced enthusiasm. 'My boyfriend is here. We're getting on well.'

'Excellent. Best get back. See you later.' Tom thought she was just telling him things were going well to save face, but at least it took the pressure off him. He could concentrate on Vicky for now.

As Tom rejoined the others, Hugh was still complaining about the heavy tactics of the police. Vicky again changed the subject so she could proudly boast about Tom's new job. As Vicky, Tom, Andrew and Hugh discussed the risk to academic performance posed by part-time employment, Brian was distracted by a fly on the table.

He was leaning forward with his cheekbone resting on his right fist. His right elbow rested on the table next to his fresh pint of Fosters and he kept very still while his eyes followed the fly. It walked up to his glass, back towards the ashtray and through some spilled beer. It then stopped to rub its front legs together before changing direction and headed back towards the glass. It went up the side of the glass, back down, rubbed its legs together again and walked just inches past Brian's elbow towards a beer mat.

Brian followed it with his eyes until it passed in front of his fist by the length of Brian's fore-arm, at which point he slammed his fist down on the fly with alarming speed and ferocity, jolting, but not quite spilling, everybody's drinks. He wiped the dead fly on the edge of the table and, without changing his blank expression, addressed the others. 'I went to the hospital yesterday.'

Tom already knew but was the only one.

'How did it go?' asked Andrew. He was a little upset that he hadn't been told.

'Well. It shouldn't be called Southside District Hospital. It should be called Southside District Waiting Room. I spent most of the day waiting.'

'How long?' asked Andrew. Tom had already heard Brian's rant, but Brian was so disgusted by how long he had waited that he wanted more people to share his anger. Andrew was happy to listen.

'I got up early to be there on time and was kept waiting for half an hour before I was called. All they did then was move me to a second waiting room for another 45 minutes. Then I got a backwards-have-a-look-at-my-bum gown on and was kept waiting for the doctor in a cubical for another half hour.'

'What then?' Andrew was following with interest.

'The doctor fondled my nads for three minutes and left without saying anything.'

'He must have said something.' Vicky thought Brian must be exaggerating.

'Well not to me he didn't. He mumbled a few things to the nurse and, reading between the lines, I think the doctor I saw last autumn was spot on and I need a small operation.'

'When?' asked Tom, now worried about whether Brian would be fit for the end-of-season run-in. The university had won through to the cup final, to be played at the home of Southside Wanderers in Thief Lane, and Brian was a vital player. The league title was out of their reach now, but the cup final was against a team they had already beaten twice earlier in the season, but with Brian at his best.

'Don't know. All they would commit to was "as soon as possible, but there's a waiting list". Tells me nothing.

Could be tomorrow or next year.' Brian wasn't happy. 'The future of my bollock is out of my hands.'

Andrew had been listening carefully, but had still been able to keep a lookout for Pink Socks over Brian's shoulder and, as soon as he picked her out, Brian's bollock was forgotten. 'Tom. You won't believe this, but I've just spotted Pink Socks and I'm sure she was looking at me … I am.'

Everybody looked across the room at Pink Socks, except Andrew, who put his hands in his pockets and squirmed, thinking this could be his moment. She must have worked out the flowers were from him.

Tom, who was sat alongside Andrew, had other ideas about who Karen Fisher might be looking at, but kept them to himself not wishing to upset Andrew, or Vicky. 'Best get over there Andrew.'

'Mmm … not just yet.' Andrew couldn't think of a reason why not, but still thought it wise to be cautious.

'Come on Andrew.' Even Vicky was getting a little impatient with him. 'You've already spoken to her a couple of times. It won't hurt to go and have a quick chat.'

'Do you think I have any chance Vicky … do you?' Andrew, without knowing it, was fishing for compliments to give him a boost in confidence. Tom usually made some up, Brian usually changed the subject, Hugh would happily tell him she was out of his league, but Vicky dug deep to find something positive to say.

'Of course you have. You are a good looking boy with a heart of gold.'

'You're on,' Colin shouted to the Hill brothers on his return from the snooker tables with Ian.

'Who won?' asked Brian.

'Wanker on the black ball. Lucky bastard,' replied Colin. 'Pinball Hugh?' Colin suggested.

Brian and Tom went to play snooker while Colin, Hugh and Ian crowded round the pinball machine, leaving Vicky and Andrew sat at the table.

'What should I say to her?' Andrew asked Vicky for advice.

'Just tell her you sent the flowers and ask if she liked them.'

'She'd probably just tell me to get lost.'

'I doubt it. That would be very unkind. If she were that unkind, you're best not getting to know her anyway.'

'What next?'

'Then ask her out. She probably wouldn't say no. If she didn't want to, she would make an excuse, but she wouldn't tell you to get lost.'

Andrew thought for a moment. 'How did Tom ask you out?'

'Well. He didn't really. You were there when we met at the photo shop. We just got talking, but he did ask me on a proper date a few days later.'

'And you said "yes"?'

'Well actually I said "no", but he assumed it was because I didn't want to waste his money, so he insisted and we went to The Pepper Pot for a meal.'

Andrew stood up. He was ready to talk to Pink Socks.

'Too late Andrew,' said Vicky. 'She's gone.'

Andrew sat down again, almost relieved that he had avoided a tense situation. At least not asking her delayed her turning him down. 'Missed my chance.'

'Never mind.'

'I wish I were more like Tom.'

'One Tom is more than enough,' joked Vicky.

Andrew had drunk enough beer to have lost his nervous echo. Vicky was a good listener. Andrew was happy talking to her when Tom disappeared, which he often did. In fact, thought Andrew, he probably spent more time with Tom and Brian's girlfriends than they did, so maybe he was becoming more like Tom. The thought gave Andrew a warm glow.

'Tom's the best friend I've ever had.' Andrew told Vicky. 'I'm happy he has such a nice girlfriend and you get on so well.'

Vicky was starting to think Tom would never love her and had no close friends to talk to. She had also drunk a few beers and Andrew seemed like a good listener. 'Things aren't always what they seem though Andrew.'

'There's nothing wrong is there?' Andrew was shocked and genuinely worried for his friends.

'No. Not really, but I love him so much and I'm not sure he feels the same way about me.'

Andrew was lost for words. A girl had never been so open with him on such a delicate subject and he didn't know what he should say and he had no comforting words to offer. 'Can I get you another drink Vicky?'

'No thanks. I'm fine.' She had a full glass and realised Andrew only asked to hide his embarrassment. 'I'm sorry. I didn't mean to burden you with my troubles.'

'No. No. I don't mind at all.' He did. 'I just don't know what to say.' That was obvious.

'I think you're supposed to say, "don't worry, these things take time. He'll come round." That's what I've been telling myself.'

'I'm sure you're right.' That was the best Andrew could do.

Two hours later, Colin, Hugh and Ian staggered to the coffee bar, while Tom, Brian, Vicky and Andrew headed back to Dickens court. They sat in Andrew's bedroom while Tom made coffee. It was instant and not even coffee. It was a budget jar containing mostly chicory.

Brian sat in the soft chair while Andrew sat at his desk. Vicky sat on the bed with her back against the wall, leaving enough space for Tom to sit next to her.

The last time they had shared a coffee in Andrew's room was when Frank and Maureen Leopard had come to meet Karen Fisher and discovered their son's best friend kissing Karen Fisher, who wasn't actually Karen Fisher. Tom was a shade anxious that the subject wasn't bought up in case Vicky heard about Tom's kiss with Greenpeace Badge.

In an effort to steer the subject safely away from Sanita Harrison, Tom raised the subject of Andrew's relationship with his father. 'So Andrew. Last time we were in here for coffee, your father left in a hurry. Have you heard from him since?'

'Yes, but only to make travel arrangements for Easter.'

'Has he banned you from talking to me?'

'No. He didn't even mention their visit.'

'Is he waiting till he's got you at home?'

'Possibly, but I'll be ready. What you said to him during their visit was right. He does treat me like shit, and he has chipped away at me for years, so I don't have the confidence to defend myself.'

Tom thought he was at last getting somewhere with Andrew. If he could start thinking for himself instead of doing what he thought his father wanted, he would be much happier. 'You're talking a good game Andrew, but he's going to try and re-establish his hold on you over Easter.

It's a six-week break. That's a long time. But if you can see what he's doing to you, you've more chance to break free. Trouble is, he truly believes he knows best, and he doesn't want you to think for yourself.'

'I know you shocked him.' Andrew was hugely proud of Tom for standing up to Frank on his behalf. 'He's not used to people standing up to him. I've got to do it now though.'

Chapter 26

Action on the squash court

Three weeks later, March 16, 1984: It was the last day of term before the six-week Easter break. Vicky Owen was going home tomorrow. Tom Hill was staying at college with his brother for the holiday; they had nowhere to go. It would give them chance to do some studies for the first time, catch up on course work and prepare a few answers for the exams at the end of the year. The grades weren't important as they didn't effect the final grade of the degree. It was just pass or fail and if you passed, you progressed to the second year.

Tom had high hopes of making progress with Vicky on their final night. He wasn't going to see her for ages. Surely she would give in. He had booked the final session on the squash court behind the Dickens Court reception. There were a number of squash courts alongside the sports hall, but each accommodation block had its own court near their reception building.

He had taken her to see a romantic film at the Odeon for the first part of the evening to set the mood with a vigorous game of squash to follow. Tom had booked the final session of the evening at 20 past eleven. The warden left at 11.30 so Tom agreed to lock up and push the key through the letterbox outside reception.

Vicky changed first and began warming up, hitting the ball against the far wall. Each time she hit the ball, she muttered under her breath. 'He loves me … ping … he loves me not … ping … he loves me … ping … he loves me not.' The ball hit the frame of her racket and fell to the ground. She picked it up, disappointed. 'This time. He loves me … ping … he loves me not … bother.' She missed the ball and it rolled towards the door, ending at Tom's feet as he came in.

'You ready for a good tonking?' Tom was glad he hadn't made a Freudian slip.

'We'll see about that.' Vicky had improved, but Tom still won every game.

The first game ended nine zero in Tom's favour. He put his racket down at the end of the game and took his shorts and shirt off.

'What are you doing?' Vicky asked anxiously.

'I was giving you a chance. I had my clothes on backwards.' Tom chuckled to himself as he dressed correctly.

Vicky managed a smile. 'It won't be so easy this time. I'm just getting warmed up.'

The next game was a little longer. Tom's co-ordination wasn't so good, Vicky took advantage and served a few times, but still scored nothing, the game ending nine zero again.

'I nearly had you there,' Vicky said with determination.

Tom theatrically tossed his racket from his left hand to his right hand. 'You should have beaten me. I was playing left handed.'

Vicky playfully punched Tom in the chest.

Tom replied with a playful squeeze of her buttock.

'I'll get at least one point this game. You see if I don't … and play properly. I don't need any favours.'

Even though Southside was a relatively modern university, the squash courts were shabby, probably not redecorated since the day they were built around 20 years ago. The markings on the floor were almost worn away and multi-coloured streaks filled the corners from countless racket heads thrust desperately towards the wall to keep the rally alive. The strip lighting was mostly good, but in one corner it flickered and hummed. The gallery overlooking the court had been taken over as storage. It was filled with spare beds, desks and chairs.

Ping, thump, ping, smash. 'Nine zero. What happened to those points you were going to score this time?' Tom mocked, rubbing his right eye with the palm of his hand.

'What's wrong with your eye?' Concern from Vicky.

'Oh nothing … nothing really … it's just a bit sore.'

'Let me have a look. Have you got something in it?' Vicky reached up to Tom's face to get a closer look.

'No. No. There's nothing in it. It's just a bit sore because I played the whole game with it shut.'

Vicky pushed his face away in light-hearted protest. Tom beamed a triumphant smile. She gave him another playful punch in the chest.

'I told you not to give me a chance.'

'So what are you going to do about it?' Tom was still smiling and turned his bum towards Vicky. 'Are you going to smack me?'

Whack. She swiped him on the backside with her racket.

Tom howled in pain and fell to the floor. She had caught him with the frame and it hurt.

She bent over him full of apologies. 'Are you okay Tom? I'm sorry. I didn't mean to hit you that hard.'

'I will be in a minute.' He was still writhing in agony. 'But I need something for the pain.

'What do you need?'

'A good snog.' Tom pulled her on top of him.

She battled a little, but conceded to his advances.

The coin-operated lights switched themselves off. It was midnight. The time slot was over. But Tom and Vicky's passion continued despite the darkness and strange surroundings, which were turning out to be quite inspirational despite the cold hard floor.

Tom pushed Vicky against the door, still kissing her and still entwined on the ground. He wanted to make sure nobody could get in and also it hid them from the balcony above.

It was the last night of term. Vicky was deeply in love and desperately hoping Tom would declare his love so that their passion could reach its natural conclusion.

Tom was also hoping this would lead to full sex, but he was hoping he would not have to declare his love. He wanted to, but it would be a lie. He was very fond of Vicky, but no more, but she was responding with great enthusiasm. Perhaps they could skip the love thing.

They had both got used to the dark and could see each other in the soft amber light which lit up the top part of the room from two windows at the back of the balcony.

Vicky was wearing a short blue skirt and light blue polo shirt, and Tom's hands found their way under the loose fitting clothes. 'You're so beautiful Vicky.' He helped her off with her shirt and kissed her neck before working his way down.

She helped him off with his shirt. 'I love you Tom.'

'You're the nicest girl I've ever known.' Tom replied.

'The floor's very cold.' It had been cold through Vicky's shirt. Now it was very cold on her naked back and her bra fastener was pushing uncomfortably into her soft skin.

The thrill of the moment dulled the pain and she resisted only a little as Tom pulled off the rest of her clothes. She knew she wanted him badly but she kept hearing the voice in the back of her head telling her to wait. Tom tossed his own clothes in the corner. The heat of the moment hid the chill in the air. They had been hot playing squash and the passion had kept the temperature up and there was plenty of passion after ten weeks of holding back.

Tom paused to reach for his condom and lay back down beside Vicky and held her tight but her enthusiasm had faded. She no longer responded. The moment had passed. In the faint orange glow, Tom could see a tear trickle down her cheek. Suddenly the room seemed cold.

'Do you love me Tom?' she asked with desperation in her voice, hoping he did, but knowing he didn't.

'You know how I feel about you Vicky. You mean the world to me.'

'But do you love me? I need to know.'

Tom sat up and faced away from Vicky. She hated the silence. He hated the silence. He carefully considered his words before speaking. 'You're always in my thoughts and I'm ever so fond of you, but I'm only 18. I don't know what love is. It's for serious people, working people, settled people. I'm young and looking for adventure. Why can't you just come on an adventure with me? That's all I want, but I can't say I love you.' Tom now had desperation in his voice.

He knew he was upsetting her, but he couldn't think the way she did. 'You know I adore you. I want to be with you and, whether you think it's morally right or wrong, I want to have sex with you. It would be fun … for both of us.'

The flow of tears increased. 'It would be fun,' she repeated. 'That's not enough for me Tom. It has to mean something.' After another pause, she added, 'Whenever I'm with you Tom,' she was looking down now, unable to look him in the eye, 'I always think of that Meatloaf song you play all the time.'

'All revved up?' Tom suggested cruelly.

'No.' A slightly bitter response. 'Two Out Of Three Ain't Bad.'

Tom felt guilty now, first for his All Revved Up jibe but secondly as he thought of the words Vicky must have ringing in her head. 'I want you, I need you, but there ain't no way I'm ever goin' to love you. But don't be sad, 'cause two out of three ain't bad.'

Chapter 27

Temptation

Three weeks later, April 6, 1984: The Horse And Groom wasn't as busy as it had been on bonfire night, but it was busy enough to keep Tom Hill, the landlord and his wife all working hard. Tom had been doing shifts at the pub for just over a month and had most of the prices in his head. He could change barrels but still needed help with some drinks and duties. He enjoyed the work mostly, although some customers could be unpleasant.

'Two pints of your best bitter young sir. Jugs. None of those pansy lager glasses with no handles … what will you have darling?' demanded a moustached man in his fifties as he turned from Tom to face his wife.

'Make mine a G and T,' replied the woman, also in her fifties, age and waistline.

'And Doreen?' shouted the moustached man to a second woman. There were two couples together. All about the same age, very expensively, yet casually dressed and all four of them spoke loud enough for the people surrounding their group to hear what they were saying, which mostly included name dropping and descriptions of their latest saloon cars or long-distance holidays. They were from the wealthy residential corner of Southside near Royal Avenue, where Hugh has been ousted by the police after climbing a tree.

Tom repeated the order to avoid mistakes. 'Two pints of bitter and two gin and tonics?'

'Is there a problem young man?' said the moustached man tersely. He didn't like saying anything twice and didn't like menials keeping him waiting. He adjusted his pale yellow lambs-wool V-neck golf jumper before asserting himself. 'A man could die of thirst here. Jump to it my lad.'

Tom thought what an obnoxious man he was but kept it to himself. He was prepared to tolerate the awkward customers because some of the others were quite nice. 'Not at all … coming right up.' Tom hoped he had got the order right.

Tom placed the drinks on the bar. 'That'll be four pounds and six pence please sir.'

The customer handed him a five pound note without looking at him. Tom placed the man's change next to his drink and turned to the next customer. Before he served them, the moustached man shouted over. 'I say young man. I gave you a ten pound note. You've only given me change for a fiver.' He was adamant.

Tom knew it had been a five pound note. The landlord had warned him about people like the moustached man and told Tom that is was often the richer customers who would try it on. Tom remembered his boss's words. 'It's always the rich bastards try to rip you off. Arseholes the lot of 'em. Don't budge an inch. They'll back off if they see you're determined.'

Tom held his ground. 'I'm sorry sir, but you gave me a five pound note.'

The man was alone now. The other three had moved away from the bar. He twisted the ends of his moustache. The barman's impertinence had taken him aback and he wasn't having it. He puffed out his chest with great authority. 'Are you calling me a liar sonny?'

Tom maintained his cool. He was comfortable with conflict, almost enjoyed the challenge. Again he spoke calmly, looking the man directly in the eye. 'Not at all sir, but you gave me a five pound note. Would you like me to get the landlord?'

The man's strategy would have been to ask for the landlord next, but Tom had called his bluff. He twisted the ends of his moustache once more before pointing a finger at Tom in warning. 'You have a serious attitude problem young man. You can keep my five pounds this time. Fortunately I am sufficiently wealthy to not notice the loss, but if you try it again, I will have you in front of a magistrate … you mark my words.' He stormed off.

Tom returned to the other customer, an unshaved scruffy, yet intelligent-looking man in his late sixties with small wire-framed glasses sat on the end of his red nose. He was average height and, despite being a little scruffy, wore a shirt and tie, although the tie was stiff with the dirt of many years. It was Tom's favourite customer, Old George. He sat in the same seat every night and always bought Tom a drink. During quiet moments, Tom would listen in awe to the old man's tales. He had been a corporal in north Africa during the Second World War, responsible for maintaining a fleet of trucks.

'Evening George. How are you? The usual?' Tom asked with a smile, the conflict already forgotten.

'Yes please my boy and one for yourself.' He winked at Tom and settled in his favourite chair at the end of the bar.

'Most generous George. I'll join you with half a stout.' Tom had developed a taste for Guinness. George had told him it would darken his hair and keep the girls interested. 'Lager sends you blond like the Aussies,' George had told him. Tom doubted it, but was happy to humour his new friend. George was always quick with advice, on any subject. Often his thoughts were unsolicited but always well intended and well received. Tom thought tonight may be a good chance to ask his opinion on Vicky Owen.

A small aggressive man shouted down the counter. Tom went to serve him. The short man had a scarred right cheek and ordered through narrow lips with such a strong dialect that Tom couldn't work out what he had said. The delivery made it even harder. His small eyes burned with anger and his words shot across the bar like they had been fired from a gun. 'Um beb.'

'I'm sorry. What was that?'

The man's eyes closed slightly as he spat his order over the bar with fresh venom. 'Um beb.'

Tom was fine with conflict but this was something new. The man wasn't being unpleasant, but Tom feared he may appear disrespectful if he couldn't give the man what he wanted. He stood back and ran his hand past the optics, hoping the customer would shout when he passed the correct drink. The customer just repeated his order with obvious frustration and impatience.

Just as Tom reached for a pen and paper to ask the man to write down his order, the landlord came to his rescue. 'That's not a good idea Tom. He can't read or write. He wants a rum and peppermint. That's all he drinks. He's one of the Irish workers from the building site. I'll take care of him.'

Tom returned to washing glasses.

'Pint of lager barman and make it snappy.'

Tom's smile returned and he placed a pint of lager on the bar for his brother Brian Hill, who had popped down for a quiet drink and grabbed a seat next to Old George. He had also got to know the friendly old bloke and ordered him a drink. Brian had a bit more money than Tom. He had no girlfriend to entertain.

'How are our studies going Brian?' Tom asked. He said 'our' instead of 'your' because they were on the same course and shared the work.

'Sorry. Fell asleep watching the news.' Brian was supposed to do half the work, but was easily distracted.

As Tom handed Brian his change, he looked beyond his brother to the entrance and a big smile spread across his face.

Brian saw the smile and turned to see what he had seen. 'Yoopy do,' said Brian with great satisfaction. Two girls walked into the bar and the landlord served them at the far end of the counter before they settled at a table in the bay window overlooking Southside Common. It was two of the girls Tom and Brian had met on bonfire night, Gaudy Ear-rings and Polo-Neck. Tom and Brian had made a good impression on the two girls before Hugh's clumsiness had caused the girls to leave early.

Tom had been very keen on Gaudy Ear-rings at the time, but was now trying not to show too much interest with his mind focussed on Vicky. Brian, on the other hand, was delighted to see the girls. He had got on very well with Polo-Neck before the spilled beer caused her early departure.

Tom disappeared to serve a young couple with matching white anoraks.

'You should give Guinness a try young Brian. It'll darken your hair and get the girls interested. Lager's a girls' drink,' Old George told Brian.

'I'm sure you know your stuff George but I've tried Guinness and it tastes like shit. Besides, I'm a good looking chap and have no problem with the girls anyway.' The two friends laughed together.

'The Aussies all drink lager. All blond surfers.' Old George was leading up to a story. 'I had an Aussie mate during the war.'

Brian turned his chair more towards George and leant a little in his direction. He enjoyed the old man's tales.

'Me and the Aussie nearly died one day.'

Brian nodded, impressed so far.

'It was in the desert. We were taking cover from dive bombers by the trucks. It was a blistering hot day and the sand was burning my flesh as I crouched down. Then this Stuka came out of the sun heading straight for us. They always came from the direction of the sun to make it difficult for our gunners.' George paused to take a sip of his whisky. 'The howl of the engines, high pitched, revving free in a steep dive, is horrifying.' George paused again, now looking into the distance with fear in his eyes, as if he were back in the desert re-living his ordeal.

'Then it pulled out of its dive and the squeal of its motor dropped to a cry of pain as it clawed itself away from our machine gunners. Then I saw a tiny black pinhead in the clear blue sky where the bomber had been. The small black dot began to grow. As the spot grew larger, a whistling sound began. Then the two of us both knew we were about to die. The Stuka's bomb was heading straight for us. We froze, couldn't move a muscle, as the spot grew larger and larger.' He took another sip of his whisky.

Brian followed his lead and had a gulp of his lager, but couldn't help asking, 'Why didn't you run?'

'It all happened a lot quicker than I can tell the story. It was a matter of seconds, but when you know you are about to die, time seems to run in slow motion. I felt like I'd been watching the bomb fall towards me all day.'

'So what happened?' Brian asked in awe.

'The bomb landed three yards from us.'

'So why aren't you dead?'

'Defective bomb. Never went off. But it made a hell of a noise when it hit the ground. That's what did my Aussie mate. Pushed him over the edge. The noise and the fear sent him gaga. He couldn't speak. I took him to the hospital tent and never saw him again. He would probably have been alright if he hadn't drunk so much lager when he was your age. Guinness and he'd have had nerves of steel.'

'Nice try George, but I'll stick to lager.' Brian wasn't going to be persuaded.

Smash, tinkle, curse. Tom broke a glass.

The landlady, a full figured woman in her late thirties, rushed to reprimand her young barman. As she hurried along the bar, her low cut blouse strained at every seam to contain her ample breasts. She tossed back her wiry blond hair as she squared up to Tom. 'You students don't have the common sense you were born with. I don't know. Really.' She took a deep breath before continuing. 'If I've told you once …' It was a familiar speech. 'Never leave a glass on the brush. You always forget it's there, then, sure as eggs is eggs, you smash the next glass on top of it.'

The glass-washing bowl had a rotating brush fixed in the middle pointing upwards and you pushed the dirty glasses over the brush.

The landlady squeezed Tom's cheek and gave him a warm motherly smile. She had grown quite fond of him and enjoyed any opportunity for an exchange of words, even if it was to correct her part timer.

Tom smiled kindly back. He didn't have the heart to tell her she had been the last to wash glasses.

Old George waved Tom over. 'Usual please, a pint of Guinness and whatever you're having.' George wasn't giving Brian any choice.

As Tom placed the drinks on the bar, he looked beyond his brother. The two girls were still there and had been looking over at Tom and Brian every now and then. Brian had smiled at them a couple of times. George had noticed.

'You should get over there boy.' George gave Brian an encouraging slap on the back. 'You're only young once.'

Brian didn't need pushing. 'Alright I'll give it a go.' He walked past the man with the moustache, past the couple in matching white anoraks and sat down at the girls' table.

George and Tom watched with interest. Thirty seconds later he was still there. He'd made a good start. Thirty minutes later, George ordered another drink.

'I think I'll squeeze one more whisky down. Your brother's got the gift Tom. He's still going strong. I expect he's saving one for you.'

'Actually, I'm spoken for. I'm seeing a girl called Vicky up at the college.'

'You married to her?'

'No.'

'Are you in love with her?'

Tom paused a little before giving the same answer. 'No.'

'Well then. Like I told your brother. You should get over there boy. You're only young once. If I were 50 years younger ...'

'But George.' Tom stopped him. 'Vicky loves me and it would break her heart ...'

'Not if she didn't find out.' George's wry grin widened.

'But I'm too honest. She would see it in my face and I'd end up telling her. We're really good together and I don't want to spoil it.'

George looked over at the two girls laughing and joking with Brian. 'Look at that pair of legs Tom.'

'Yes. Yes. They're very nice.'

'I can see you're tempted.'

'That's not the point.' Tom looked at George before turning away to serve a customer.

When he returned, George was pulling on his tired old tweed jacket. He shook Tom's hand vigorously and squeezed his shoulder. He leant forward and whispered a final word of advice. 'I've seen you watching those girls and I can tell you something. If you don't break Vicky's heart tonight, you will soon enough.' With that, he waved over to Brian and left.

As the landlord rang the bell for last orders, the angry Irish builder attracted Tom's attention.

'Um bay bab?' The words ricocheted around the bar.

Tom repeated the words in his head but couldn't see any meaning. Before Tom answered, the moustached man butted in. 'I say young man, two more pints of your best bitter and two G and Ts.'

'I'll be right with you sir,' replied Tom, while still facing the small builder. 'Rum and peppermint?'

The short scarred man shook his head and repeated, 'Um bay bab?'

Moustache Man was getting impatient. 'Are you going to serve me or not.'

'Um bay bab?' screeched the builder.

Moustache Man had had enough. He pushed the little builder gently to one side in order to get Tom's full attention. The builder was very angry now and shouted a string of indistinguishable expletives at the moustached man, who was not used to having his authority questioned and pointed his finger towards the builder. 'Now look here my good man …'

That's as far as he got. One swift punch from the builder square on the jaw knocked him out cold and he slumped to the floor against the bar. At that moment the landlord appeared from the cellar. He couldn't see the flaccid man on the floor and thought all seemed as it should be.

The builder turned back to Tom and calmly repeated himself. 'Um bay bab?'

The landlord once again came to Tom's rescue. 'I'll take care of him. He wants you to order him a taxi.'

The moustached man reappeared above the bar, a little groggy and shook his head. He faced the builder. 'I'll have you in front of a magistrate for that. Assault. And I have a witness. The barman saw everything.' He turned to face Tom and repeated himself. 'You saw him hit me didn't you boy?'

'Sorry. Didn't see a thing.'

The single punch had been so fast and so unexpected that Tom was the only person who had been watching. Moustache Man thought making an issue of the assault may prove futile and chose to make a scene instead, loudly gathering his wife and friends, vowing never to return to the Horse And Groom and making wild threats based on his close friendship with one of the local magistrates.

As the pub emptied, Tom busied himself wiping tables and clearing glasses. Brian was still entertaining the two girls, whose laughter filled the smoky air. Tom's thoughts drifted to Vicky. It was three weeks since he had seen her and another three until he would see her again. It was a long Easter break and, although Tom missed her, he felt some relief. The pressure of being a dutiful boyfriend could be hard work.

His sexual urges towards her seemed to have gone home with her. He expected them to return when she did, but he had his doubts. Maybe she wasn't the right girl for him.

The matter had been taken out of his hands. Brian called him over.

'Tom, Sarah, Anita, Anita, Sarah, Tom. They're coming with us to The Skin Shop.'

An hour later, Tom and Brian sat at a table in The Skin Shop while Sarah, formerly known as Gaudy Ear-rings, and Anita, formerly known as Polo-Neck, went to the bar.

'Look at that bum Tom,' urged Brian with great enthusiasm as Sarah swayed gracefully to the bar with Anita. They were at a table next to the main dance floor in the night-club.

'Yes Brian. Nice. But I've got a girl.' Tom had made it clear to his brother that he would only go to the club to keep the party atmosphere going and give Brian more chance of pulling. But he found himself following Sarah's hips as they swung with each step. Her short red dress hugged her body leaving very little to the imagination. Anita wore a similar dress, but in white, and walked with the same grace as her friend.

The girls and Brian had already had a few drinks and Tom was a long way behind. He had enjoyed a few halves during his shift, but was not as buoyant as the others. Angry builders, pompous golfers and thoughts of Vicky had kept him sober, but the lively mood of the others was infectious. The girls returned with two blue cocktails and two pints, one of Guinness and one of lager.

Tom had only exchanged small-talk with Sarah on the way to The Skin Shop and the conversation had flowed easily. He had obviously made a strong impression when they met on bonfire night. She had fully accepted his reasons for not calling her. He remembered the insurance company she worked for, but didn't know her name, otherwise he would have tried to contact her.

Sarah flashed her bright eyes in Tom's direction and addressed him with a wave of the hand. 'What do you think of my new dress?' She jumped to her feet and twirled around, running her hands down the front of her body and bending her knees first to one side and then the other.

'Stunning Sarah.' It was an honest answer from Tom.

'It's a peach,' added Brian, before sticking out his broad chest. 'How do you like my T-shirt?' He was wearing the shirt Tom had bought him on his birthday.

Tom noticed Anita's eyes light up as Brian stuck his chest out. 'Nice,' she said following the outline of the pattern with the tip of her finger.

A couple of drinks later, Tom had put Vicky briefly to the back of his mind and suggested a dance. The girls giggled their way to the dance floor followed by the brothers. It was Love Cats by The Cure and Brian and Tom playfully bumped into each other. Between the four of them, they had drunk enough to find their slapstick antics quite funny.

Brian slipped his arm around Anita's waist. Tom followed his lead. He didn't want Sarah to feel left out and it couldn't be classed as cheating on Vicky. They both placed their hands firmly in the middle of the girls' backs, but as they jostled on the dance floor, Brian pushed Tom's hand down over Sarah's bottom. Tom moved it immediately. 'I'm sorry. It was Brian,' he quickly told her.

'Don't be,' she replied and pushed his hand back down.

Tom thought he might return the favour to his brother. He turned towards them. No need. Brian had already planted both his hands on Anita's bum. She laughed and draped her arms around his shoulders, still dancing. Tom was feeling slightly guilty now. This could possibly be counted as cheating on Vicky. He went to the bar. Another drink would keep his hands off Sarah. Then again, it may push him the other way.

Sarah joined him at the bar. The conversation bubbled along as they flirted and watched Brian and Anita on the dance floor.

Brian grabbed her around the thighs and lifted her above his head. She threw her arms in the air and Brian kept rhythm to What Difference Does It make by The Smiths. As that song finished, the final slow song of the night started, He put her down and held her close for In The Air Tonight by Phil Collins.

Sarah jumped off her seat, grabbed Tom by the hand and pulled him to the dance floor. Tom was close enough to smell Sarah's perfume and felt her warm breath on his face, but he didn't kiss her. Tom was still holding back. Sarah knew nothing about Vicky and assumed Tom was available.

Brian had no doubts about Anita. He liked her a lot. He pressed his stubbly cheek against Anita's. He hadn't shaved for two days. Lazy. He kissed her cheek softly. She looked deep into his eyes. She brushed her lips against his neck, pinching his rough skin between her lips. She worked her way up to his chin and round to his mouth. She kissed him gently on the lips. Moments later they had stopped dancing and kissed with vigour as the other clubbers danced around them.

The song finished, the house lights came up and the DJ urged Brian and Anita to 'get a room'. Instead she went with Sarah to get their coats from the cloakroom, giving them chance to talk. They quickly agreed they didn't want the night to finish yet.

Tom and Brian were waiting by the exit.

'We have a bottle of wine back at our flat. How about sharing it with us?' Anita asked the brothers. The two girls had a flat close to town centre.

Brian didn't need to think about it. 'Sounds great.' He turned to Tom.

It was not such an easy answer for Tom. He was very fond of Sarah, but was also very fond of Vicky. He didn't want to let his brother down either. Eventually he convinced himself that he had met Sarah before Vicky and if things had turned out differently, she could have been his girlfriend, so he should keep going and see what happens. 'Yes. Excellent idea. Shall we get a taxi?'

'No need,' replied Sarah, 'It's only a five minute walk along the river.'

Tom held out his arm for Sarah. She took it and they left the nightclub arm in arm. It was a very mild night for April and there was no wind. There were a few clouds, but the bright moon peeped through every now and then, its soft rays flickering on the ripples of the narrow river.

Brian slipped his arm around Anita's shoulder and she snuggled up against him. Tom and Sarah were behind the others. Tom thought he might appear distant if he didn't follow his brother's lead and, for the sake of group harmony, he slipped his arm around Sarah.

She responded by turning to face him. She reached both arms around Tom's neck, stood on her tiptoes and kissed him gently on the lips. Tom didn't want to appear insulting and the kiss lingered. After a warm hug, they began walking again.

Things were getting difficult for Tom now. A kiss was definitely cheating on Vicky, but it had been rather nice and he was strongly attracted to Sarah.

Pop, gurgle, clink, cheers. The girls had a stylish two-bedroom flat in a smart courtyard development by the river. With a glass of wine in her hand, Sarah showed the boys around the flat followed by Anita. The boys were impressed and said so. Anita put some music on, a tape she had put together of seventies disco classics, which began with Play That Funky Music by Wild Cherry followed by Boogie Nights from Heatwave.

They had a soft cream leather three piece suite arranged around a pine coffee table and sheepskin rug with plants and books filling three tall pine shelving units from Habitat in town. Sarah lit a few candles and turned off the main lights. There was a tall standard lamp in one corner with a shell-like multi-coloured shade on a long chrome-plated shaft. This also came from a department store in town and cast soft coloured light across the room.

They played Trivial Pursuit on the coffee table. The brand new quiz game over from Canada, which had become very popular very quickly.

'Yellow question Brian,' said Anita.

'Which is England's largest castle?' Brian asked.

'No idea.' Anita went for a second bottle of wine.

'Who had their biggest hit with God Save the Queen in Her Majesty's silver jubilee year,' Sarah asked Tom.

'Sex Pistols thank-you very much. Pink pie piece please,' Tom took the lead as Sylvester played You Make Me Feel Mighty Real.

'We could make this game more interesting,' Brian said with a big smile.

'How's that?' said Anita.

'Have you ever played strip Trivial Pursuit?'

'No. Have you?'

'All the time,' joked Brian.

'I'll give it a go,' Sarah was keen.

'And me,' said Anita.

'Tom?' asked Brian.

Tom thought he was better at general knowledge than his brother and hoped he would be better than the girls. So he felt quite safe. 'Yeah. Go on. How do you play?'

'Every time you get a pie piece, the other three take off an item of clothes.' Brian was making it up as he went along, but got nods of approval from everyone.

'Go on then,' Anita was keen to start.

'You should all take something off now. I've already got a pie piece,' said Tom hopefully.

'I don't think so,' replied Sarah. 'We should all start again.'

'That's fine, as long as I can start.' Tom took out his pie piece.

Shake Your Body by The Jacksons played in the background.

'Orange. Which bird is fair game from August 12?' asked Sarah.

'Grouse,' said Tom as he rolled the dice again.

'Yellow. Whose kidnapping started the Trojan Wars?' Sarah didn't think he'd get this one.

'Helen,' said Tom as he rolled again. 'Wooah,' shouted Tom with delight. 'Brown question for a pie piece please.'

The other three groaned.

'Which bit of a newt goes into the witches' brew in Macbeth?' asked Sarah. 'No chance. You're not getting this.'

Tom had done Macbeth at school. He sang along with Lipps Inc. 'Don't you take me to, Funkytown. Clothes off. Eye of newt. Thank-you. I'm so clever. Pie Piece please.'

The girls squealed. Brian groaned.

They each slipped off one shoe.

It was Tom's turn to groan. 'Three questions in a row and I only get three shoes. That was worth a dress.'

Sarah, Brian and Anita both got their questions wrong. Tom won another pie piece and got three more shoes.

The wine was all gone, but the girls had some vodka. Donna Summer was next on the tape; I Feel Love.

Sarah got two questions right but no pie piece. Brian got one right and landed on a blue pie space. 'Come on baby. Hit me with a blue. Your dress is coming off.'

'Which canal flows through Gatun locks?' asked Anita with an anxious frown, which returned to a smile when Brian didn't answer straight away.

He didn't have a clue. The only canals he knew were Panama and Suez. He took a guess. 'Panama?'

Anita screamed. He looked like he was guessing and got lucky.

Her reaction told him it was a good guess. He cheered and clapped. 'Dress next,' he encouraged her.

She slipped her tights off. So did Sarah. Tom took off one of his plastic shoes.

Anita then got one question right but no pie piece.

Back to Tom. The drink had slowed his movements down but his mind was still sharp. Two correct answers put him on a green pie space.

Sarah knew another pie piece would cost her a dress. 'Do pigs suffer from sunburn?' she asked.

Tom had no idea. 'Yes?' he asked.

Sarah smiled demurely, stood up, slipped her red dress slowly over her head, sat back down on the rug by Tom's feet, took a sip of her vodka and leant back against Tom's legs with just her pink chiffon bra and knickers left.

'What an excellent game.' Brian couldn't hide his appreciation. 'Your turn Anita.' She did the same. Brian took his sock off, quietly pleased that he hadn't been too lazy to have a shower that morning.

Tom and Sarah smiled at each other.
'Starting to get interesting,' Tom said, trying to be cool, but unable to hide a smile. The soft flicker of candle light glowed on Sarah's deep brown flesh. She had Tom's full attention now.

'I'm getting the next ten pie pieces though. Just watch me,' she said defiantly.

Sarah rolled the dice, got a blue question right, then landed on an orange pie space.

'Which head of state opened the 1976 Montreal Olympics?' asked Tom.

'I know this,' Sarah said, but couldn't remember.

'I hope you don't,' said Anita, who would lose her bra if Sarah remembered.

'I watched it with my parents. Oohh. Oohh. I know … The Queen,' she shouted triumphantly.

'Yes,' shouted Tom, delighted that she had got a pie piece.

'Yes,' shouted Brian, delighted that Anita was about to take her bra off.

'Oh no!' screamed Anita.

'Bra,' urged Brian, before joining in with KC And The Sunshine Band. 'That's the way. Uh huh, uh huh, I like it.'

Tom and Sarah looked at each other wondering if Anita would do it.

Anita waited, looking at Brian, who was bobbing his shoulders in time with the music and sipping his vodka.

Tom came to her rescue. 'You can do it in your bedroom if you want.'

She was happy with that, stood up, grabbed Brian by the hand and led him to her room.

Sarah had Tom to herself now and topped up his drink. She reached into the Trivial Pursuit box and pulled out two pie pieces. She handed them to Tom. He placed them in his pie, put his drink on the coffee table, scooped Sarah up in his arms and carried her into the other bedroom.

Chapter 28

Revelation

The next day, April 7, 1984: 'I've still got a nightmare of a headache,' said Brian Hill holding both hands to his head. The brothers were in their Dickens Court kitchen sat with a cup of tea the morning after playing strip Trivial Pursuit. Despite the sore head, Brian was buzzing. 'It was worth it though. What a night!' Brian wanted to know how bad the infidelity had been. 'So Tom … Did you?'

Tom Hill stared into the distance. His feelings were very different from his brother's. Guilt was the most powerful, not just for being unfaithful to Vicky Owen, but for not letting Sarah know about Vicky. He felt like he had the morning after sleeping with Greenpeace Badge. As if he had used the girl. He turned to Brian. 'Yes. Yes I did. How about you?' He had to ask. If his brother had lost his virginity, he should share his joy, regardless of how low he was feeling himself.

'I most certainly did Tom. And I'm not just a god of football. I'm the man.' He stuck out his chest with pride, but could see his brother, although pleased, was unexpectedly thoughtful. 'Why the long face?'

'I think I've made a big mistake. Sarah is a babe and last night was special, but when I woke up, sober, I felt physically sick with guilt. Worse than I could have imagined.'

'Vicky doesn't have to find out.' Brian couldn't understand the problem.

'It's not just Vicky. Sarah thought I was single. She told me she had been hoping to see me again after bonfire night. I don't suppose she had a one-night stand in mind.'

'She was willing enough. You've got to get a grip Tom. You are not responsible for everybody else's feelings. You should put yourself first now and then. I really don't think there is a problem.' Even Brian didn't believe that last sentence.

'Shit Brian. I shouldn't have done it and now I don't know what to do.'

'Do you want to see Sarah again?'

'It would be nice, but not nice enough to give up Vicky. And I wouldn't want to lead Sarah on any more than I already have.'

'Maybe it would be more unkind to cut Sarah off completely after just one night.' Brian was almost serious for a moment, but added, 'She does have extremely nice tits.'

'I know. I know, but a clean break is kindest I think.' Tom's good intentions were speaking, but his instincts had to be heard. 'Oooh, but what a body.'

'And you'd walk away from that for a tame fumble with Vicky.' Brian's good intentions always took a back seat to his instincts.

'Yes. I think I would. At least I'd sleep at night.' Tom was trying to convince himself as much as Brian.

'You'd have no choice,' Brian unsympathetically pointed out. 'Vicky won't keep you awake shagging.'

'But Brian. It's not all about sex.'

'Isn't it?' Brian said, half joking, half serious.

'Vicky loves me. I have a responsibility towards her because her happiness is in my hands. Can't you see what I'm saying?' Tom screwed up his face in agonised appeal for understanding.

'Yes. I suppose I do,' Brian had to admit, but as he was saying it, in his head he was picturing Sarah curled up against Tom's legs in her bra and knickers, with the soft light playing on the curves of her body. 'But I can't believe you are going to turn your back on Sarah, and, knowing you, probably tell Vicky all about it as well.' Brian thought that a little foolish, but admired his brother's misguided chivalry.

'Yes. You're probably right. I will need to tell her. No secrets.' Tom felt a little selfish for not asking his brother more about Anita. 'How about you? Have you arranged to see Anita again?'

Brian half laughed. 'No chance,' he said quickly and with very little feeling. 'And I have you to thank for making that decision for me.'

'How's that?' Tom was missing something.

'I don't want to work in a pub serving pompous golfers. You're only there because you've spent all your money on having a steady girlfriend. I can't afford a girlfriend and I'm certainly not giving up football nights out or anything like that just so I can buy gifts for a chick.'

Tom knew Brian meant what he said, so it was pointless challenging him on it. 'What did you say to Anita then?'

'I said we had exams coming up and we'd be studying all the time, but if I got a chance, I would try to call her. At least that way, I might get another shag without all the slushy, expensive, time-consuming stuff in between.'

'You're all heart,' Tom said with sarcasm, but still put his arm warmly around his brother's shoulder.

During the Easter holidays, the kitchen had been unusually tidy. The other students had all gone home, so the cleaner had made an extra effort. She had no choice. The university held conferences during the holiday breaks and guests often stayed in the halls of residence.

As they prepared two omelettes for lunch, one of the conference visitors came in and opened the fridge. They took little notice of him. Students didn't mix much with the temporary residents. Both brothers were surprised when the newcomer spoke to them. He had a slight lisp, a very wide face and closely cropped blond hair. He had unusually big blue eyes and wore eccentric clothes; a kind of white Arabian tunic, almost like a dress. He was a shade below average height, but had a presence that made him seem taller.

'How are you today boys?' A slightly mocking smile, but the voice was carefully manicured. The final 's' was stressed and lingered.

Tom was first to respond. 'Good thanks. How about you?'

'As well as can be expected,' he lisped cordially. 'One struggles to find a quiet corner in today's commercial world.'

'You sound like you have the world's troubles on your shoulders.' Tom tried to get on the man's wavelength. He put him in his mid twenties, thought his accent very London and noticed a slightly camp twang in some of his inflection.

'Only as much as the next man,' he replied with a sigh. 'Although I do sometimes feel I'm swimming against the tide. It's the me, me, me culture of twentieth century Britain that gets me down sometimes. But today I'm up.'

'Are you here for a conference?' asked Brian as he flipped his omelette over.

'Oh, no, no … heaven forbid.' He sounded almost offended. 'I'm a post-graduate student in the music department.'

Tom suddenly twigged. 'Do you live in room number one?'

'That's correct. Do you boys live on this floor? I'm so seldom in the building, I hardly have time to meet my own neighbours.'

Both brothers were rudely staring, without realising. This was The Invisible Man. He hadn't been seen for more than six months and here he was saying he should get to know his neighbours. The stranger noticed they were staring and looked down at himself. 'I say … do I have some food on my chin?'

'I'm sorry.' Tom shook his head, realising his loss of manners. Brian was still staring. 'I'm Tom Hill, room number five. This is my brother Brian, room four.' Tom noticed his brother was still staring. 'Brian,' he said sharply to encourage him to shut his mouth and join the conversation.

Brian regained his composure eventually. 'Hi. I'm Brian, room four.' He thrust out his hand to greet The Invisible Man.

'Delighted,' he replied and held Brian's hand more than shook it. 'Eckhart … Rupert … you must call me Rupert.' He bowed his head slightly and held his hand out to Tom. 'Will you be terribly busy after your breakfast?'

The boys looked at each other. They had no plans until their football match in the afternoon.

'Nothing that won't keep,' replied Tom.

'Then would you care to join me for a coffee? I discovered an interesting new blend in London yesterday. It would please me if you could give me your opinions.'

'Lovely.' Tom could think of nothing else to say.

Brian belatedly added his acceptance. 'Sounds great. Thanks.'

'Then I wish you bon appetit and look forward to your company.' With that he floated out of the kitchen and disappeared down the corridor.

The brothers stared at each other. They had nothing to say. Rupert Eckhart was not what they had expected. He was far too nice. A bit gay Brian thought, but anyone who didn't play football was a bit gay in Brian's opinion. The smell of burning egg broke the trance. Brian turned to rescue the food.

They were still deep in thought as they crunched through their meal with a weak cup of tea. They had shared the last tea bag. Finally Tom spoke. 'Well?'

'Well what?' replied Brian.

'What do you think of Rupert?' Tom was a shade irritated at having to spell out his question. He thought 'well' had been more than enough.

'I don't think he plays football.' Irony from Brian.

'You could be right.' Tom had hoped for something more insightful. 'How can somebody we haven't met in six months be so friendly? That's what I can't work out.'

'Why don't you ask him over coffee?' Always a simple answer from Brian.

'Did you notice the speech impediment?' asked Tom.

'No. He did sound a bit strange though. Bit of a weirdo.'

'Nothing wrong with that,' Tom replied with feeling, jumping to the man's defence despite only knowing him for ten minutes.

'True. True.' Brian agreed.

'Let's go and find out a bit more then,' Tom instructed and they left their dirty pots on the table. The door to room number one was open and they cautiously popped their heads around the door. Rupert was lighting a small cone of incense. At least that's what the brothers thought it was. This man was strange. Maybe it was a weird drug.

'Nobody allergic to sandalwood is there?' Rupert enquired thoughtfully.

They shook their heads, while their eyes took in the detail of the room. It was pretty much the same as Tom remembered from his sneak preview; framed prints on the walls, the tapestry with nymphs and shepherds, art books and the bust of Napoleon with a single black tear under one eye.

Rupert handed them coffee in gold-coloured porcelain cups with matching saucers. They took a sip. It had a very rich taste, like nothing they had ever tasted before. They had only drunk instant coffee from a jar and had no idea whether this new blend was good or bad.

'How's your coffee?' asked Rupert, his eyes dancing from one brother to the other and back.

'Quite different from the stuff I'm used to, but it's nice ... I like it,' replied Tom with enthusiasm.

'What are you used to?' Rupert asked with genuine interest.

'Whatever is cheapest in the supermarket,' replied Tom.

Brian was much more fussy. 'I prefer to drink something I've at least heard of,' added Brian, thinking he was being more sophisticated than his brother.

'Is advertising important to you?' Rupert asked Brian, again with genuine interest.

'No. Not really. I suppose.' Brian felt belittled.

'Well. Each to his own and let no man wink at a cyclops,' replied Rupert profoundly.

Brian no longer felt belittled. He felt thoroughly confused.

Tom's curiosity got the better of him. 'What do you mean?' he asked as inoffensively as he could.

'Excellent question,' replied Rupert quickly, offering both boys a biscuit from a porcelain pot, in the same gold as the tea cups and saucers.

Rupert sat back down without answering. 'You were saying,' Tom urged him to continue with his answer.

'I'm sorry. I was distracted. Lovely biscuits.' He took another bite before going on. 'A cyclops has only one eye, so a trivial wink is insulting. Such a trivial gesture cannot be reciprocated, much the same as patting a snake on the back. So don't do it.'

Tom and Brian looked just as confused, so Rupert continued.

'The sentiment is that we must respect each other's differences, rather than mock them. There is as much quality in a cheap instant coffee as there is in the finest ground coffee. It is just that the qualities are different.' Rupert smiled warmly.

The brothers nodded slowly, half understanding what he had said, but still not sure.

Rupert watched with interest as the brothers gorged themselves on the mysteries of his room.

Again Tom's curiosity got the better of him. 'Why does Napoleon have a tear under one eye?'

'Symbolic Tom,' Rupert replied as if no more explanation were needed.

There was a pause of about ten seconds before Tom asked, 'symbolic of what?'

'Aah. Glad you asked. Fascinating thought. Napoleon was responsible for the deaths of thousands of men in pursuit of his own ambition. A cruel, heartless, single-minded machine of a man and yet he was humble in some ways, the same as you and me. He fell over and cried when he was a child. He laughed, loved, joked and played. He must have felt some compassion for those who died in his wars, not enough to stop him doing it, but enough to shed a single tear to remind us he was still human. It's a powerful contrast. It is only the difference between good and evil which drives the world forward.'

'I'm with you.' Tom followed that one a bit better. 'Good strives to overcome bad. The tear is good. Napoleon is bad.'

'In a nutshell. Yes. But I prefer the flowery explanation. It's more poetic. It works better with feeling.'

Brian was completely lost and sipped his coffee slowly. He thought it was vile and wished Rupert had some cheap instant. He also had unanswered questions. 'So Rupert. How come we haven't seen you in six months?'

'Just turned out that way I suppose. I promise I've not been avoiding you. I do a lot of composing and I need studio time for that. Under-graduates book the studio time during the day and most of the evening, so I take what's left, often through the night. It's the only time I can get near the equipment.'

'Do you sleep during the day then?' Brian was filling in the gaps.

'Sometimes, but I have no lectures. I don't need to be on campus much. My work often takes me to London and other places for concerts, to meet experts and to extend the scope of my research. So … you see … I'm hardly ever in Southside, and when I am, I work through the night.'

Both boys nodded slowly in understanding, but Brian had one more question. 'So what brings you to Southside today, in the middle of the holidays?'

'I thought you may ask,' he said, still smiling warmly. Then he jerked his head to one side, raised both eyebrows and lisped mysteriously, 'there is no mystery.' He paused before continuing. 'There are very few under-graduates on campus at the moment. I have unlimited access to the studio and must make hay while the sun shines.'

The brothers had expected a strange oblique answer and were almost disappointed with the simplicity of the truth.

'So what keeps you boys on campus through the holiday?' asked Rupert.

The brothers never liked telling anybody about their parents, but Brian had an answer ready, which avoided the subject.

'I had to stick around because I'm waiting for an operation. Tom stayed to keep me company.'

'Do you have a date?' Rupert asked.

'Got it in the post this morning. They cut me open in six days time.'

Chapter 29

The final straw

Four days later, April 11, 1984: It was cup final day, 48 hours before Brian Hill's operation and there was heavy rain. The temperature was as low as it had been in January. A piercing and constant wind blew from the north. It had been raining when the brothers woke up and hadn't stopped all day. It was an evening kick-off under floodlights at the home of Southside Wanderers in Thief Lane.

Southside University's football team had won through to the final largely as a result of fast, tidy football played on dry pitches with no strong wind. The whole team relied on a careful and composed passing game. None of them was particularly big, but they could usually outplay bigger stronger sides in the right conditions. Thick mud and strong wind was the last thing they wanted. It would give their more physical opponents a chance to bully them off the ball.

All morning, the brothers had looked anxiously out of the window hoping for a break in the rain, but, if anything, it got heavier. If it were still winter, the pitch would have been waterlogged and the game called off, but a recent spell of warm dry weather had left the ground quite hard. The pitch would be muddy but playable.

They sat in the Dickens Court kitchen eating their tea; sausages, baked beans and instant mash, watching the rain thrash against the window.

'Shit Brian. We're in trouble. Southside YMCA will love this. They're a bunch of thugs.' Tom chewed slowly. He didn't want indigestion during the game. The university had already beaten the YMCA twice in the league but on nice days.

Brian was more positive. 'If we are solid at the back, one goal is all we need and if I can't find the back of the net at least once in 90 minutes, I may as well give up football.'

It didn't help much. They both sat in the gloom staring out at the rain with blank faces.

Two hours later they were in the changing rooms. The smell of liniment was strong. The buzz of confident banter was electric as the students proudly pulled on their red shirts for the biggest game of their season. Leaps Like A Salmon was busy putting in new studs to cope with the mud. Who Me was polishing his boots. They would be covered in mud within seconds of leaving the changing room, but it was part of his routine and sticking to the routine gave him confidence.

Slogger sat quietly in the corner, pulling on his boots. He had been called in as substitute at the last minute after a fine season as second team captain. The heavy rain had led to his call-up. Slogger was a big lad, a no-nonsense grafter. He was a little nervous, however, he hadn't been with the first team before and he knew his first touch was inferior to his team-mates. He hoped, if he got the chance, to make up for that with aggression and commitment.

I Got The Last Touch was loudly slamming his boots on the concrete floor. The mud from previous games was packed between the studs. It fell out eventually, leaving two hard cakes of mud with neat sets of holes in each where the studs had been.

Brian and Tom sat next to each other.

'Anybody got any spare tie-ups?' shouted Who Me.

The Hard Man, who was team captain, threw a roll of tape at him. It caught him in the tummy. The Hard Man played alongside Tom in the centre of midfield. He did most of the tackling while Tom was the playmaker. With the 7.30pm kick off looming, Tom started his stretches in the changing room. He went through the same routine before every match, to make sure he didn't pull any muscles in the early stages of the game.

The tension in the dressing room was growing as the minutes ticked by, but the rain still fell and the wind still blew. The Hard Man clapped his hands loudly. 'Right. Listen up.' The room went quiet. Who Me made a joke. 'Shut it Who Me. Let's start thinking about football now. The joking's over. Get your minds on the game. We've worked hard to reach this final, so don't let yourselves down.'

There were murmurs of agreement. 'The pitch will cut up. No prisoners tonight. Hit 'em hard. Ask questions later.' He thumped his fist on the table in the middle of the room and snarled with genuine aggression. 'Hit the bastards hard. They won't hold back. We've done 'em twice in the league. They want revenge and they think we're a fair-weather side, so let's prove 'em wrong.'

The Hard Man paused briefly. 'And,' he said, turning to Brian with a steely glare. 'No fancy shit. You got that Brian?'

Brian smiled. He said nothing but was thinking, 'Your job's to stop them scoring. I'm the magician. Leave the heroics to me. I know what I'm doing.'

The Hard Man continued. 'Keep it tight at the back. Listen to the call. Go with it. Any shirkers and you're off. Slogger's on the bench. He's fired up and I won't hesitate to bring him on. He'll do a job if we need him. Right. Let's get interested. I want to hear a bit of desire. Come on. Let's do it.' He smashed both fists on the table now and the players clapped loudly and stamped their studs on the hard floor in an adrenalin-charged crescendo.

They jogged onto the rain-soaked, flood-lit pitch in front of almost empty stands. Around 200 students and YMCA supporters formed a noisy group in the seats around the players' tunnel.

Seven free kicks in the first ten minutes confirmed The Hard Man's opinion that it would be a physical game. The rain now fell so hard that it was difficult to see the whole length of the pitch. The biting wind sapped the students' strength and made it hard to follow the flight of the ball accurately.

No goals after 15 minutes and very few goal-mouth incidents. YMCA had forced a corner, but it was into the wind and fell short. A tame hooked shot went well wide. From the resultant goal kick, which sliced off to the left as it caught the wind, Brian picked up the ball and set off on a run, only to be chopped down from behind sending him face first into the mud.

The referee's whistle blew for a free-kick. Brian picked himself up and set off on a run down the left. Leaps Like A Salmon saw his run and chipped the free-kick into his path. He took the ball in his stride and took it forward to the edge of the penalty area. With the defender about to lunge at his feet, he turned sharply and ran along the edge of the 18-yard box. He hoped he might have a shot and waited for a clear view of goal, but waltzing past further tackles pushed him to the far side of the area, at which point he stopped, rolled the ball back under his right foot and clipped it with his heal gently in the direction of the penalty spot.

The change of direction sent all the defenders the wrong way, but Who Me read the pass and strolled through unmarked for a simple tap in to the keeper's left. The boys were jubilant and celebrated loudly with due credit to Brian for his inspired defence-splitting pass.

With five minutes to go before the break, Brian made a similar jinking run followed by a beautifully weighted pass, which gave I Got The Last Touch a clear shot on goal. He drilled the ball top left giving the keeper no chance. Again there was jubilation and again Brian was rightly given a great deal of credit.

The half-time whistle blew and the students were glad of the chance to warm themselves with a cup of tea in the changing room. Spirits were high, but The Hard Man was quick to urge caution as the players congratulated Who Me and I Got The Last Touch for their goals.

'The fat lady isn't singing yet. There's another 45 minutes to go. If we can score two, so can they. So we've got to dig deep and give it everything.' The unfortunate table was thumped repeatedly. 'We're 45 minutes away from glory, but it won't come easy. Keep it simple and play the easy ball … every time Brian. No room for fancy shit, right?'

'Give us a break. That's why we're winning,' Brian appealed light-heartedly.

The Hard Man was stern. 'I'm not arguing with you Brian. Keep it simple or you're off. If you passed a bit sooner more often, we could have been three up, home and dry by now. Right. Get out there and do it.' If the table were a small dog, it would have cowered in the corner. After more table thumping, foot stamping and loud clapping, they jogged back out into the rain.

The YMCA manager had inspired his players to fresh levels of aggression. The free-kick rate reached new peaks. Four YMCA players were booked in the space of 20 minutes, but there were no more goals. The students were starting to feel the impact of the tackles and the flowing football had become more frantic.

Brian tried to unlock the defence with a delicate chip, but the heavy mud and hard tackles had weakened his legs. The pass fell short and was easily intercepted. From the resultant YMCA attack, Tom made a desperate goal-line clearance.

Minutes later Brian was tackled after twice failing to play a simple pass and again Tom came to his rescue with a well-timed tackle just moments before a clear shot on the students' goal.

Brian was again tackled, but chased the YMCA player all the way back to the penalty area and slid at his feet with a reckless challenge. The whistle blew. Penalty. Thump. The lead was cut to a single goal.

With 15 minutes to play, YMCA scored a second goal after a goal-mouth scramble.

'Ref,' shouted The Hard Man. 'Substitution please.' The referee nodded. 'Brian.' The Hard Man was taking off Brian for Slogger.

Brian was shocked. Just when his side needed some inspiration, the captain was taking off their most gifted player to be replaced by their least talented plodder. This was too stupid for words. He trudged off and sat in the dug-out.

Tom dropped to sweeper and Slogger made an extra man in the centre of defence.

With two minutes left to play, YMCA played a long hopeful ball forward, which deceived Slogger. He missed the ball completely and it ran towards goal. Tom had stepped forward expecting Slogger to make the clearance, leaving space for the YMCA striker to nip in and tap home the winner.

The students' heads dropped as the final whistle blew.

Nobody spoke in the changing room. Water dripped from their muddy bodies. Matted hair fell over disappointed eyes. A bemused tension filled the air. They had thrown away a two-goal lead and the captain had taken off their star player. The players had mixed thoughts on the wisdom of The Hard Man's decision. Still nobody spoke.

Brian's adrenalin was coursing through his veins, no longer pumped up with the desire to win, now driven by anger. He pulled off his red kit and left it where it fell. His movements were jerky and hurried. He needed to get out of the room as quickly as possible, if only to avoid hitting someone. He was inwardly telling himself he had just played his last game for the university. He wanted nothing more to do with a club run by a captain who was prepared to commit cup-final suicide as The Hard Man had just done.

He didn't bother with a shower and pulled his jeans on over the thick layers of wet mud. He slipped his trainers on over his bare feet. He jumped up and headed for the door, taking a route past The Hard Man. With his face held only a few inches from the captain's face, he passed judgement with great menace and bared teeth. 'Dickhead.'

The Hard Man wisely refrained from reacting, knowing Brian would probably need very little excuse to throw a punch. Brian turned away and stormed out. Tom quickly dressed, apologised for his brother's outburst and chased after him through the rain. Brian was walking purposefully back towards the college.

'Hold up Brian,' Tom had to run to catch him.

Brian ignored him and kept up his brisk pace, staring hard at the path in front of him. As Tom caught up, Brian's glare remained fixed on the path in front of him.

'Dickhead,' Brian repeated, with the same venom shown in the changing room. 'What a complete dickhead. How could he possibly have thought that taking me off, the top goal scorer, for that donkey Slogger, would help us win the cup? What a total pratt.' Brian's pace quickened as they crossed the railway bridge, but he continued to stare straight ahead, teeth grinding, lips taut, eyes narrowed. Brian's tirade ebbed and flowed as the boys passed the union building and turned towards Dickens Court.

As they passed Dickens Court reception building, Tom tried to calm Brian's anger. 'Maybe he had good reason to take you off.' His words were poorly chosen. They only sparked a fresh volley of anger.

Brian stopped in his tracks, turned to face his brother and pointed his finger sharply at Tom as he switched his fury on his brother. 'Good reason? Good reason?' he shouted. In the darkness, their faces were softly lit by the lights pouring out of the reception windows. The rain could be seen clearly against the amber path lights, still falling hard and the boys were shouting, partly through anger and partly to be heard over the howling wind. They were soaked to the skin but had long stopped caring.

It was years since the brothers had argued. There had been plenty of heated exchanges, but they had been no more than playful banter. This was different. Tom felt the malice in Brian's words cut like a knife. He wasn't sure how to respond and again his choice of words only inflamed the situation. 'Let's face it Brian. You did give the penalty away, I cleared off the line following one of your mistakes and I blocked another shot after you gave the ball away.'

They were still face to face outside the reception. The rain was relentless and the drains had flooded. Water now flowed around their feet as the paths ran like mountain streams.

Brian was livid. There was only one thing worse than The Hard Man weakly conceding the cup by taking him off and that was his brother agreeing with the fool. The one person he expected to stand by him in any situation was stabbing him in the back. He pushed Tom's chest with the palm of his hand, almost daring him to take a swing. 'Yes. Let's face it Tom.' He repeated Tom's choice of opening words to give his reply added bite. 'It was no way a penalty and I worked bloody hard to get back and make the tackle. And you are supposed to tidy up after my mistakes. That's your job. Mine is to score and make goals. I did. Twice. That's usually enough to win any game.'

Brian paused for breath. 'And if Donkey Slogger hadn't come on, we'd have probably won, even if it went to penalties. Don't suppose you noticed their third goal came from his mistake?'

Brian pushed Tom in the chest again. Tom, felt he was being blamed for Brian's substitution and was starting to lose patience. 'There's no point standing in the rain. That's not going to solve anything. Let's go inside,' Tom appealed.

'I'll stand wherever the hell I want Tom.' Brian shouted. He was well past the point of reason.

'That's up to you Brian. I'm going in the kitchen for a cup of tea. Want one?' with that Tom turned and headed for block F.

Brian stayed motionless outside the reception building, rain dripping from his clothes. The anger wouldn't go away. He couldn't believe his brother had turned against him. Tom never did that. It was his duty to stand by him. Memories raced through Brian's mind. How often had he swept Tom's failings under the carpet? How many times had he been generous and forgiving, all to have it thrown back in his face in his hour of need.

Their father, Norman Hill, sat on his bench watching Brian stand in the rain taking deep breaths. He wanted to help. He couldn't. He didn't know how. He didn't feel the wind. He didn't notice the rain. He wasn't cold. He watched as Brian turned and walked purposefully towards block F, and was gone.

Brian took the steps two at a time and marched into the kitchen. 'What's the matter with you? You're supposed to be my brother. Why are you being such a bastard?' Piercing eyes. Sharp accusing looks.

Tom poured his tea, walked over to the soft chairs in the corner and sat down. Brian stood over him waiting for a reaction. He got it in calm but determined words. 'You're the bastard Brian. You're the one speaking without thinking, expecting everyone to bend over backwards for you. You've been like that all your life. To be honest Brian … I'm sick of it and it's time you took a good look at yourself.'

Brian's voice leapt an octave. 'Look at myself? What about you?'

Tom came straight back, his expression blank but serious. 'You have no humility Brian. You can only see things from Brian's point of view. What's best for Brian? That's how you approach everything.'

Brian's disappointment over the football was no longer the issue. This was a stinging and thoroughly unreasonable personal attack. The anger had gone. It was replaced by a sense of betrayal. The only person whose opinion he genuinely valued thought he was a selfish bastard.

Before Brian could come back, Tom continued his onslaught. 'You shagged Anita and walked away without even kissing her goodbye in case she cost you a few gifts. Don't tell me that wasn't selfish. You even lied to her so you could go back for another session at a later date. Studying for exams my arse. You haven't opened a text book since the day you got here.'

Brian fought back. 'You might have kissed Sarah goodbye, but you still shagged her behind your girlfriend's back. Just because you felt bad about cheating on Vicky, doesn't make you a nice bloke. You still cheated on her. And you walked away from Sarah at the same speed I walked away from Anita. You've no intention of seeing Sarah again. At least I considered seeing Anita again, even if it was just for sex. Maybe that's all she wants.'

Brian had the upper hand again and pressed his advantage. 'And what about Vicky? You'll probably tell her all about Sarah when she gets back and it will break her heart. And why tell her? I'll tell you why … to ease your own guilt. Not to put her mind at ease, just for your own benefit; the warm glow of confession for Mr Superior Tom Hill. At least I'm honest with myself, even if that makes me selfish. You hide behind a mask of good intentions.'

'So you're honest with yourself Brian?' Tom retaliated. 'But that's as far as it goes. What happened to your simple honesty when Black Lips invited you to meet her parents? You were too busy boozing with the football club to even take five minutes to phone her.'

Brian had no answer for that and thought he may do better by narrowing the scope of the argument. 'Let's just say we're both out of order when it comes to girls. That's not what this is about. This is about you and me. So who was the selfish brother when Vicky came along. We did everything together until you started seeing her, but did I complain? Not a bit of it. I was happy for you. And now you call me selfish.'

The blackness of the night filled the kitchen window. The rain had eased to drizzle. The wind had blown itself out. Both brothers had run out of steam. They sat side by side looking at the black window, their own reflections staring back at themselves. They said nothing for five minutes as the dust settled. They both felt bad. Suppressed tension had exploded and they had both said painful things, the truth, but painful nevertheless, to the person they loved the most.

Tom broke the silence. 'Of course you're right. We probably would have won if he hadn't taken you off, but he's the captain and we have to respect his judgement … even if he is wrong.'

Brian was calm now and appreciated that his brother was offering an olive branch. 'I know. He did what he thought was best. Maybe I did give the ball away once too often, but he was wrong all the same. I had a goal left in me. The cup was ours.'

They stared at themselves a while longer in the black window.

Brian was starting to feel guilty. He had used his brother as a punch bag and taken his anger out on him. He turned to face his brother. 'Okay Tom. I was out of order. I'm sorry. I said some nasty stuff.'

'No need Brian. I did too and I'm sorry too.'

'If I didn't care about your opinions, I wouldn't have defended myself so fiercely.' He edged towards Tom and gave him a hug before adding. 'Mind you. If anyone else had spoken to me like you did, I'd have decked them.'

Chapter 30

Making the cut

Two days later, April 13, 1984: In the days leading up to Brian Hill's operation, he had successfully put thoughts of sharp knives and needles to the back of his mind, but as soon as he started walking through Southside towards the hospital with his overnight bag, he was gripped with fear. His whole body felt drained and weak. He consoled himself with the thought that it would be over in a matter of hours. All he had gathered from his fleeting moments with the doctor was that they would give him a general anaesthetic, cut him open and pull out a few surplus veins from his ball bag. Sounded awful. Sounded painful. In the days running up to the operation, he had been told a number of hospital horror stories.

Old George told him of operations done in field hospitals during the war with no anaesthetic other than a swig of brandy and a piece of wood to bite on. Rupert Eckhart had told him about a man who had woken up during an operation. He regained consciousness and all feeling, but couldn't speak or move. He felt the pain and saw everything they did but couldn't tell them he was awake.

Rupert's story played over and over in his mind as he walked through the arched entrance of the hospital and headed for reception.

'Mr Hill did you say?' asked a large nurse behind the counter. She smiled up at Brian.

'Yes. Brian Hill.'

'Ah yes. I have you here.' She fingered through a list of papers. The formalities of filling out forms took Brian's mind off Rupert's story briefly. She then ushered him down the corridor to a room full of equally apprehensive patients. Many of them had family and friends to share their fears. Brian was alone. Tom had offered to go with him, but he didn't want to look weak and had been too macho to accept. He could have done with him now. He must be only minutes away from being cut open.

A book or newspaper would have been a good distraction. Others were reading, some wore pyjamas, some wore hospital robes. Brian noticed a man's bottom through the split at the back of his robe as he shuffled off to the toilet. The waiting room was about 30 feet by 20 feet with seats running all around the outside edge. A spiky haired boy of around seven years old ran from end to end pushing a large red truck. He made engine noises and allowed the truck to smash into furniture at the end of each run. If you run into my ankles, I'll kick you into the next county, Brian unkindly thought to himself.

The clock on the wall told Brian he had only been in the waiting room five minutes. It seemed more like half an hour. A name was called by a nurse with a clipboard. The family of the truck-pushing child followed the nurse with their noisy child. Brian and all those around him breathed a sigh of relief. The man in the robe returned from the toilet, delighted to see the boy gone. He sat back down next to Brian and addressed anyone who was interested. 'Little bugger. Needs a good smack. No discipline these days some parents.'

Nobody replied. Brian nodded in agreement but couldn't manage a smile. Brian's mind wandered back to Rupert's story. He looked up at the clock almost every 30 seconds. His wait agonisingly stretched to half an hour before the nurse with the clipboard returned and called his name. He was taken to a desk in the corridor outside the waiting room. He could feel his heart race. People were talking but the words echoed around his head.

'Have a seat Mr Hill.' The nurse pointed to a hard plastic seat by the desk. He sat waiting while the nurses discussed their plans for the weekend and talked about their children. Brian thought the seat rather uncomfortable and wondered why he couldn't have stayed in the soft chairs of the waiting room. After another five minutes, Brian was introduced to a young doctor who directed him to a small consulting room.

'Good morning Brian. I'm the anaesthetist. I just need to fill this form in with you. It will help me with the anaesthetic.' When the form was complete, the young doctor added, 'You're a lucky boy. You have the consultant today. He always does a very tidy job.'

Brian nodded nervously while wondering to himself whether one of the cleaners might have picked up the scalpel if the consultant hadn't been available. What a strange thing to say. Surely whoever went near his balls with a sharp knife would be highly skilled and well trained. Brian was ushered back to the waiting room. Nobody looked up. Another 15 minutes later, Brian was called back to the desk in the corridor and handed a hospital robe. The nurse explained he must wear nothing underneath and the robe must be open at the back. She also gave him a bag for his belongings and assured him it would find its way to a locker next to his hospital bed.

Then she handed him two disposable safety razors, pointed in the direction of the toilets and told him to remove his pubic hair on the left side of his groin.

'What about my scrotum?' Brian asked using the correct words. He didn't want any risk of misunderstanding.

She assured him that wouldn't be necessary and he went to the toilets wondering how the surgeon was going to remove veins from his ball bag by cutting into the bottom of his tummy. The hospital gown felt quite degrading and shaving your pubic hair in a public toilet with a dry disposable razor felt equally degrading.

The anaesthetist had drawn a black arrow on the left-hand side of his tummy, presumably to show the doctor where to cut. Brian studied the arrow, clumsily drawn and thought how basic it all seemed. He hoped the surgeon had a few more details about his case in addition to one hurriedly drawn arrow. He put his clothes in the bag and returned to the nurse, who directed him back to the waiting room where his gaze returned to the slow-moving clock.

He waited another tense five minutes. He must be close now he thought. The clock had stopped. The nurse with the clipboard walked in again. She appeared to be moving in slow motion and her words were slow and drawn out as she looked in Brian's direction. 'Brian Hill please.'

She led him to another room, half the size of the waiting room. He entered through double doors at one end. Two other doors at the far end with round windows appeared to lead to, what Brian thought must be, the operating theatre. Brian had images in his head of his blood veins being cut and pulled from his body. In a short time, he would be lying naked on the operating table. The doctor would be stood over him with Brian's dick in one hand and a very sharp knife in the other.

The nurse instructed him to place his footwear in the corner and lie on the trolley in the middle of the room. He also undid the opening at the back of the robe and lay on his back, making sure he wasn't on top of the loose flaps of the robe. As the anaesthetist entered the room, Brian could feel every muscle in his body pulling hard.

He was told to relax, but that seemed the most unnatural thing to do in the circumstances. He concentrated on a roll of what appeared to be two foot wide toilet roll hanging on the far wall.

'This won't hurt a bit. You're doing fine. Next thing you know, you'll be a new man.'

A nurse held Brian's hand as the anaesthetist did his job.

'You're a stupid son of a bitch. No balls and no brains.' Brian thumped The Hard Man in the face, which imploded with surprising ease. Brian's fist was sucked into the captain's brain. He felt his hand tangle with eye balls, blood veins and fragments of skull. As he pulled away, the head sprang back to its original shape, like a rubber ball. But it was no longer the face of The Hard Man; it was Anita and she was crying.

Brian's first thought wasn't about the curious rubber qualities of the face, but why Anita was crying. Maybe she had lost a close relative or even a favourite pet. It didn't occur to him that he might be the cause of her distress. While he considered the problem, a throbbing sensation, not quite pain, but still a little uncomfortable, distracted his attention. It came from his groin. Strange. There was bright light. He was in a well-lit room.

Brian opened his tired eyes. He was only semi-conscious and he couldn't understand where he was or why he was there. He appeared to be in a large store cupboard, twice the size of the Dickens Court kitchen. He was lying on his side and he had no energy at all. It took him all his strength to lift his eyelids. He couldn't possibly move anything else. The dull sensation from his groin returned. That must have something to do with his unusual circumstances he thought. He was on a narrow bed with chrome-plated bars running down each side to stop him rolling off.

Someone bumped into the end of his bed. The jolt cleared his mind a bit and when a nurse appeared, he remembered he was in Southside District Hospital.

'Are you alright Brian? How are you feeling?' The nurse smiled.

Brian felt like shit. 'I'm fine thank-you. Were there any complications or was everything as it should be?' The success of the operation was the first thing Brian could think of when he realised why his groin was throbbing.

'The doctor will be able to tell you about that, but all's well as far as I know.'

Brian slipped back into a light sleep. He woke a few moments later, or at least it seemed a few moments. His bed had wheels. A man was pushing him along the corridor followed by a nurse. He was wheeled into an extra-large lift, which went upwards, very slowly. He was pushed down more corridors and into a ward, where the side bars were dropped, the top portion of the bed lifted off like a stretcher and he was eased into a bed. The nurse gave Brian a couple of pain killing pills and left. He fell into a deep sleep.

When Brian next opened his eyes, Tom was beside him reading The Sun. Tom saw his brother wake up.

'I've brought you your favourite paper Brian. Nice pair of tits today.'

'Bastard. Don't make me laugh. It hurts.' Every word was hard work for Brian. Staying awake was exhausting.

He thought this must be what it feels like when your 90 years old and tired.

'I spoke to the nurse. She said it went well and you'll feel great within a week.'

'I don't feel great now. I feel like I've been in a fight … and lost.' Brian tried to sit up but it was too much. He gave in.

'I wasn't sure whether I should bring The Sun. I don't want you to pull your stitches.' Tom smiled warmly and looked around the ward.

Six beds filled the room, three on either side. One was empty, but the others were occupied by a wide selection of patients. Opposite Brian was a man of around 50, surrounded by bickering members of his family. One woman of similar age, probably his wife, had a deeply furrowed brow, which showed great distress. Tom listened to their conversation. It wasn't difficult. The discussion was heated and the level of consideration for other patients was low. Her concern, expressed to a pale-faced girl in her mid twenties, had nothing to do with the bed-ridden man's double hernia operation. Pale Face had an equally furrowed brow although the lines were not as deep as the older woman but ran in the same direction. Presumably she was the daughter.

The subject was decoration and refurbishment. Another man, also in his mid-twenties, contributed nothing to the debate. He had an unfortunate nervous twitch. His head appeared to be nodding agreement every few seconds. Tom thought, at first, that he was agreeing with the others all the time, but when the nodding continued during a pause in the row, it became clear that it had nothing to do with what was being said.

From what Tom could gather, Pale Face and Nodder had just bought a flat, which needed a great deal of modernisation and improvement. Their plans had been put on ice when Pale Face's father had been rushed to hospital for his operation. Solving the problem of replacing the father, who had been due to carry out all the work on the flat, was the subject of the heated debate. The father was clearly delighted to have escaped a lot of work and his cheerful smile had sparked the exchange.

In the next bed, a thin-faced man in his late thirties, possibly early forties, read a paperback. He looked the picture of health. Tom wondered what was wrong with him. The third bed on the opposite side of the room was occupied by an elderly grey-haired man. He had no cards, flowers or gifts. There were no visitors around his bed and he was fast asleep. Tom couldn't see any movement at all and wondered if he was dead.

Brian's immediate neighbour was the only other patient in the ward. He was asleep but snored a little. Tom turned back to Brian. He was asleep again.

When Tom returned the next day, Brian was sat up in bed reading The Sun.

'You look a lot better today Brian.'

'I am. I can even walk to the toilet myself, but it takes a while.'

'Good. They said you can come home tomorrow, but you need a week in bed, then back to have your stitches out.'

'I haven't got stitches,' Brian corrected him. 'I've got clips holding me together, and they're not in my ball bag.'

'Where then?'

'My tummy, where my pubic hair used to be before they made me shave it off.'

'I thought it was veins in your sack though.' Tom looked puzzled.

'It was, but they cut my tummy open, grabbed the right vein and pulled it up from my bag.'

'Have you got loads of bandages like a nappy?'

'No bandages.'

'How come?'

'No dressing at all.' Brian pulled back the covers and pulled down his pyjamas to show Tom the wound.

Tom, slightly embarrassed, took a quick look around the room, but nobody had taken much interest, so he leant forward for a closer look. The surgeon had cut a tidy straight line, almost two inches long. It ran diagonally from Brian's hip to his crotch. It ran parallel with the natural creases of the body. Tom was impressed with the tidy work. Very few signs of blood at all. Four large clips, which looked like staples, straddled the scar.

'Don't those staples hurt?' Tom found himself pointing.

'I can feel them. They don't hurt, but they itch like a scab that needs picking.'

As he pulled the covers back, a scruffy elderly man walked into the ward. When he saw Brian and Tom a warm fatherly grin spread across his face.

'How's it hanging?' shouted Old George as he headed in their direction.

Brian waited until he was a little closer. He didn't have the strength to shout back. 'Mustn't grumble thanks. How are you?'

'Here you go. This should take your mind off your pain.' George handed Brian a brown paper bag. Brian peered into the bag without taking out what was in it. It was a dog-eared girly magazine.

'What's up with you both? I've had my sack cut open and you bring me pictures of tits.' Brian said with good humour. It was nice to see his old friend.

'You're probably feeling the same age as me right now,' said George as he pulled up a chair.

'Well. Yes. I suppose I am, but yesterday was worse. When I first came round, I felt about 90 years old. Today I only feel about 70.'

'Sounds about right.' George nodded. 'You're looking well.' George then smiled for no obvious reason. His own words had reminded him of a story. He pushed his glasses further up his nose.

Brian and Tom knew that meant he was about to tell one of his stories.

'That's how you greet old people.'

'How's that George?' asked Tom.

'My … you're looking well.'

Tom and Brian looked at each other confused, then looked back at George for an explanation.

'You see boys. There are three stages in life.' He looked at them both in turn before continuing. 'You are young, middle aged or "my … you're looking well".'

Tom smiled as he caught on. 'You've never looked better George.'

Brian would have twigged as well if he hadn't fallen asleep again.

An hour later he was woken by a nurse. She had his lunch. Tom and George had gone. As soon as he finished his food, he laboured to the toilet. He climbed back in bed feeling good. Visits to the toilet, much to his relief, had been easy. As he settled down to a spot of light reading, courtesy of George's brown paper bag, he heard a camp voice talking to the ward nurse. He knew that voice. Rupert had come to visit.

The music post graduate student from room number one minced his way along the ward to Brian's bedside. 'How are you today Brian? I've brought you a Mars bar to build up your strength.'

'Thanks Rupert. Have a seat.' Brian gestured to the bedside chair. Rupert sat down and looked around the room. The family decorator opposite was enjoying a book on gardening. The healthy looking thin-faced man was still reading his book. The elderly man in the next bed, who seemed dead the day before, had still not moved, but an unhappy looking lady sat quietly by his bed. Brian's immediate neighbour, the snorer, was awake now and making a lot less noise. He was sat up in bed staring at the man with the gardening book.

'Can I see the scar?' Rupert asked.

'The bandages haven't come off yet,' Brian lied. 'How are your studies going?'

Brian had chosen the right question. Rupert spoke for almost 15 minutes without stopping for breath. He explained his latest composition, the drawbacks of multi-track recording and the limitations of the primitive equipment at Southside University. Brian could feel his eyes closing but bravely kept them open and nodded agreement in all the right places.

Rupert finished his rant about composing and looked around the ward again. The snoring man was now staring at the thin-faced man.

'Well Brian. Society is a hospital of incurables.' Rupert said profoundly. Brian looked at him confused. 'Ralph Waldo Emerson,' Rupert added by way of explanation. Brian's confused expression was unchanged. 'American poet,' Rupert added in a slightly higher voice, which indicated it was his final attempt at explaining himself.

Brian smiled acknowledgement, half understanding. That was enough for Rupert. He stood up, wished Brian a speedy recovery and glided out of the ward, sunlight from the window catching the folds of his Arabian tunic.

Brian closed his eyes. The visit had tired him, but seconds later, a tall bald, wide-eyed young man with a tattoo of a lizard above his ear and a pair of red glasses perched on his nose, made himself at home in the bedside chair.

'Brian, you old tart. How's your twig?' Hugh Grundy's loud voice didn't just wake Brian. The dead man even stirred briefly.

Brian's startled eyes opened. 'Hugh. Didn't expect to see you. How are you?'

'I'm good. Back early to prepare for second year finals.' Hugh was on the edge of his chair. Brian could see he wanted to tell him something. He guessed correctly. During his Easter break, Hugh had finally come up with a successful scheme for making money.

Hugh didn't wait to be asked and launched straight into it. 'I'm in the money Brian. Don't know why I didn't think of it before.'

Brian had endured 15 minutes of music jargon from Rupert and now got 15 minutes from Hugh on how he was paid to deliver free newspapers, but kept them for a couple of weeks before selling them to his uncle who ran a fish and chip shop.

'Got the idea off my old ma. She's always complaining about the papers coming through the door. "Half stuffed in the letterbox. Lets all the cold air in," she said. So I said, "At least it's a free newspaper." And she said, "No Hugh.

It's full of crap. All adverts. I wish they'd do us all a favour and keep their junk." So I'm getting paid for delivering them and getting paid again by my uncle at the chippy.' Hugh waited for Brian's praise.

'Good job Hugh.' Brian couldn't help thinking their must be a catch. 'What if people complain they're not getting a paper?'

'Would you complain if the flu was going round and you didn't get it?' Hugh had thought of that one.

'Aah, but what if somebody working for the paper doesn't get it delivered?' Brian asked.

'My boss would say number 22 hasn't had their paper and I would keep one back each week for number 22.' Hugh smiled with pride.

'So are you going to try it in Southside?' Brian played along.

'If I can find a friendly chippy.' Hugh then leaned over to Brian and whispered. 'But could you do me a favour?'

'Go on,' Brian nodded.

'Don't tell Colin. He'll want to do it with me and he mucks everything up.'

'Sure. No problem,' agreed Brian.

Hugh sat back up and returned to speaking very loudly. 'You get some freaks in here don't you?'

'Where are you looking?' said Brian, glimpsing at the staring man, the healthy man, the dead man and the family decorator.

Hugh saw him looking around. 'No. Not this room. Just as I was walking down the corridor, looking for the right ward, I saw a man in a white dress.' Hugh pulled a face to show his disapproval.

Brian had a fairly good idea who Hugh had seen and thought it a little strange that a bald young man with a tattoo above one ear should think a man with an Arabian tunic was any more strange than himself. 'Did this man have short blond hair?' Brian asked.

'That's right. And he walked like a girl.'

Brian smiled. 'That man had just been to visit me.'

'What?' Hugh squealed. 'How do you know him?'

'He lives in Dickens Court, block F.'

'Which floor? I've never seen him.'

'Our floor.'

Hugh's mind was working hard. Ten seconds later he put two and two together and shouted, 'No?'

Brian nodded.

'Room number one?'

Brian nodded again.

Chapter 31

Did you miss me?

Twelve days later, April 25, 1984: It was six weeks since Vicky Owen had seen Tom Hill; the boy she loved, but, sadly for her, the boy that didn't feel the same way about her. He had been in her thoughts every day during the long Easter break, and, as the days passed, she ticked them off her calendar. She hoped that he had missed her at least half as much as she had missed him. During the holiday, she hadn't looked at another boy. The fact that there were other suitable boys did not cross her mind. Tom was the only boy for her and the wait was over. She unlocked the door of her room in Dickens Court, block B, and dumped her stuff on the bed.

She unzipped her big suitcase and pulled out the bag of groceries her mother had carefully packed for her. She hurried to the kitchen and placed the fresh food in the fridge. She had intended to unpack her clothes before the creases became fixed. She didn't want to have to iron everything again, but she couldn't wait. She left her luggage on the bed, locked the door and set off at a fast pace towards Tom's room.

She knocked gently on his door and stood on her tiptoes with her eyes shut and pouting lips ready for a kiss when he opened the door and saw her.

'Come in,' shouted Tom.

She opened the door. Tom was sat at his desk reading.

'Hi Tom,' she said shyly and very quietly. She walked over to his chair hoping for a kiss and a cuddle.

'How's it going Vicky? You look good.' Tom stood. 'Have my seat. Want a cup of tea?'

Vicky didn't want a cup of tea. She wanted a kiss. 'Yes please. That would be lovely.' She sat down. Tom went to the kitchen and returned five minutes later with the drinks and a packet of biscuits.

Vicky stood up and hugged Tom. She pecked him on the cheek. His response was more formal than affectionate. She was starting to sense that things were not as they should be. Tom was cold towards her. She sat on the bed and patted the space beside her to encourage Tom to join her. Instead, he passed her tea and sat in the soft chair at the end of the bed.

Her fringe still followed the line of her eyebrows, but her hair was shorter. Tom didn't notice, or if he did, he chose not to comment. She had a new jumper in a floral pattern, slightly more daring than usual. Again Tom chose not to comment. Vicky hoped Tom's mind was on Brian's recovery from his operation. It certainly wasn't on her. All the euphoria she had felt in the last few days as the new term drew close, had withered away in a matter of minutes. Something was wrong and Vicky feared the worse.

She felt a sense of great loss. Empty space filled her mind where once there had been love, optimism and joy. For six weeks she had thought of nothing but Tom. The good memories had dominated. The disappointments had been forgotten. She had built him up in her mind to something far greater than he was or ever could be. She felt let down and vacant. She loved him deeply but he looked as if he would rather be playing football.

Tom could feel the tension. In the six weeks he had been apart from Vicky, the good times had been forgotten. He had dwelled on the problems and disappointments. His opinion of Vicky and their relationship had spiralled steadily downwards. He thought when he saw her again, the magic would return, but when she opened his door he felt revulsion. He couldn't handle the responsibility for her feelings. It was too much for a boy of 18 with a spirit of romantic adventure. He no longer liked the idea of a steady girlfriend. Or maybe he no longer liked the idea of Vicky as his steady girlfriend. He wasn't sure which, but, either way, as soon as she walked through the door, he knew it was over.

While Vicky sat on the bed sipping her tea, Tom stared out of his window across campus. There was a middle-aged man in a suit sat on the bench at the far side of the lawn looking up at him. As Tom turned to Vicky, he thought he recognised the man and took another look, but he had gone.

The silence told its own story. Vicky's empty feeling grew stronger with every silent moment that slipped by, and she was first to break the quiet, more through embarrassment than a genuine belief that she could put things right.

Her voice was soft and trembling as she looked at Tom through watery eyes. 'Did you miss me?' In more joyful circumstances, the irony of her question would have been funny.

Tom looked her in the eye and was bluntly honest. 'No.'

The silence returned. Vicky dare not even blink. The simplest movement may signal her acceptance of his rejection. The tears started to flow faster. She felt desperate. Tom was so cold. She didn't deserve this. Was it so bad to have denied him sex? Or was there another girl? She edged towards him and sat on the arm of the chair with her arms around his shoulders. She didn't want to lose him and pleaded. 'But Tom, I love you. I've missed you so much. I need you.' She pressed her cheek against his shoulder but nothing came back. Tom's hands remained at his sides.

'I'm sorry Vicky, but that's just it. You need me. I don't want to be needed by anybody. It's too much responsibility and I don't love you. I was very fond of you. Very. But … but it's over.'

She was sobbing now and gripped him tightly around the shoulders not wanting to let go.

Tom thought back to his argument with his brother. He had accused Brian of always putting Brian first. 'What's best for Brian? That's how you approach everything,' he had said to him.

Brian had replied, 'And what about Vicky? You'll probably tell her all about Sarah when she gets back and it will break her heart. And why tell her? I'll tell you why … to ease your own guilt. Not to put her mind at ease, just for your own benefit; the warm glow of confession for Mr

Superior Tom Hill. At least I'm honest with myself, even if that makes me selfish. You hide behind a mask of good intentions.'

His mask of good intentions had slipped and he felt enormous guilt. He could have tried harder with Vicky, but he had taken the easy way out and ended things. He looked at himself through Vicky's eyes and he didn't like what he saw.

She still clung on sobbing. Tom wanted to comfort her, but it would give her false hope. He needed a clean break. Yes it was selfish but it's what he wanted. And why shouldn't he have what he wanted sometimes? He couldn't always put others first.

She cried on his shoulder for a good five minutes in silence, still sobbing, before renewing her appeal. 'I love you Tom. I can't live without you. You're all I think about every day. Can't we give it another try? I'll change. I'll try and see things your way. Let's give it another go.' She knew she was starting to show her desperation but she didn't care. Without Tom, she had no use for dignity and pride.

She continued to plead while Tom repeated how sorry he was. She fell silent again, still crying on his shoulder. She needed answers. 'What did I do wrong?' she blubbered. 'Tell me and I'll put it right.'

Tom resisted the temptation to say 'It's not you, it's me', opting instead for, 'You haven't done anything wrong Vicky. It's just not going to work. We want different things.'

Tom was thinking on his feet. He hadn't thought this through because he didn't know how he was going to feel until she walked through his door, so he dwelled on his own words almost as much as Vicky did. He asked himself if the lack of sex had been a factor and concluded that it definitely had not. It was the intensity of the relationship that had been too much. The triviality of sex with Sarah had been fun. He didn't want to replace Vicky with Sarah, but the night of passion with Sarah had helped him realise that a steady relationship with Vicky was not what he wanted.

After another painful silence, Vicky asked the question she didn't want to hear the answer to, but she had to know. 'You've met someone else haven't you?' She spoke as calmly as her crying allowed.

Tom looked back out of the window. He thought about Sarah. It had been fun, but Sarah had only helped him understand his own feelings. She had not changed his feelings. Again he thought back to Brian's words. It would hurt Vicky more to tell her about Sarah. She didn't need to know. 'I meet someone else every day, but no, I haven't replaced you. I just don't want a girlfriend now. I don't want you Vicky. It's over.'

There was another knock at the door. Vicky and Tom looked at each other. 'Come in,' shouted Tom.

Andrew pushed the door open and walked in with a big smile, which turned to a frown as soon as he saw Vicky crying. 'Oh sorry. Shall I come back later.'

'No Andrew,' Vicky replied as she stood up. 'I have to unpack. See you both later.' With that she left.

'Why was she crying?' asked Andrew.

'We just split up.'

'Oh. That's a shame. What went wrong?' Andrew asked with genuine concern.

'I'm not totally sure myself, so why don't I make you a cup of tea and you can tell me all about your holiday.' Tom couldn't face going over it all again with Andrew, not yet anyway. He disappeared for five minutes and returned with two more cups of tea.

Andrew had taken the seat by the desk, leaving Tom the soft chair at the end of the bed. He was feeling good and couldn't wait to share his news with Tom. He had struggled through some difficult exchanges with his father and stood up for himself.

Tom handed Andrew his tea and settled back down in the soft chair. 'So did Frank give you a hard time?'

'Sort of. It was like you had never said anything to him at first and he treated me the same as normal, but things changed after I challenged him one night.'

Tom had noticed Andrew's echo had gone. Tom had been expecting Andrew to say, 'Things changed after I challenged him one night … they did.' But there was no 'they did'. It seemed strange, but nice. Tom was genuinely pleased to see that Andrew had made some progress. His confidence was starting to grow. He would have said something about the echo, but thought it best not to draw attention to the green shoots of progress for fear of squashing them. 'Go on. What happened?' Tom asked.

'He arrived home from work and handed his coat to my mum. He sat in front of the telly and said, "I think I'll have a whisky." Instead of going and getting him one I said "excellent idea", then carried on reading my book.'

'Nice one. Good so far,' Tom nodded for Andrew to continue.

'After a couple of minutes, he said, "Jump to it boy." And I replied, "Jump to what?" So he said, "The whisky won't pour itself will it?" I said, "I thought you were getting it." And he said, "No I'm not. You are. I asked you." So I said, "No you didn't. You're exact words were, 'I think I'll have a whisky.' And he replied, "Well then.

You know what that means don't you?" And that's when it got a bit heated.

'Excellent. What did you say?' Tom was delighted that Andrew had finally stood up to his father.

'I said, "I know exactly what it means. It means you have no manners and you treat me like shit. Just like Tom told you when you came to dinner at Southside. You sit down in front of the telly, expecting mum to hang your coat up and me to run around pouring you drinks when you haven't even got the manners to ask me nicely. I'm your son, not your butler." At first he just stared at me but you won't believe what he said next.'

'Knowing your father, I think I will,' said Tom.

'He said, "I know what's going on here. I had a friend at work in a very similar situation. He was a young man in his first job and had moved away from home. He was under a lot of stress and it affected his mind. Couldn't think straight. Started being rude to people when things got on top of him, lashing out and not showing his senior colleagues the respect they were due. Had to go home, signed off with stress by his doctor. Going to Southside University has been a big step for you. Angry young rebels like Tom putting dangerous ideas in your head. You've probably got a mental disorder. I'll get your mum to take you to the doctor tomorrow." Unbelievable. He's the rudest man in Britain and when I question him, I have a mental illness.'

'I hope you didn't let him get away with that.'

'No I didn't. I said, "It's nothing to do with Southside. You are a rude man with no manners and before I started at Southside, and for as long as I can remember, you have been a rude man with no manners. The only mental disorder I have is that I have allowed you to walk all over me for my whole life, but that stops now. From now on, if you treat me unkindly, I shall say so." And then I left the room.'

'To get him a whisky?'

'No. To read my book in my room.'

'Well done Andrew.' Tom leant over and squeezed his shoulder. 'So how was he after that?'

'Just as rude and bad mannered as he had been before but only to my mum. He steered clear of me until last week.'

'What happened then?'

'I told him I was dropping the politics element of my degree and concentrating on economics. He said, "Now you're just being foolish. The politics is important to you." And I said, "No. The economics is important to me. The politics is important to you. But I'm taking the degree, not you. So I'm dropping politics." He's not spoken to me since.'

'And how do you feel about that?' Tom asked.

'I really don't mind, because I know he's only blanking me to try and guilt me into doing what he wants. But he can sulk all he likes. It's my life and I'm living it for me, not for my father. I'm going to make my own decisions from now on.'

'I bet he mentioned road-works on the drive back though?' Tom couldn't help making a small joke, despite the serious subject.

'Actually he didn't, but I could hear him muttering angrily to himself while we were sat in a tailback on the motorway.'

'I'm pleased for you Andrew.' Tom offered Andrew a biscuit.

'Thanks.' He took one. They were his favourite. 'So I've finally broken free from my father's influence,' said

Andrew proudly, but added, 'Do you think I've done the right thing?' He wanted Tom's approval and Tom immediately had the feeling that, although Andrew may have mentally pulled away from the influence of his father, he appeared to have replaced Frank Leopard with Tom Hill. Tom had just ditched Vicky because he didn't want responsibility for her hopes and fears and life in general, and now Andrew appeared to have made Tom his new official mentor. Why couldn't they all be more like Brian, and just selfishly take care of themselves?

Chapter 32

Janet Hill

Ten days later, May 4, 1984: 'Ipso facto, we achieve equilibrium once again,' Professor Mumbles concluded and closed his book.

As the students filed out of the lecture theatre, Andrew caught up with Pink Socks. 'Hi Karen. How's it going?'

'Hey Andrew. Good thanks. Bit worried about the end of year exams though,' Karen replied with a kind smile.

'I've been reading through the text books over and over. Haven't had chance to go out much for ages. Been too busy.' Andrew had been advised by Tom to bring up the subject of going out without asking her directly to see how the conversation went. 'Opportunities always come up naturally,' Tom had said.

'I've been going through all my essays and re-writing them,' Karen Fisher replied. 'I've not been out much either, but I usually go down the Coffee Bar at the end of a night with Emily and Charlotte. Maybe I'll see you down there.'

'Sounds good. I'll see you in the Coffee Bar.' With that, Andrew headed in the other direction towards Dickens Court.

After a couple of steps, Karen shouted after him, 'Will you be with Tom and Brian?'

'Yeah, probably,' shouted Andrew, thinking nothing of it.

It was a lovely sunny morning, very warm for a spring day and Andrew walked along with a new confidence in his stride. Not only had he stood up to his father, but he was making some progress with the girl he loved. The new-found confidence had also affected his complexion. He still had spots, but they seemed less prominent these days. They probably weren't, but when things go well, Andrew worried less about them.

He arrived at the entrance to Dickens Court as Tom and Brian Hill came out, both wearing their suits.

'How's it going Andrew?' asked Tom.

'Excellent thanks. Pink Socks just suggested I meet her in the Coffee Bar some time. I think I'm winning her over,' Andrew said with a huge smile, but switched immediately to a serious face when he remembered why the brothers were smartly dressed. 'You off to the?' Andrew didn't finish the sentence. He just raised his eyebrows and nodded in the direction of town. He was uncomfortable using the word 'graveyard'. Things always seemed worse when they were spelled out.

'Yes. Should be back for lunch. See you later,' said Tom, with an equally serious face. The brothers were on their way to the graveyard beyond Southside Common. They took flowers every year on the anniversary of the car crash to commemorate their loss.

On the far side of the lawned area, their father Norman Hill sat on his bench and watched his sons discreetly from a distance. He couldn't see himself ever talking to them. It didn't seem right. He'd been out of their lives for too long. After watching them for many months, he felt great pride seeing them so happy, but his feelings of loss never seemed to change. They were just as they had been on the fateful day of the crash. He couldn't understand why nothing changed with the passing of time. The boys turned the corner and were gone.

Half an hour later, and following a visit to the flower shop in Royal Avenue next to The Pepper Pot restaurant, the boys arrived at the iron gates of the graveyard. There were headstones almost as far as the eye could see spread across the gently sloping field with Oak trees dotted around and benches by the side of the gravelled paths which ran between the graves.

Tom and Brian walked, in silence, through the older headstones by the entrance, to the far corner with the mid-day sun on their backs. The only sound was a dog barking in the distance and the deep rumble of traffic on the main London road over a mile away. They stopped and bowed their heads. The past eight years had been difficult but they had helped each other through them.

The boys had a bunch of flowers each. Tom placed his red roses on their mother's grave while Brian put his purple tulips alongside them up against their father's headstone. They had died together on the same day. A cruel twist of fate had left them both travelling separately to collect their sons from football training.

Janet had agreed to collect the boys because Norman had been held up with a meeting, but the meeting had finished early. If Norman could get there quick enough he would still be able to see his boys playing together at the back end of training. His car had been blocked in at work, so, not wishing to lose any time, Norman had taken one of the white delivery vans.

As the routes converged just around the corner from the football pitch, Norman had been in collision with his own wife's car. They had both died. The impact could be heard from the football pitch and the players had all rushed over, buzzing with curiosity and excitement. Something big had happened right next to them and they would be first on the scene.

The young brothers' smiles had turned to screams of anguish as they recognised the car. Their football coach saw both drivers and could see there was very little hope of saving them. He dragged the boys away from the scene and sent his assistant to the payphone to call the emergency services.

Now, eight years later, the boys hugged each other as they grieved for their parents. They had been devastated by their loss and their education had suffered having been thrust into boarding school after the comfort blanket of cosy family life in Southside, but as their first housemaster had told them, 'What don't kill you, makes you stronger'. He had been right. Before the accident, they had been confident and happy boys and, after the accident, with each other's help, they eventually bounced back and learned to rely on themselves.

Their inheritance had been placed in trust and paid their education costs while providing a modest allowance to supplement their university grants. There would also be a lump sum for each brother when they turned 21, but nothing could ever replace the love of their parents. They had been a close family and as the boys stood over the two graves, they both shed a tear before walking slowly away.

Janet Hill sat on one of the benches about 20 yards from her boys and watched them walk away. She thought how handsome they had become and what good boys to remember their parents with flowers. She missed being with them so much but, although shorter than it should have been, they had made her life special. She had her memories and they were all good. She waved and, as they disappeared over the crest of the hill, she started to look forward to next year's anniversary, when she hoped to see them again.

Chapter 33

Swimming against the tide

A week later, May 11, 1984: 'And I haven't seen him since,' Brian Hill told Andrew Leopard, who had been asking about The Invisible Man. Since the hospital visit he had not been seen again. Apart from Hugh, the other residents of floor three had their doubts about the existence of Rupert Eckhart. Some thought it an elaborate wind-up by the Hill brothers. The music post-graduate student was unusual and hard to believe, but as Brian repeated his description of Rupert, the story became so exaggerated that it went beyond belief.

'He was a nice bloke though,' Tom Hill told Andrew.

The three boys were in the Coffee Bar after a rare evening of drinking in The Red Lion. The end-of-year exams were only a few weeks away and there was a lot of studying ahead, so they were having a final Friday night out. They each had a toastie and a hot chocolate. Andrew had drunk less than the brothers but they were all in high spirits. It was a month since Brian's operation and he was feeling good. Tom's feelings of guilt towards Vicky had started to ease, although she had been unable to accept the split and pleaded for a second chance every time she saw him. Andrew was looking out for Pink Socks with high hopes of making more progress.

It was a warm spring night with very few clouds and the Coffee Bar was packed. There was an even split between those who had been on a night out and those who needed some light relief after an evening of study. But it was so busy that the customers had spilled out onto the terrace around the entrance and they sat around on low walls and leant against the cherry and silver birch trees. The sound of the juke-box mingled with conversation and laughter as clusters of students enjoyed the buzz of student life in the soft moonlight.

'Thirty six,' shouted a red-faced girl behind the counter. Two bearded mature students made their way through the crowd. Excuse me, oops, I'm sorry, pardon me. They collected two hot dogs and the red-faced girl pressed their ticket over a spike and busied herself preparing the next order.

Tom saw The Hard Man making his way through the crowd. He looked drained. Tom assumed he was one of those who had been studying all evening; he was in his final year. Since the cup final, Tom had spoken a few times with the captain, and apologised again for Brian's outburst. But since calling his leader a dickhead, Brian had not spoken to The Hard Man, despite encouragement from Tom to do so.

Andrew had heard about the cup final substitution from Brian a few times already, but when Brian saw The Hard Man, he couldn't help telling Andrew the story all over again. As Brian reached the part where he gave away the penalty, Tom noticed, over his shoulder, Pink Socks. She had been watching him and, as he picked her out, she quickly looked away; embarrassed at being caught out.

When Brian arrived at the part of his story where Slogger missed the high ball to allow YMCA in to score the winning goal, Tom found himself once more looking in the direction of Pink Socks. Again she was looking at him, but this time, she held her gaze with an inviting smile. This time Tom was a shade embarrassed and quickly looked back to his own companions.

Tom faced an awful dilemma. His best friend Andrew was 'in love' with Pink Socks, but did very little about it. Tom, on the other hand, had picked out Pink Socks on the first day of the first term and was strongly attracted to her; an attraction he had fought against repeatedly even though he got all the signals from Karen Fisher that she would respond to any advances he might make.

Even when he was seeing Vicky Owen, he could see Pink Socks was keeping her eye on him waiting for her moment. There was a chemistry between Tom and Karen which Tom had ignored for the benefit of his best friend, but however much Andrew 'loved' Pink Socks, Tom could see it was never going to happen. Andrew was swimming against the tide. Pink Socks only had eyes for Tom.

The sexual energy between Tom and Pink Socks had been building up for the whole year and Tom felt himself almost physically drawn towards her. He fought against his urges by trying once more to end Brian's feud with the captain. 'I still think you should apologise to him.'

'He was wrong though. He cost us the cup. And worse than that … he pissed me off.' Brian was still angry a month after the cup defeat.

‘So he was wrong. Is that such a crime? We all make mistakes.’

‘But in this case, I, and the whole team, suffered because of his mistake.’ Brian could accept that people made mistakes but not when he was the one who suffered as a result of the mistake.

‘So if you were a magistrate would you fine a man £100 for stealing a car, but jail another man for six months if he stole YOUR car. The crime is the same. Get over yourself and forgive the bloke.’

Brian had no answer. He turned and begrudgingly looked at The Hard Man. The captain saw Brian scowling at him and nodded acknowledgement, not a smile, but friendly enough.

‘Go on Brian. Swallow your pride. You know it makes sense.’ Tom pushed his brother gently in the direction of the captain and kept pushing slowly until they were face to face.

‘Brian.’ The Hard Man nodded.

‘Hard Man.’ Brian nodded back.

‘How’s your wound?’

‘Fully recovered and ready for action thank-you.’ Brian kept a straight face, not wishing to show any emotion.

The small talk bumped along slowly until it died out. They both looked down at their plastic cups, equally reluctant to raise the subject of the cup final. The Hard Man eventually gave in and broke the silence. ‘Listen Brian. I’m sorry. Looking back it’s easy to say I got it wrong, and maybe I did. But at the time, I thought it was the right thing to do. We were struggling to hold on, let alone score a winner. I just wanted to hold out for penalties. I think we’d have done them in a shoot-out. If you had to make the call, you may have done the same thing. Who knows? It's the …'

Brian cut him short. 'No. I'm sorry. I was out of order. You're the captain and I should have respected your decision, but I do think I still had a goal left in me.'

'Maybe you did Brian.' The Hard Man reached out and shook Brian warmly by the hand. 'Who Me and I Got The Last Touch are outside. You coming out.'

'Yeah. Why not? Coming Tom?' asked Brian.

Tom followed Brian and The Hard Man towards the door and gave his brother and The Hard Man both a firm pat on the back.

Before the brothers had edged towards The Hard Man, Andrew had gone in the other direction towards Pink Socks and tapped her on the shoulder. 'Hi Karen. How's it going?'

'Andrew. Not too bad. What've you been up to?' she replied, looking around to see where Tom had gone.

'Had a few in The Red Lion. You been out?' Andrew was feeling confident. He beamed inwardly. A simple conversation with Pink Socks was all he had dreamed of since he started at Southside University. Andrew, for the first time in his life, was proud of himself. He had picked out a beautiful girl and patiently, with his best friend Tom's help, finally become her friend, and who knows what his new friendship could lead to. She could be the one, and he now dared to dream that she could, one day, be his girlfriend, and love him as much as he loved her.

The conversation flowed. Andrew offered her another coffee and toastie. They took them outside and sat under a cherry tree in the moonlight on the opposite side of the terrace from where Brian was talking his team-mates through his best goals for the university team. It was quieter outside and easier to talk. The juke-box was playing Ballad Of A Teenage Queen by Johnny Cash. Andrew thought he was doing well to have got Pink Socks on her own out on the terrace.

Andrew told Pink Socks all about Tom and Brian staying for the Christmas holidays. He told her about The Invisible Man from room number one and Hugh Grundy's money-making schemes. They laughed about the penny for the Guy incident on bonfire night and the last bottle of milk in the supermarket they had both reached for at the same time.

Andrew had a permanent smile until he saw Vicky Owen and her friends coming towards the Coffee Bar. Vicky greeted Tom briefly, waved at Andrew and went inside. 'That was Tom's old girlfriend,' Andrew said.

'The one with the fringe?' asked Karen, trying not to let on that she knew exactly which girl was Tom's girlfriend, but she had to hide a smile on discovering that they were no longer together.

'Yes. That's the one,' replied Andrew.

'What went wrong?' Karen couldn't help herself fishing for information. She had been waiting all year for half a chance to get close to Tom. She had seen him on the very first day of the first term at the Third World Collective shop in town and couldn't believe her luck when one of the boys on her economics course turned out to be his best friend. She had sent him a Valentine Card and had been given some roses which she hoped were from Tom, but she suspected they were from Andrew.

She quite liked Andrew as a possible friend, but there was only one boy she wanted as a lover and she felt that he had started to show signs of taking an interest in her. And now he had dumped his dowdy girlfriend. She was filled with anticipation of what might happen. There was electricity between her and Tom and she felt almost physically drawn towards him.

'They just weren't right for each other,' Andrew repeated. Pink Socks seemed distracted. She was looking over at the footballers. They were a bit noisy. Andrew wondered if now was a good time to invite her back to Dickens Court for a chance to talk in peace, but the beer was working its way through him fast and he was desperate for the toilet. 'Must visit the gents. Back in a minute.' Andrew rushed to the toilets at the back of the Coffee Bar.

He was not the only customer in a hurry. There was only one urinal in the gents and the queue was three deep. A few minutes later he washed his hands as quick as he could and rushed for the door. As he passed through the coffee bar, he saw Vicky in floods of tears. She was by the exit so he couldn't avoid her. 'Vicky. What's wrong?'

She was inconsolable and couldn't speak for sobbing. Andrew felt as if everyone were watching them as he and her two friends tried to comfort her. They led her outside but she was crying too much to speak.

Andrew didn't want to be held up too long. He had to get back to Pink Socks. And as much as he shared Vicky's pain, he had waited all year for his chance with Pink Socks and he had to get back. He looked over to where he had been sat with Pink Socks, but she was gone. He looked all around but could not see her. He went back inside but could not see her there either.

This was strange. Maybe she had also gone to the toilet. He would ask Tom. He would have seen where she had gone. He went back out to the footballers, but Tom wasn't with them. He looked around for him, but couldn't see him either.

'Brian. Have you seen Tom or Pink Socks?' Andrew asked, almost frantic.

Brian didn't answer straight away.

Andrew could see in his eyes, he knew what had happened.

Brian knew exactly where they were and was angry with his brother for placing him in the difficult position of breaking the news to Andrew.

Andrew looked into Brian's eyes with horror as his mind raced towards the truth, but, even though he had worked out what must have happened, he couldn't believe his best friend could do such a thing to him. He wouldn't let the painful truth even pass through his mind until he heard it from Brian.

He repeated his question slowly and with menace in his voice. 'Have you seen Tom or Pink Socks?'

Again Brian didn't answer straight away. He put his arm around Andrew's shoulder and led him away from the other footballers. 'I'm sorry Andrew. They left together.'

Chapter 34

And

The next day, May 12, 1984: Andrew Leopard sat in the back of the car with his head resting against the window. As the car hit bumps in the road, Andrew's head bounced away from the window before thudding gently back against the glass. It wasn't very comfortable, but if he sat up straight and didn't rest his head against something, he felt sick, so he suffered the odd bumped head to avoid feeling ill.

Maureen Leopard sat in the passenger seat with a road atlas on her lap. A set of notes was attached to the left-hand page with a paperclip. The notes showed her the route Frank Leopard wanted to take on their journey to Wales.

'Move over you pillock,' shouted Frank, as he came up behind a slow-moving car in the middle lane of the motorway. There was nothing on the inside lane and nothing in the third lane. Frank didn't want to undertake the slow car because it was against the Highway Code. He couldn't overtake the slow car because cars towing caravans weren't allowed in the third lane.

Frank sounded his horn. 'Unbelievable. What's the matter with some people?' The slow car stayed in the middle lane and slowed down to about 30 miles an hour.

Frank sounded his horn again and kept the palm of his hand pressed firmly on the switch. There were still no other cars in either of the other lanes, or up ahead, or behind them. The car in front stayed in the middle lane and slowed down to about ten miles an hour.

Frank was livid. He flashed the slow car, but still they didn't move over. Frank stopped to allow a gap to grow and then accelerated to about 50 miles an hour, ramming the slow car so hard that the driver lost control and skewed sideways into the third lane allowing Frank and his caravan to pass. 'Idiots,' blasted Frank through his open window. He threw a copy of the Highway Code at the stricken car. It landed, open, on the front windscreen.

Andrew looked over at the crumpled slow car. Tom Hill was the driver and Pink Socks was in the passenger seat. They smiled and waved at Andrew. With the road to himself, Frank accelerated through the gears until he reached almost 100 miles an hour.

He kept looking in his rear-view mirror. 'What's the matter Frank? Is there a police car behind us?'

'No Maureen, you fool. Look at the caravan.' It was slewing from side to side in an alarming fashion. Frank was still driving down the middle lane but the caravan was sliding across all three lanes. 'I think we are going to have to stop.'

Frank pulled over and got out for a look. Andrew and Maureen followed him wondering what the problem might be. 'Right. There's our problem. Flat tyre. Get the pump Andrew.'

'Sorry. It's at home.' Andrew had put it away after blowing the tyres up before the journey. 'A place for everything and everything in its place.'

'You didn't pack the pump. You stupid boy. What were you thinking? No wonder Pinks Socks would rather go out with Tom. You'll never amount to anything.'

The cutting words woke Andrew with a jolt. He sat up in bed and the horror of what had happened the night before filled his head once more. The reality was far worse than his nightmare. There was a pain in his throat like hunger, but it was worse and nothing would make it go away.

His best friend had left the Coffee Bar with the girl he loved and Vicky Owen had seen them leave together. Her sobbing left no room for doubt. Tom and Pink Socks left arm in arm.

Andrew's green shoots of confidence had been crushed. He could stand up to his father, but that counted for nothing now. Since he started at Southside University, Andrew had aspired to be like Tom; the kindest, coolest, most loyal friend he had ever had. Tom had been like a brother to Andrew, sharing his deepest secrets, hopes and fears.

For almost a year, Andrew had dreamt of being with Pinks Socks and when he finally got close to his goal, Tom had stolen her from under his nose. Tom had a massive choice of girls compared to Andrew, so why take Pink Socks away from him? She was all he ever wanted and Andrew had been talking with her for nearly an hour. He nipped into the toilet for two minutes and in that time, Tom made his first move and disappeared into the darkness with her, probably for a night of endless passion.

The images in Andrew's head compounded the betrayal he felt. If a stranger had left arm in arm with Pink Socks Andrew would have been gutted. If Tom had let Andrew down for any other reason, he would have been utterly deflated, but the double blow of losing his reason for living as a result of his best friend's action was unbearable. He had lost the best two things in his life in the space of two minutes.

Andrew could no longer sleep. He couldn't eat. He had no energy or motivation to dress, or even get out of bed. He kept going over what had happened. He only left his room twice in the whole day, on both occasions to visit the bathroom. He saw nobody and quickly returned to his room and locked the door.

During the morning, Brian went in the kitchen for some breakfast. He expected to see Andrew, but the kitchen was empty. Brian knocked on Tom's door, but there was no reply. He knocked on Andrew's door, but there was no reply so he made his own cup of tea and sat on one of the soft chairs in the corner of the kitchen eating his cereal.

His peace was broken as the door slowly opened. Tom walked in with an embarrassed smile. 'Brian.' He nodded.

'Tom. You sly bugger. You left me with a very difficult situation.'

'I'm so sorry. I really am Brian, but it all happened too fast.'

'I take it by your smile that you slept with her.' Brian couldn't hide a smile.

'Yes. We spent the night together. She didn't need me to tell her I loved her. We just clicked. We'd hardly spoken and were in bed together. We were at it for ages and then we spent the rest of the night talking.'

'What happened at the Coffee Bar then?' Brian asked.

'She was sat on her own looking at me. I couldn't take my eyes off her and I just found myself walking towards her. She stood up, linked arms with mine, and said, "Let's go". I didn't need to think about it. We just went back to her place.'

Tom's smile was permanent. Brian had never seen him so happy. Greenpeace Badge, Vicky Owen and Sarah had made Tom happy, but this was something quite new. Before this moment, Brian had never seen such joy in Tom's smile. But Brian had been left to pick up the pieces and Tom would need to face the consequences of his actions.

'You realise Andrew and Vicky are both suicidal thanks to you?'

Tom still smiled. He couldn't help himself, but he did feel bad for Andrew, not so much for Vicky, because he hoped she would move on. He had been fair to her all the time and could do no more, but Andrew was very different. Despite not wanting to, Tom did feel responsible for Andrew and he knew his shy friend would be hurting now.

'What happened after I left?'

'Vicky cried like a baby. Andrew just sat on the wall and stared blankly into the distance.'

'Ooh dear.'

'Vicky's friends eventually took her home, but Andrew didn't move. He said nothing and kept staring at nothing.' Brian finished his drink. 'Want a cup of tea?'

'Yes please.' Tom had been so swept away by Pink Socks that he hadn't stopped to think about Andrew, but the bad feeling was growing now. He had no regrets at all, but wanted to do what he could to rescue his friendship. He valued Andrew as a friend and was prepared to do whatever he could to pick him back up. But he didn't want to turn the clock back. He had found a girl that he wanted to be with for a long time and they had already started making plans.

Brian handed him his tea. 'He was still there when the Coffee Bar shut. I sat with him for a bit but we didn't speak and we walked home in silence. He went in his room and I haven't seen him since. I've tried his door but he's not answering.'

'I'll have a try.' Tom left the kitchen with his drink, but returned two minutes later. 'No answer.'

Andrew stayed in his room for three days, even missing lectures. Hugh saw him visit the bathroom on the third day, but thought nothing of it, having not been told what had happened. It was only when Pink Socks came to eat in the Dickens Court kitchen with Tom, that Hugh, and the others on floor three, realised what had happened.

'You bastard Tom,' Hugh smiled. He was impressed with how unkind Tom had been to his friend. 'How could you do that to Andrew?'

'It's not like that,' Tom defended himself. He had already told Pink Socks how much she meant to Andrew. He didn't feel he owed Hugh an explanation for anything, but didn't like being accused of trampling all over his friend's feelings. He had. That was true. But not intentionally.

'If it's not like that, why hasn't he come out of his room for three days?' Hugh pointed out.

Colin Dean had seen him. 'He has been out of his room. I saw him sat on the bench across from the grass.'

'What? The grass outside Dickens Court?' Tom asked.

'Yeah. He was there ages. Just staring into the distance.' Colin laughed.

The next day, Andrew woke again at six in the morning, had a cup of tea and a piece of toast before walking downstairs, across the grass and sitting on the bench. He no longer wanted the solitude of his bedroom. He felt no better and could not stop his mind going over the events of the previous weekend time after time, looking for a positive explanation, but nothing came. He preferred sitting on the bench because he could watch people walking past.

There were all sorts of people of many ages. He studied their faces. Some were happy, some were sad and others had expressions which told Andrew nothing. He sat and wondered what their lives were like. Did they have girlfriends, wives, children, pets? He imagined many things and wondered if he would ever find happiness. His confidence was shattered, but he felt a new strength. He had broken free from the control his father had over him and that had given him the strength. When previously he would have needed somebody else to tell him what he should do next, he now asked himself the big questions.

'Bollocks to them all,' he told himself. 'So I've no friends and Pink Socks isn't interested. Bollocks to them all. I'm still here. I'm not that bad looking, I'm bright. Look at all these people walking past me. They have wives and girlfriends. If they can find somebody, why can't I?' He was feeling defiant.

Four hours later, the same pattern of thoughts was still running through his mind as Brian sat down with him.

'Andrew. I'm not used to sitting on the bench.' Brian couldn't help starting with a joke. He hoped it might get a smile out of his friend. It didn't.

Andrew's expression was unchanged and he carried on facing forward.

'I haven't seen you for four days.'

'I've been thinking.' Andrew was still staring forwards.

'Has it helped?' Brian asked, genuinely concerned.

'I don't know. Maybe.' Andrew paused. 'I would have trusted Tom with my life and he betrayed me. I can't understand why he would do that? That's the sort of thing my father would do to me. Knock me over and kick me when I'm down.'

Brian thought for a moment before continuing. 'I think, possibly Andrew, that you expected too much of Tom. You had issues with your father that Tom helped you with and you dealt with them eventually. But, I think, maybe, that you replaced your father with Tom. And so you expected Tom to give you what you never got from your father.'

Andrew turned and faced Brian now, finding his theory a little hard to swallow. 'I don't think so. I loved Pink Socks and when I nearly had her, he took her. It's as simple as that. He's no friend of mine. He's a git, so father figure bollocks. I don't think so.'

'Just a minute. That's not fair. Let's just suppose he fancied Pink Socks just as long as you but never said anything. Maybe he backed off for your sake. And let's just suppose she fancied him all year and just used you to get close to him. I'm pretty sure that's what happened, but he still helped you. Would you have done that for him if it were the other way round?' Brian had a point.

Andrew had been thinking about Pink Socks and Tom for four days, but this was a completely new way of looking at things. It was possible that he was so wrapped up in what he wanted that he completely discounted Tom's needs, or even Pink Socks. 'Okay. You have a point Brian. Doesn't mean you're right. But I still feel like shit and I still think Tom's a git.'

'No you don't Andrew. He treats you better than he treats me sometimes and you know it. I've got a lecture. I'll see you later.' Brian left Andrew on the bench.

He stayed there all day and returned the next morning.

After his conversation with Brian, Andrew's thoughts had changed. He still felt utterly depressed, but ready to pick a fight with the whole world. He wanted to hate Tom, but Brian had sowed the seeds of doubt in his mind. He watched the people going past. Being so close to so many people was helping him. He didn't speak to them, but just watching the emotion in the faces of strangers gave him a sense that he was sharing their lives.

Tom had been a good friend. Why was he directing all his anger on him but still feeling love for Pink Socks? Brian was probably right. Maybe he had broken free of his father only to replace him with Tom. He needed to break free from Tom now and the best way to do that would be to accept what had happened and set new goals.

The wind was picking up. As Andrew did up the zip on his anorak, Tom sat next to him on the bench. They sat side by side, both facing forward. They said nothing. It was five days since they had been in the Coffee Bar together, but it seemed like five months to Andrew. For Tom, it seemed like five minutes. He had never been happier and the only thing he needed now was to see his friend smile.

It was ten minutes before Tom broke the silence. He faced Andrew. 'I'm sorry.'

Andrew also turned to face Tom and they looked at each other for a moment before Tom went on. 'I must have had the hots for her since the first day of term. I ignored it because you liked her.' He waited for a reaction, but Andrew still didn't speak. 'I've got to be honest though. I don't think you ever had any chance. She's felt the same about me for just as long.'

Andrew faced forward again. He wasn't feeling angry. He could see Tom felt bad and that meant a lot to Andrew. If Tom didn't care about him as a friend, he wouldn't be sat next to him on the bench struggling to explain himself.

'You're right. I've thought about it and you're right. I thought I loved her, but I knew nothing about her. Until the night in the Coffee Bar, I'd never even spoken to her properly. I think I was in love with the idea of being in love. It could have been anybody. It just happened to be Pink Socks.'

'I think you're spot on Andrew. And when you do meet the right girl, I think you've got a lot of love to give.' Tom squeezed him affectionately on the shoulder.

At that moment, Pink Socks walked up to the bench.

'You alright Pinky?' said Tom with a big smile.

'I'm fine thanks, but I do have a problem. Maybe you could help me Andrew,' she said.

Andrew looked up at her surprised.

'My friend Charlotte hasn't had a date all year and she's a bit down. I told her I knew somebody who may go on a blind date with her.'

They both waited for a reaction. Andrew was a bit slow. After a couple of seconds, he said, 'Me?'

'Yeah. Why not Andrew? She's a nice girl.' Pink Socks raised her eyebrows to push for an answer.

'Excellent. I'd love to,' he replied. He couldn't help a small smile. Tom patted him on the back.

'We're late for lectures. You coming?' asked Tom.

'Thanks. I'll just stop here for a bit though. I'll see you later.' Tom and Pink Socks walked away holding hands. Andrew felt pleased for Tom. Andrew's confidence was coming back. He had expected too much of Tom. He must try to be a better friend from now on. He remembered Charlotte. She was a nice looking girl. He was already looking forward to his blind date.

There weren't many people walking past now. They were mostly in lectures, but the odd straggler walked past.

One of them was Hugh Grundy. He saw Andrew sitting alone on the bench. He hadn't seen him since Tom had taken Pink Socks from under his nose and here he was, on his own, a perfect opportunity to poke fun. Hugh strolled up and sat down next to Andrew. 'Andrew. I understand you have had a small problem with Tom. Is there anything I can help with?'

Andrew slowly turned to face Hugh, looked him straight in the eye and spoke with the assured confidence of a young man who believed in himself. 'Fuck off Hugh.'

Garry Kay is self-published and will only succeed if his readers spread the word. If you enjoyed the book, please pass on your copy or buy another for a friend. A review on Amazon (good or bad) would be fantastic, however short.

Break Free is Garry Kay's first novel. Garry is 48 and lives in Cornwall with his wife Ginny and two teenage children, Hannah and Sam. Break Free is set in the fictional town of Southside near London in the early 80s. It was inspired by Garry's first year at the University of Surrey in Guildford. The book is in no way biographical and all characters are entirely fictional. In 1986 Garry started as a trainee reporter on the West Sussex County Times in Horsham. After the County Times, Garry joined the Yorkshire Gazette & Herald in York as sports editor. He then took a career break with Ginny to work in a bar in Lanzarote while she worked as a holiday rep. He returned to York as chief sub-editor before joining The West Briton in 1995 as deputy editor. In 2000, he joined the Press Association in Leeds as new media chief sub-editor, but missed Cornwall so much that he returned. Since then he has made a living through property investments and writing novels. During his time at the Yorkshire Gazette & Herald, the paper won the coveted Press Gazette national award for Newspaper of the Year, a success Garry repeated at The West Briton in Cornwall.

www.garrykay.com

Printed in Great Britain
by Amazon.co.uk, Ltd.,
Marston Gate.